For more than forty years,
Yearling has been the leading name
in classic and award-winning literature
for young readers.

Yearling books feature children's
favorite authors and characters,
providing dynamic stories of adventure,
humor, history, mystery, and fantasy.

Trust Yearling paperbacks to entertain,
inspire, and promote the love of reading
in all children.

sammy KEYES

and the COLD HARD CASH

WENDELIN VAN DRAANEN

A YEARLING BOOK

Text copyright © 2008 by Wendelin Van Draanen Parsons
Illustrations copyright © 2008 by Dan Yaccarino

All rights reserved. Published in the United States by Yearling, an imprint of Random House Children's Books, a division of Random House, Inc., New York. Originally published in hardcover in the United States by Alfred A. Knopf, an imprint of Random House Children's Books, a division of Random House, Inc., New York, in 2008.

Yearling and the jumping horse design are registered trademarks of Random House, Inc.

Visit us on the Web! www.randomhouse.com/kids

Educators and librarians, for a variety of teaching tools,
visit us at www.randomhouse.com/teachers

The Library of Congress has cataloged the hardcover edition of this work as follows:
Van Draanen, Wendelin.
Sammy Keyes and the cold hard cash / Wendelin Van Draanen ;
[illustrations by Dan Yaccarino].
p. cm.
Summary: Thirteen-year-old Sammy meets a mysterious man who dies of a heart attack after telling her to get rid of the large amount of money he is carrying, leading her to investigate who the man was and how he came to be carrying so much cash.
ISBN 978-0-375-83526-1 (trade) — ISBN 978-0-375-93526-8 (lib. bdg.) —
ISBN 978-0-375-89148-9 (e-book)
[1. Wealth—Fiction. 2. Counterfeits and counterfeiting—Fiction. 3. Death—Fiction.
4. Veterans—Fiction. 5. Mystery and detective stories.] I. Yaccarino, Dan, ill. II. Title.
PZ7.V2857Sabm 2008
[Fic]—dc22
2008020643

ISBN 978-0-440-42113-9 (pbk.)

Printed in the United States of America
10 9 8 7 6 5 4 3 2

First Yearling Edition

This book is dedicated to
Becky Bendele, Caradith Craven, Roberta Hough, and Kate Schoedinger,
who make me realize I've been rich all along.

sammy
KEYES
and the COLD HARD CASH

PROLOGUE

After two years of sneaking up the fire escape and stealing down a hallway of old people's apartments to get to my grandmother's, you'd think I'd have it down. You'd think I'd know just where to duck and how to hide and what to say if some ornery old guy sees me tiptoeing down his hallway.

You'd think.

You'd also think I'd relax a little about living illegally in a seniors-only building. I mean, come on. I'm thirteen now, not some scared-to-death eleven-year-old worried about being tossed out onto the streets.

And the truth is, I *was* sort of used to it. I *had* started to relax a little. Slipping in and out of the apartment had become routine. The Senior Highrise was my *home*.

But then one night I was doing my usual sneak up the fire escape when something happened.

Something that had never happened before.

And now I *really* know what it means to be scared to death.

ONE

Holly Janquell is one of my best friends, and she happens to live right across Broadway from the Senior Highrise in an apartment above the Pup Parlor. I love going over to the Pup Parlor. You never know what crazy canine creation you'll find getting groomed there.

As far as the Pup Parlor *humans* go, you can expect to find either Meg or Vera, or both. Meg is Vera's daughter, and they were both friends of mine way before they adopted Holly. Grams describes them as "salt of the earth," but I don't really get that expression. I just know that they're hardworking and kind and trustworthy. They put it together about me living with Grams back when the only other person who knew was my friend Marissa. They never made a peep about it, either. They just minded their own business.

When I first met her, I thought Vera was, like, ninety. She's got wrinkles galore, she's missing teeth, and she's wiry. Her forearms look like stretched-out, overroasted chicken legs. You know, where all the fat's been burned away and what's left are tendons, shrively muscles, wrinkly skin, and bones.

But I don't think anyone who's ninety could wrestle a bulldog into a bathing tank the way Vera does. It's like seeing an Italian greyhound take down a mastiff. Those wiry arms go into action, and watch out! She'll have a dog tubbed and sudsed before you can get across the shop to offer help.

Meg's taller and stockier than her mom, but they let the world know they're related by the way they do their hair. They both have pouffy poodle dos decorated with little clip-on bows: red, pink, purple, polka-dotted. . . . They seem to have a different pair of bows for every day of the month.

I used to go hang out at the Pup Parlor just to kill time before going home, but now I go there because Holly lives there and it's fun to do homework together or help around the shop.

This time, though, I hadn't just dropped by. And, it being summer and all, I sure wasn't there to do homework.

This time I was there by official invitation.

Holly had called me at home Tuesday morning and said, "Hey! I'm inviting everyone over tonight to see pictures of our trip. Seven-thirty to nine-thirty. Can you come?"

I squinted at the phone. "You've got two hours of pictures?"

"No! It's a party. We're having pizza and salad, and dessert, too." Then she laughed. "But Vera did get a new digital camera before the trip, so expect to be bombarded."

I laughed, and after I cleared it with Grams, I said, "I'll be there!"

Holly also invited Marissa and Dot, so it was a real best friends reunion. "Sammy!" they cried when I entered the apartment. I hadn't seen Dot all summer because she and her family had been in Holland visiting relatives. She sorta blinked at me and said, "You're so tan!"

"Just my arms and face. It's a total backpacker tan."

She bounced up and down a little. "Did you bring pictures of your camping trip? I heard you saw condors!"

I snorted. "And snakes and scorpions and ticks and a dead boar and—"

Her face pinched up. "Eew."

I grinned. "So be glad—no pictures."

Dot shrugged, then looked kinda embarrassed as she said, "I brought some pictures of our trip to Holland." Then real fast, she added, "Meg and Vera said it was fine."

I eyed Marissa and asked, "Did you bring pictures of Las Vegas?" because her family had already taken three trips there this summer.

Marissa scowled. "You can't take pictures in Las Vegas. Everything's too . . . *big*."

The doorbell rang. "Pizza's here!" Meg called from the kitchen. So we all swarmed downstairs, got the pizzas, and pounded back up to the family room, where Vera was setting up a slide show on a laptop computer.

Meg brought in a salad, more drinks, and plates, and we all got comfy on the floor around their oversized coffee table and dug in. Meg usually gives off a pretty serious vibe, but having an apartment full of teenagers seemed to agree with her. She sat back in a recliner with a piece of pepperoni pizza, reclipped one of her royal blue bows, and let out a happy sigh. "Ready, Mother?"

"I believe so," Vera said, then started the slide show.

"Bombarded" doesn't even begin to describe it. We

saw pictures of Holly in the motor home, Holly at a meteor crater, Holly in the Painted Desert, Holly at the Grand Canyon, Holly cooking dinner, Holly next to a buffalo, Holly nose to nose with a chipmunk, Holly asleep, Holly waking up, Holly watching a Wild West show, Holly shopping for arrowheads, Holly standing by a pack of Harley-Davidsons, and Holly at Mount Rushmore. Fifty gazillion pictures of Holly at Mount Rushmore.

It might have been a real snooze, only luckily, Vera clicked through the shots fast and Holly had enough funny stories to go with the pictures to keep us entertained.

Plus, it was really good pizza.

When the slide show was done, Dot produced her photo album, and we saw another bunch of pictures, this time of Dot and her family by windmills, in oversized wooden shoes, by old churches, and on bikes. "We rode bikes everywhere!" she said. "Holland's really flat, so that's what everyone does. My brothers and I rode all the way into Germany. It was awesome!"

Now, when we neared the end of Dot's photo album, I noticed that Marissa had gotten very quiet. So while we were cleaning up, I kinda pulled her aside and whispered, "You okay?"

She nodded, but I could tell she wasn't. "What's going on?"

She shrugged. "Dot's got the coolest family, don't you think? And Holly had a blast with Meg and Vera. And you had that amazing backpacking adventure. What have I done this summer but get dragged to Las Vegas?"

"I thought you liked Las Vegas."

She frowned. "I am so over Las Vegas." Then she eyed me and said, "My parents have been fighting so much lately. Going anywhere with them is a total drag."

Holly and Dot were coming toward us, so Marissa put on a smile and said, "But Brandon's pool party is this weekend. *That*, at least, will be fun." Then she said to Holly and Dot, "You guys have to come to my cousin's pool party on Saturday. It's always such a blast." She turned to me. "Huh, Sammy?"

I nodded. "It's no sit-around-the-pool party, that's for sure. It's war."

"War?" Dot asked, and she looked worried.

Marissa laughed. "Water hoops to the death!"

Holly's eyebrows popped. "Water hoops?" And Dot said, "Oh, *that* sounds like fun. But . . . are you sure it's okay if we come?"

"Absolutely," Marissa said. "Brandon told me to bring whoever I want—if you guys come, it would be awesome!"

So we hung around talking about the pool party for a while, and when things started winding down, Dot called her dad to pick her and Marissa up, and we went downstairs and hung out on the sidewalk.

When Dot's dad pulled up to the curb, he leaned across the bench seat of his DeVries Nursery delivery truck and called, "Hello, girls! You had a good time, *ja*?"

I laughed because Mr. DeVries puts *"Ja?"* at the end of practically every sentence, and it always cracks me up a little. *"Ja!"* we said, then told him their trip to Holland looked amazing.

As they drove off, Marissa leaned out the window and

shouted, "I'll call with details about the pool party!" but when they were gone, Holly kinda shook her head and said, "I don't know if I'm going to that, Sammy."

"You do *not* want to miss it, Holly." I looked at her and added, "We'll go over together, okay?"

She hesitated, then gave a little smile. "Okay."

It was already ten o'clock, so I thanked her for inviting me, and when there was a break in traffic, I snugged down my ball cap, said, "See ya!" and jaywalked across the street.

Now, on my way home, I did what I always do: I took a roundabout route to the fire escape, hung back in the shadows a few seconds to make sure nobody was watching, then started up the steps.

By the second-floor landing, I was on automatic pilot, because really, what is there to do besides zigzag up to the fifth floor? It was nighttime, I was wearing dark clothes, there were no floodlights giving me away, and it's not like anyone ever *uses* the fire escape. I mean, can you imagine creaky old men and women hobbling up or down switchback after switchback of stairs by choice? Even in a fire, most of the ones I know would just stay put.

Anyway, there I am, trucking up the stairs, and for the first time in all the years I've been going to Brandon McKenze's summer pool party, I'm actually worrying that I don't have a decent swimsuit to wear, when all of a sudden it happens.

A fire escape door starts to open right in front of me.

For a split second I freeze, not knowing what to do.

If I go up, I'll be seen.

If I go *down,* I'll be seen.

So I do the only thing I can think to do—I dive behind the opening door and suck up to the wall like a coat of lumpy paint.

The door shoves open slowly.

And not very far.

And then it just *stays* like that.

Even in the cool night air, my whole body's sweating—my hands, my armpits, my forehead—I can practically hear the cotton band inside my cap slurping up sweat.

Then my knees start wobbling and my heart decides to try to bang its way out of my body as my mind scrambles around for a believable excuse. I mean, what's my story? Why am I up here on the fourth-floor landing of an old folks' fire escape at ten o'clock at night?

But with all that sweating and wobbling and banging and scrambling going on, I'm also thinking, Why isn't anyone coming out?

What are they doing?

Just looking?

But for what?

For *me*?

I start willing the door to close. Close! Close! Close! I say in my head.

Unfortunately, the power to move large metal objects with my mind is not well honed, because the opposite happens.

The door swings open.

And then suddenly there's a man stepping through the doorway and onto the fourth-floor landing.

TWO

Light from the hallway shines on the man as he starts across the landing toward the steps going down. He's wearing a dark blue jacket, dark pants, a hat pulled down low, and *white* Velcro-close shoes.

Old-guy shoes.

Then the door swings closed, and I relax a little because he is definitely not the building manager. Mr. Garnucci is skinny, and this guy's stocky. And whoever he is, he doesn't notice me. He's just some old guy who's sure to have bad eyes, bad ears, and a focus on the ground instead of what's ahead of him.

Or what's behind him.

But then, before he takes his first step down, he glances over his shoulder. Maybe to check the door, I don't know. All I know is that his glance turns into a double take, and the double take turns into a look of terror.

He's spotted me, all right, and from the look on his face, he thinks I might *mug* him or something. And then all of a sudden his face wrenches up and he makes a horrible *choking* sound and slowly collapses onto the fire escape.

"Are you all right?" I ask, going toward him.

His face is still all contorted, but he blinks at me, then chokes out, "You're . . . just a . . . *girl*."

"I'm sorry I scared you. Are you . . . all right?"

He shakes his head, licks his lips, pants, pulls another awful face, and clutches his chest. And that's when it finally hits me—this guy is having a heart attack!

"I'll call an ambulance!" I tell him, but he gasps, "Wait!" and it looks like he's trying to take something out of an inside coat pocket.

"Do you have heart medicine?" I ask, because somewhere in the back of my brain I remember seeing something like that on TV.

His face pinches up hard and he closes his eyes.

So I dive down and start digging through his coat, asking, "Which pocket?" only I stop short because what I run into instead is a big fat bundle of money.

"Get . . . rid of it," he gasps.

I hesitate. "The money?"

He nods and pants, "All . . . of . . . it."

"The *money*?" I ask again, then dive back into his pockets, looking for pills. "Don't talk crazy. Where's your medicine?"

He doesn't answer. And when I find a second bundle of money, and then a *third*, he says, "It's not—" but he can't seem to get the rest out. He just folds up in pain.

"Where's your medicine?" I cry, and when he doesn't answer, I stand up and say, "I'm getting an ambulance!"

"Throw it!" he gasps. "Get . . . rid of it!"

"The *money*?"

"Please!" he wheezes. "Throw it!"

So I pick up the bundles of money, but really, tossing them away is not something that comes naturally to me. I mean, with Grams' limited income and my *zero* income, money is always an issue.

But what am I supposed to do? It's not *my* money, and something about it being there sure seems to be making his condition worse.

Then he pulls a terrible face and wheezes, *"Please,"* so I take a deep breath and heave the bundles over the railing and into the bushes below.

He seems to relax a little, so I say, "Look, do you have medicine or not?"

He shakes his head.

"I'm getting an ambulance!" So I power up the stairs to the fifth floor and shoot down the hall to get Grams' help, only before I get there, I hear her voice coming through the open doorway of our neighbor's apartment. "Rose, honestly," she's snapping. "I can't do this alone. I'm going to have to call for help!"

I stop short, thinking, Uh-oh, because I know what this means.

It means what it always means.

Our supersized neighbor has fallen off the toilet and can't get up.

My plan, as I was charging down the hall, was to have Grams call 911. *I* sure didn't want to do it! Those 911 people ask you stuff like who you are and where you live, and what you're doing on a seniors building fire escape giving people heart attacks.

But now I knew that Grams was dealing with Mrs.

Wedgewood, so my choice was to either go into the Wedge's apartment and get Grams to call 911 or go into our apartment and call 911 myself, pretending to be Grams.

I've learned the hard way that a split-second decision can affect you a lot longer than the split second it took to make. In this case, my split-second decision was to go inside Mrs. Wedgewood's apartment and head straight for the bathroom.

The place was dripping with steam. The mirrors were completely fogged up, and there was an actual *cloud* hanging in the air. "Oh, thank heavens!" Grams said when she saw me, her hair in sweaty curls, her glasses milky with steam.

Mrs. Wedgewood hadn't fallen off the toilet. It was actually worse. She was on the floor of the shower, looking like a big blob of blubber.

I tried to wave Grams out of the bathroom, whispering, "Quick! You've got to call an ambulance!"

"She's not hurt," Grams says, pushing her glasses back up her nose. "She's just slippery!"

"Grams!" I whisper. "It's an emergency!" But for some reason she can't seem to see that I'm dealing with a crisis bigger than a soaped-up whale. So in another split-second decision, I run into the kitchen, pick up Mrs. Wedgewood's phone, and dial 911.

"It's a real emergency," I say in my best old-lady voice when they answer. "A man collapsed on the fire escape of the Senior Highrise!" And since there are two fire escapes for the building, I add, "The Broadway side! He's on the fourth-floor landing! I think he's having a heart attack! Send an ambulance quick!"

Then before they can ask me any questions, I slam down the phone, turn around, and nearly slam into Grams.

"What was that?" she asks me.

So real fast I tell her about the guy on the landing having a heart attack.

She shoves hair off her forehead with the back of her hand and gasps, "Oh dear! Let's go!"

She calls, "I'll be right back, Rose!" and after she grabs a flashlight from home, we both hurry over to the fire escape.

Grams was amazingly quick on the stairs, and when we reached the fourth floor, she knelt down by the man and took his pulse.

It was too late, though. I could just tell—he looked way too peaceful to be alive.

"Oh dear!" Grams says over her shoulder. "I think he's gone!"

Sirens are screeching down Main Street, so Grams shoos me off, whispering, "Go! I'll take care of this. See if you can help Rose."

So up the stairs I fly, feeling shaky and sick to my stomach.

No matter how much I didn't want to believe it, it was still true.

I'd scared a man to death.

THREE

Rose Wedgewood knows I live with Grams. I've never actually *admitted* it to her, but she knows. And she's turned out to be the biggest sweet-talking blackmailer the world has ever seen. Early on she said, "Don't worry, sugar. I'll keep your little secret," then immediately started asking me to do all sorts of errands and chores.

The thing about Mrs. Wedgewood is, I don't think she *wants* to be a sweet-talking blackmailer. Underneath it all I think she's probably a nice person. But she says that moving to assisted living—which, believe me, she needs—would be like "opening the coffin and steppin' in," so instead, she blackmails us into helping her stay at the Highrise. She calls us on the phone to send us on errands and have us do her laundry and stuff like that, but for emergencies she doesn't bother with the phone. No, for emergencies she bangs on her bathroom wall.

Now, that's probably because most of her emergencies happen in the bathroom.

And her definition of "emergency" can be pretty broad. Sometimes she's dropped her wig on the floor and can't pick it up. Sometimes her walker's out of reach and the bathroom floor's wet and she's afraid of slipping and crashing through to the apartment below. Sometimes the toilet paper roll's run out and she needs us to get her a refill from under her sink.

Usually, though, she bangs on the wall because she's fallen off the toilet.

I don't want to get into the gross details of how or why this happens, but man, is she good at it. And it takes both Grams and me to hoist her back onto the throne.

In all the times I'd been inside her bathroom, though, I'd never seen her in all her bald, naked glory on the shower stall floor. I didn't even think she took showers. From her usual, uh, *aroma*, I figured she sponged off maybe once a week and called it good.

"Sammy!" she gasped when she saw me. "Where's Rita? I thought she'd left me here to die!"

I whipped the double-sized beach towel she'd made me sew together off the rack and covered her body. "Are you kidding? She wouldn't do that." I studied the situation a minute. She was sort of on her side, with her back end toward the door.

"I should never have tried a shower," she moaned. "What got into me?"

"Let's just get you out of there." I knelt in front of the shower and put out my hand. "Here. I'll help you sit up, and then maybe you can get on your knees. Then I'll get the walker and . . . we'll go from there."

So she takes my hand, making it practically disappear inside of hers, and after I wedge my knees up tight against the curb of the shower, I go, "Ready? One, two, three!" and pull back as hard as I can. Trouble is, instead of her moving anywhere, my knees slip out from under me and I go *flying* into the shower.

I land with a sloppy *thump* right on top of her, and even though the towel's between *some* of us, it's not between *all* of us. And I'm sorry, but being sprawled out over all that flubbery blubberyness freaked me out.

"Aaaah!" I cried, and quicker than a cat tossed in ice water, I backed *out* of there.

"You almost had me! Try again," she says.

I did *not* want to try again, but I knew there was no escaping it. So finally I take a deep breath and lean in, and this time I brace myself by putting one foot against the curb of the shower.

I pull, and she swings up, up, up, until she's sorta sitting, using one arm to prop herself up.

"Okay, both hands right here," I tell her, tapping on the curb of the shower. "Then get up on your knees. Can you do that?"

"I'll sure try, sugar," she says, panting hard. "But first can you hand me my wig? I am so embarrassed to have you see me like this."

I want to say, You're kidding, right? because her bald head's *nothing* compared to her bald body. But I can tell she's serious, so I get her curly black head-mop off the counter and wrestle it onto her head.

When I'm done, she looks like one of those enormous beached seals with a wig on. It seems to give her confidence, though. "All right, sugar," she says, "let's do it."

So with big groans and moans she finally gets up on all fours.

I drape the towel over her back, and as she's peering at me through the shower door opening, she now reminds me of one of those maharaja elephants.

"Okay!" I tell her. "Good job." I grab the walker and put it up to the curb. "You're almost there!"

"Give me a minute," she pants. "And I'm going to need your help getting up."

I just stare at her, because helping her up means I've got to get in the shower.

It means I've got to grab her under her armpit and heave-ho.

It means . . .

I try to block the grossness of it all from my mind and squeeze past her into the shower.

"I really need to get me one of those shower seats," she says. "And one of those spray nozzles on a hose. And maybe you could come by and help me bathe, rather than my trying to do this all myself."

The thought of that makes me shudder. I mean, come on! How far is this blackmail stuff going to go?

I don't say a word, though. I just get her to grab the walker, then I take a deep breath and scoop an arm into the flubbery abyss between her arm and her body. And as I'm straining to help her up, I'm wishing Grams would hurry back. I mean, what was taking so long? Were the police quizzing her? Was she telling them that she found the guy passed out? Dead?

What else could she say?

And there were a gazillion other questions running through my head. Who was the guy and what was he doing using the fire escape? Did he live in the building? And why did he have fat bundles of cash? You don't live in the Senior Highrise if you have fat bundles of cash! You live here because you *don't* have fat bundles of cash.

And why had he been so worried about getting *rid* of the money? He obviously didn't want anyone to find it on him. Had he robbed a bank? Had he stolen it from an apartment?

But who in this place had fat wads of cash?

"We did it, sugar, we did it!" Mrs. Wedgewood panted as she stood outside the shower in all her naked glory. "Oh, bless you, child. Bless you!"

I was panting, too. "Okay. Well, there you go." I wrapped the towel over her shoulders.

"That's okay, sugar, I'm not cold," she said, shrugging it off. And as she clomped out of the bathroom and into the living room, Grams came hurrying into the apartment, closing the door tight behind her.

"Oh, good!" she said when she saw that Mrs. Wedgewood was out of the shower. And even though she blinked pretty good at her as she clomped along, from the flush of her cheeks and her darting eyes I could see that Grams had bigger things on her mind than Mrs. Wedgewood.

"So, Rose, are you going to be all right?" she asked, giving me the let's-get-out-of-here nod.

"I am famished," she said, clomping toward her bedroom. "Would you mind fixing me some eggs? And toast. Buttered."

"Uh . . . sure," Grams said, eyeing me.

"I think I'm out of eggs," Mrs. Wedgewood called over her shoulder. "Do you have any? If not, maybe you could run to the store?"

Grams pinched her lips together and counted to ten through flared nostrils. "I'll see what I have."

Grams gave me the nod again, so I followed her to our apartment and whispered, "What happened?"

"He's dead," she whispered back. "But it's all very strange. His name's Buck Ritter and his driver's license shows he was from Omaha, Nebraska. And there was a receipt from the Heavenly Hotel. I don't think he lived in our building at all!"

"Wait. Did you go through his wallet?"

She gave a little frown. "I wanted to know who he was! If he was a Highrise resident, his neighbors would certainly not have wanted to learn about his death on the morning news!"

"So it was your civic duty to go nosing through his wallet?"

She gave me a prim look. "I didn't nose."

"So what happened after the paramedics showed up? What did you tell them?"

"The paramedics were fine," she said. "They tried to revive him, but it was no use." She was quiet a minute, then said, "He had wings tattooed on his neck."

"On his neck?" I asked, because she was sounding . . . strange.

"On the back of it. There was a star in the middle and something written over the top. I couldn't make out what it spelled, but it was strange to see."

"Because?"

She hesitated, then said, "Because they looked like angel wings." Then very softly she added, "Like he'd been ready to be carried off . . . for a long time." She shook her head. "Never mind. It was just a strange thing to see on . . . on a dead man. After that the police showed up and I panicked."

"What do you mean, you panicked?"

"What was I going to tell them?" she said, all wide-eyed. "Why was I on the fire escape so late at night?" She held her forehead. "So I left! The fourth-floor door was unlocked, so I just slipped inside and came home."

"So . . . nobody knows it was you?"

Her head quivered back and forth. "And I want it to stay that way!" She opened the refrigerator and pulled out a carton of eggs. "The whole thing was very distressing." Her head quivered some more. "Nobody wants to die on a fire escape!"

I cringed. "I didn't mean to kill him."

She stopped cold. "Don't ever say that again. Don't even *think* that. It was not your fault. He must've had a weak heart." She frowned. "And what got into him? He didn't look like he was in any condition to take the fire escape down!"

I took a deep breath because I knew something she didn't.

I knew about the money.

And I was actually about to spill this extra piece of confusing information, when suddenly Grams *screeches* and drops the carton of eggs.

"What?" I say, whipping around, and that's when I see that my cat, Dorito, is stalking a mouse.

Now, I don't mind mice. I think they're cute, actually. But Grams has this thing about them being disease-carrying, fang-faced, pooping varmints, and most of the people in the Highrise seem to share her view.

"They promised us the problem was solved!" Grams said, watching the little gray fuzzball cower in a corner.

I turned away, not wanting to see Dorito do what he's so good at doing. Instead, I picked up the oozy egg carton and headed for the stove. And by the time Grams said, "There, that's done," I had the eggs cooking in a frying pan.

"What are you doing?" Grams asked, because I had just poured the broken eggs out of the carton and was scrambling them up, plucking out little chips of shell as the eggs cooked.

"You want to finish?" I asked, handing over the spatula. "I'll take the mouse down to the trash chute."

"No." She got cleaning gloves from under the sink. "I don't want you out in the hallway. Not with everything that's going on tonight!"

So she got rid of the mouse while I finished scrambling up crunchy eggs and making toast, and when she returned, I let her deliver the "snack" to Mrs. Wedgewood.

It was after midnight by the time we went to bed. No police had come pounding on the door, nobody had called, Mrs. Wedgewood was tucked safely in bed, and there were no more mouse sightings. Everything seemed to be settling down, but there was no way I could sleep.

Not with three big bundles of cash in the bushes!

At least I hoped they were still in the bushes.

What if one of the paramedics found them?

What if the police did?

What if some homeless guy camping out in the bushes did?

Now, I'm not going to lie and say I'd be happy for some homeless guy if he found the money. *I* wanted it! I hadn't *meant* to scare the guy to death, but really, what could I do about it?

Nothing.

What I *could* do something about was the money.

I could go get it before someone else did!

So when enough time had passed, I tiptoed up to Grams' bedroom door and listened.

And there it was—the lovely sound of Grams sawing logs.

I tiptoed away from her door and into the kitchen.

I got the flashlight from the tool drawer.

I put on my sweatshirt and ball cap.

Then I eased out of the apartment and hurried down the hall.

FOUR

I tried not to think about Mr. Buck Ritter from Omaha, Nebraska, as I went past the fourth-floor landing. I tried not to picture him clutching his heart or hear his voice gasping, "Throw it! Get rid of it!" I kept my eyes peeled for cops cruising Broadway. I kept my eyes on the late-night bums who sometimes hang out in front of Maynard's Market or the Heavenly Hotel. I tried to concentrate on what was happening, rather than on what had happened.

It was dark out. And very quiet. There were hardly any cars going along Broadway or Main. Even the pink Heavenly Hotel sign buzzing through the misty air seemed muted.

All I could really hear was my heart, pounding like mad in my chest.

I didn't really know what I was going to do with the money if it was still there. I mean, if Buck Ritter from Omaha, Nebraska, had robbed someone, I'd turn it over to the police. But this didn't feel like a stolen money situation. It felt like . . . I don't know what it felt like! But Buck Ritter from Omaha, Nebraska, did not seem like a stick-'em-up kind of guy.

I mean, had Grams or I found a gun on him?

No!

A knife?

No!

A *water* pistol?

No!

All he'd had on him were bundles of cold hard cash.

I hurried over to the bushes where I'd chucked the money, and believe me, my eyes were checking around to make sure no one was watching.

The bushes were a lot bigger than they looked from the fourth-floor landing. There were also a *lot* of them.

I turned on the flashlight and started scouring the area, and almost right away I found one of the bundles just lying there on the ground.

Talk about hitting pay dirt!

The bundle was still rubber-banded together nice and snug, and when I fanned through it, the bills snapped against each other, crisp and clean.

I felt like I was in a dream—like this couldn't actually be happening.

But it was!

I started scouting around for the other bundles. I checked around the bushes and between the bushes, and when I finally spotted another bundle, half buried under dead leaves, I picked it up and giggled, "I'm rich!"

Ten minutes later I still hadn't found the last bundle of cash. And I suppose I could have just forgotten about it and gone home, but I knew it had to be somewhere! So I searched high and low and finally spotted it wedged inside a shrub.

"Money doesn't grow on trees," I laughed. "It grows in bushes!"

Then, with a quick check to make sure no one else was around, I hurried up the fire escape and slipped back into the building.

Dorito seemed very curious about the money as I counted it on the couch by flashlight. "No!" I kept telling him as he pawed across it.

"Mrowwww," he said back, rubbing up against me, padding back across the bills.

I tossed him off but he jumped right back, so I lost track, but it didn't really matter. The bills were all twenties, and there were about a hundred and fifty of them.

It was more money than I'd ever seen before in my life.

And I couldn't believe it—it was mine!

The first thing I did in the morning was check to make sure I hadn't been dreaming.

Yup, there was the money, stashed in the bottom of my backpack.

Which meant that yup, I'd scared a man to death on the fourth-floor landing.

I tried not to think about that.

It's better to focus on the positive, right?

The trouble was Grams. She was in the kitchen humming softly as she made oatmeal, and I was feeling torn. Should I tell her about the money? What would she think? What would she *do*?

Knowing her, she'd have the money turned over to the police by noon.

But . . . why should we?

What would the police do with it?

Keep it for evidence?

For what crime?

Murder on the fourth-floor landing?

There was no way I wanted to open that can of worms!

So I casually shoved my backpack under the couch and once again tried not to think about the fact that there was a dead man involved in my hitting the three-thousand-dollar jackpot.

I headed for the kitchen. "Smells good," I said, sounding as sleepy as I could in my hyped-up, flush-with-cash state.

Grams gave me a quick kiss, then continued scooping oatmeal into a second bowl. "I barely slept a wink last night. That poor man! What a place to end your days!"

"Grams, please. I'm trying not to think about it, okay?"

She stopped midscoop, the gloppy wooden spoon looming over a bowl. "Oh, Samantha. You have got to stop blaming yourself! His heart was obviously in poor condition!" She thwacked the oatmeal into the bowl, put the pot back on the stove, and handed me the walnuts, brown sugar, and milk. "But I would love to know what he was doing there!"

I sat at the table, suddenly not at all hungry. "Can we please not talk about it?" I leaned forward and whispered, "I killed a man, okay?"

She flicked out a napkin and smoothed it across her lap. "You did *not* kill him. He obviously shouldn't have been—"

"*I* shouldn't have been there! I'm not supposed to be living here, remember?"

She zeroed in on me through her glasses. "But you *do* live here, and he doesn't! He lives at the Heavenly." She shivered a little when she said "Heavenly," then almost right away added, "Or, I should say, *lived*." She poured milk on her oatmeal. "I want to know what he was doing on *our* fire escape!"

"Stop it!"

"My," she said, passing the milk. "For a girl who is usually *too* curious, it's odd that you're not at all interested in this."

I leaned waaaay forward and said, "I *killed* him, okay?"

But she was right. It wasn't just that. It was the money. The fact that it was a dead man's money. The fact that I wanted to *keep* the dead man's money. The fact that after an entire life of having nothing to spend, I now had more than I knew *how* to spend.

Marissa helped with that little problem. She called later that morning and asked, "Can you meet me at the mall at eleven? I need to find a new swimsuit."

"Me too," I said, realizing with a happy rush that I could actually afford to buy one instead of borrowing an old one of hers.

"Cool!" she said. "You want to meet at Juicers?"

"Sure!"

I waited until Grams was in the bathroom to dig up some cash. I peeled off six twenties, not because I was planning to spend a hundred and twenty bucks on a swimsuit but because that way I'd be ready in case I wanted to buy . . . other stuff!

I folded the bills in half and slipped them in my jeans pocket. I felt a twinge of guilt, but I shook it off. So I'd caught a lucky break for once. There was no crime in that—I just wasn't *used* to it.

I felt a little nervous leaving the rest of the money in a place Grams could find it if she had the mind to snoop, but really, Grams isn't in the habit of snooping. I mean, where's there to snoop? Except for my skateboard and my backpack, which both get stashed under the couch, everything I own is hidden in her bottom dresser drawer. And believe me, my backpack is not something tidy people like Grams would voluntarily snoop through. It's tattered and kinda smelly from softball paraphernalia, and in order for Grams to find the stacks of cash, she'd have to get past my ball cap, catcher's mitt, sweatshirt, cleats, and sunblock.

So I shoved the worry from my mind, told Grams I'd see her later, checked the hallway for nosy old people, then beelined over to the fire escape exit and hurried to the mall.

Brandon McKenze was working the counter at Juicers, which at one time would have immediately flicked on the spastic switch in my head. He may be Marissa's cousin and someone I've known since the third grade, but him being a high school swim star and . . . I don't know . . . *tan* all the time used to really twist me up, if you know what I mean.

But recently I was forced to actually *talk* to him a few

times, and for some reason it helped me get over being tongue-tied around him.

"Hey, Sammy!" he said, rinsing out a blender. "Cruising for trouble?"

I laughed. "Yeah. Goes by the name Marissa. Have you seen her?"

He laughed, too. "No, but I'm sure she'll show up. Trouble always shows up when you're around."

"Very funny," I said, and I felt strangely relaxed. Almost confident. This was the easiest conversation I'd ever had with Brandon.

"Can I getcha anything?" He eyed me. "Probably not, huh?"

Now, the reason he said "Probably not, huh?" is because I never buy anything at Juicers. Who can afford six bucks for some fancy juice?

Marissa, on the other hand, *always* buys something. Marissa's got money to burn. She's even got her own credit card, if you can believe that. Grams says it's her parents' way of compensating for never being home, but whatever. It doesn't bother me because Marissa doesn't *act* like a rich girl. She's generous, but in a quiet way. She just does little things—like offer to buy me Double Dynamo drumsticks or Juicers when we're cruising around town, or she'll spring for the movies so I can actually go with her.

Anyway, the point is, I owe Marissa McKenze more Juicers than I care to think about. And all of a sudden there I was, with a fat wad of twenties in my pocket and a burning urge to buy something!

"As a matter of fact, I think I'll have a large orange-strawberry, and I'll get Marissa an orange-pineapple."

He hesitated. "I can't do it on the house, you know that, right?"

I peeled a twenty out of my pocket and laid it on the counter.

He studied me a second, then gave a nod. "Coming right up."

Marissa arrived just as I was tucking away my change. I handed over her drink and said, "Surprise."

"Seriously?" She eyed it suspiciously. Like it might be poisoned or something.

"Take it, would you?"

"Hey, Cuz," Brandon called over the counter.

Marissa and he exchanged some secret McKenze eye-twitching signals, which I think translated to no, he hadn't done them on the house. Then Brandon said, "So! Pool party on Saturday. You're coming, right?"

"That's why we're here," Marissa said. "We've gotta find battle suits!"

Brandon laughed and waved. "Sammy's on my team!"

"Then so am I," Marissa called. She slung an arm around me. "You can't break *us* up!" And as we walked off sipping our Juicers, I felt really, really good.

FIVE

Swimsuits are embarrassing. I mean, who wants to run around in what's basically just colorful underwear? One-piece, two-piece . . . they're all ridiculous. Especially the ones that have stuff added to them. For example, what's with the built-in belts? Whose idea was that? Do they think waterproof underwear looks better with a belt? Is it supposed to give you a sense of security? *Wear these belted bottoms and save yourself from diving disasters.*

Please.

And think about wearing a swimsuit as you cruise the mall. It would be mortifying! But when you're at a pool, it's just . . . normal.

Well, as normal as walking around in colorful underwear can be, anyway.

Most girls I know drape a towel over their shoulders or around their waists when they're at the pool. Me, I just get in the water and stay there.

Why else would I be in a swimsuit?

Anyway, Marissa and I went to her favorite store, and I picked out a multigreen one-piece in about seven minutes.

An hour later Marissa still hadn't decided.

"Why are you even looking at a two-piece?" I finally asked. "No one wears a bikini to war."

She laughed, then blushed, and finally confessed, "Danny's going to be there."

"You invited *him*?" I rolled my eyes. "Oh, great. So what's it gonna be? Flirting or fighting?" I pointed to the bikini. "You can't expect to play water hoops in *that*."

She cringed, looking from the one-piece in her hand to the lime green ruffle-topped, belted-bottom bikini on her body. "I don't know. What do you think?"

"You *know* what I think," I grumbled.

And I wasn't just talking about flirting versus war.

Let's just say Danny Urbanski is not my favorite person.

"But don't you think this suit looks great on me? I have never had a suit look this good on me!"

It did look great on her, but that wasn't the point. "Are you going to flirt or fight? 'Cause that is not a water hoops suit."

"Fine," she said, not sounding fine at all.

I left the dressing room to let her change, saying, "You could always buy both."

Me and my big mouth. A few minutes later she emerged from the little changing closet with a great big smile on her face. "That's exactly what I'm going to do!"

I guess when you've got your own credit card, buying whatever you want is hard to resist.

So we went up to the register, where a ratty-looking girl with a silver lip ring and a single streak of blue dye through her jet-black hair scanned in Marissa's swimsuits without a word. Marissa slid her credit card through the machine and started to say something to me, but Blue Streak cleared her throat. "Hm-hmmm."

"Huh?" Marissa asked.

Blue Streak just taps the card reader and eyes her.

"Credit denied?" Marissa asks, then runs the card through again.

CREDIT DENIED appears on the little screen again.

Marissa does it a third time.

CREDIT DENIED.

"What?" Marissa says. Then she looks at lovely Miss Blue Streak and says, "There must be something wrong with your scanner. I've never had this problem before!"

Blue Streak snorts and puts her hand out to me.

So I pass over my swimsuit and whisper to Marissa, "Don't you have cash?" because Marissa *always* has cash.

She digs through her pocket and produces ten bucks and a little change.

Blue Streak has already cleared Marissa's sale and rung up my suit, so I hand over the cash to pay for it.

"Wow," Marissa says, because even though I'd tried to be sly about it, she's spotted my wad of twenties. "Where'd you get that?"

Now, I wasn't expecting this. *Why,* I don't know. I guess I thought I'd be able to be sly about it. You know, not get noticed.

But there I am, busted with a fat wad of twenties. And I should have said something like, My mom's sending me money, 'cause that would have made sense. I mean, my mom's gone from starving actress to soap star, and she *should* be sending me money.

But I *didn't* think.

I panicked.

"Uh . . . odd jobs."

"Odd jobs?" she asks as I accept the change. "Where have you been doing odd jobs?"

So while my brain scrambles around for some believable answer to *that,* my mouth pops off with, "Over at the Heavenly."

"The *Heavenly?* Since *when?*"

My brain's screaming, The Heavenly? What kind of insane answer is that? And to avoid digging myself in any deeper, I switch the subject real fast. "Hey, why don't I pay for your swimsuits? Or . . . at least one of them."

"Really?" Marissa asks, all wide-eyed. Then she starts checking out my fast-shrinking wad of cash. "Do you have enough for both? I'll pay you back tonight!"

"Uh . . . how about just one?"

"I'll pay you right back?" she pleads.

Blue Streak is tapping her black fingernails against the counter and wobbling her head from side to side, obviously annoyed. So I say, "All right, whatever," and we go through the whole ring-up process again.

And really, over the years Marissa has sprung for so many little things for me that I should have just bought both the suits as a gift, but that would have seemed weird. *Suspicious,* even.

And although I was kinda planning to tell her about poor scared-to-death Buck Ritter from Omaha, Nebraska, all of a sudden I didn't want to. For the first time in my life, I was understanding what Marissa has been complaining about *her* whole life.

When you have a lot of money, other people want to use it.

Like, if you have extra, you should share.

Not that I minded that with Marissa, but I could see it becoming one of those it's-not-really-*your*-money deals. Like winning the lottery, when everyone comes out of the woodwork and thinks they deserve a piece of the pie.

Why do they think that?

Because you didn't earn it, that's why.

You *won* it.

So standing there at the register, it hit me that I'd won the dead-guy lottery. I may have scared Mr. Buck Ritter from Omaha, Nebraska, to death, but he'd left me his winning ticket.

Even though he'd made me toss it overboard.

Into a bunch of bushes.

Which was weird, but . . . whatever.

So I decided that it was probably best not to tell anyone about my dead-guy lottery ticket—not even Marissa Moneybags McKenze. I mean, what if she slipped up and told someone about it? Or . . . what if she thought I should go to the police? That would be easy for *her* to say. It wasn't her money!

After we left the store, Marissa and I cruised around the mall for a while, but Marissa couldn't really buy anything because at both other places where she tried to use her credit card, she got the same scanner message.

CREDIT DENIED.

"I am so embarrassed!" she said after the third time. "I wonder what's wrong with my card . . . !"

So we got burgers, and afterward she dropped the rest of her cash into games at the arcade. "You want to come over to my house?" she said when she was totally broke. "I've got to figure out what's wrong with my card."

"Nah, I'd better get home."

"Why?"

I could feel myself popping with sweat. "Uh . . . I promised Grams I'd help her clean house today." I forced a laugh. "Lame, I know, but I promised."

So we went our separate ways, and as I walked out the north end of the mall, I felt kinda guilty.

Kinda dirty.

Kinda *stupid*.

I mean, why was I lying to Marissa? Why didn't I just come out with the truth? She wouldn't care! She'd be happy for me!

But way down inside I was afraid to. It was like I'd committed a terrible crime, and if even one person found out, it'd be all over.

Somehow the money would no longer be mine.

SIX

On the way home I told myself I hadn't really done anything wrong. It's not like I'd *stolen* the money. It's not like Mr. Heart Attack from Omaha, Nebraska, had asked me to pass it along to his children or grandchildren.

He'd asked me to get rid of it.

And hey, I was doing just that! I'd managed to power through over a hundred bucks already. Of course, Marissa was going to pay me back for the two swimsuits, but still. In the morning there'd been more money in my pocket than I'd ever had before, and now—*poof*—it was practically gone.

Spending dead-guy lottery money didn't bother me nearly as much as lying to Marissa did. Which I guess is why instead of going home, I found myself walking through the front door of the Heavenly Hotel.

"If it isn't my pal Sammy," the manager growled when he saw me coming up to the counter. He put aside his newspaper and rolled the unlit cigar over to the side of his mouth. "Haven't seen you in a while. . . . How's life?"

"Hey, André," I said, sounding like life was not nearly as dandy as three thousand dollars being tossed in your lap should make it. "I'm wondering if you've got odd jobs. You know—vacuuming, dusting, taking out the trash . . . ?"

An eyebrow arched as he studied me. His cigar rolled to the other side of his mouth, then back again, like it was on some sort of invisible pulley, making deliveries. Finally he clamped it between his front teeth and said, "You're what, thirteen?"

I nodded.

"Minimum age is fifteen."

"It doesn't have to be official." I looked over my shoulder. "And you really could use help around here. This place smells like rotten potatoes, and there's dust everywhere. . . ." I pulled a face. "When's the last time someone vacuumed?"

He shrugged and said, "I don't own it, you know. I just manage it."

"So? Manage to clean it. Hire me!"

He laughed, and that cigar stump teetered on his bottom lip for a second before he clamped down on it again. "So what are you suggesting I pay you?"

I thought a minute. "Whatever you think I'm worth."

He nodded and was about to say something but got distracted by two cops stepping into the hotel. "Now what?" he grumbled through the stump.

"This should be fun," I muttered, and in my gut I knew that cops being there had something to do with the *other* reason I'd wandered over to the Heavenly.

Mr. Buck Ritter from Omaha, Nebraska.

"You know them?" André asked, eyeing the cops.

"Uh-huh."

It was Squeaky and the Chick. I don't know their real names, but I do know that they're not really ready to be cops. For one thing, they're kinda young. For cops, anyway. Squeaky's all clean-cut with little apple cheeks, and the Chick wears fake fingernails and keeps her bleached-blond hair in a long braid that goes almost halfway down her back.

She also wears enough mascara to retar a road.

But the thing that bugs me about Squeaky and the Chick is that they act like they're all smart and full of authority, when they're actually kinda dumb.

Not that I'm *complaining*. I mean, it's a lot easier to get away with stuff—like, say, living someplace you're not supposed to be living—when you're dealing with cops like Squeaky and the Chick. But still.

I stepped aside, finding a seat in one of the Heavenly's funky green pointy-backed chairs, where I could disappear but still eavesdrop.

"How may I help you?" André said when they were up at the counter.

"An individual by the name of Buck Ritter was found to have expired last night. We have reason to believe he resided here, at your establishment."

I peeked around the chair and watched as André's eyebrow arched at Squeaky. "You're sayin' Buck's dead?"

Squeaky nodded. "Unfortunately, yes, sir. That is correct."

"How'd he die?"

"I don't know that we're at liberty to disclose the details of his demise," Squeaky said.

André arched the other eyebrow, and his cigar rolled lazily to the other side of his mouth. "Then I don't know that I'm at liberty to disclose the details of his residence."

The Chick scowled at her partner. "It's no biggie." She turned to André. "He had a heart attack, all right? We just need verification that he was staying here."

André nodded. "He was."

Squeaky cut in. "Mr. Ritter's next of kin will be arriving in the morning from out of town to settle his affairs. May we have your assurance that there'll be no problem with their accessing Mr. Ritter's domicile?"

André studied him with an amused smirk, then said, "I will grant them full access to his domicile."

"Very good," Squeaky said. "Then our purpose for being here is complete."

After they were gone, André shook his head and muttered, "What's this world comin' to?"

I laughed. "Yeah, they're a little different." Then, trying to be real casual-like, I asked, "So, who was this Buck Ritter guy?"

He shrugged. "You know how it is here. They come, they go." He flipped the paper back open. "Seemed like a nice fella. Said he was a war vet, but a lot of them say that." He turned the page and eyed me. "Some of them are obviously lyin', but I don't know that he was."

"Why would anyone lie about being a war vet?"

He shrugged. "Sympathy for the state they're in?"

"That's sad," I said.

He nodded and turned another page. "It's sad, all right. All the way around. Real vets *should* get respect and sympathy." He faced me straight on, the cigar stub clamped between his front teeth, looking like the barrel of a sawed-off shotgun. "Which is why fakers are so disgusting." He took a deep breath and put down the paper. "So, when you wanna start?"

"Start?" I blinked at him. "Uh . . . how about tomorrow morning?"

He nodded, then went back to his newspaper. "Sounds good."

Unbelievable as it was, it's not like I needed the money. And it's not like I *wanted* to clean the Heavenly. As my friend Hudson Graham would say, cleaning that hotel would be an exercise in futility. I mean, everything's beyond old. It's stained, falling apart, and just plain *stinky*.

But still. I felt good. I actually had a job! And I'd definitely covered my lie to Marissa, which was a giant relief.

I was also feeling very clever because I was now in a position to find out more about Mr. Buck Ritter. My plan was to get to the Heavenly in the morning and work until his relatives showed up. Maybe I'd strike up a conversation with them while I was conveniently cleaning the hallway of the floor Buck Ritter's room was on.

Maybe I'd find out why he hadn't asked me to give the money to them.

Maybe I wouldn't feel guilty anymore about spending some of that crisp green lining at the bottom of my backpack.

But the next morning when I showed up, I discovered that Buck Ritter's relatives had already come and gone.

"His brother showed up last night and left with one measly grocery sack, only half full," André grumbled. "Left a whole heap of junk for me to deal with." He handed over a box of Hefty bags and said, "Your first job is to shove all his things in bags—I'll take them to the Salvation Army. Then strip the sheets and toss 'em down the laundry chute. The towel, too."

"What room?" I asked. "And where's the laundry chute?"

"Room three-eleven." He handed over the key, saying, "The chute's about halfway down the hall, by the fire extinguisher. Just pull down the hatch and dump it in."

So I took the box of bags and the key, and as I was heading for the rickety, old-fashioned elevator, André called, "It all looked like junk to me, but if you find anything you'd like, go ahead and keep it."

It felt a little strange letting myself into the hotel room. The only other one I'd ever really been inside was rented to a chain-smoking fortune-teller known as Madame Nashira. And Buck Ritter's room was a lot like Madame Nashira's—peeling wallpaper, a stained sink with a cracked and clouded mirror over it, a small lumpy bed, and filthy carpeting. It didn't reek of cigarettes, though; it smelled like mildew.

The place was also a mess. The bedspread was balled up at the foot of the bed, the sheets were untucked, the mattress wasn't lined up with the box spring. . . . It was like he'd tossed and turned for a month straight. The dresser drawers were hanging open a few inches—like he'd been too tired to close them all the way. There were clothes draped over the footboard, over the desk chair, and on the floor. Everything seemed . . . disheveled.

Everything except a tidy stack of Styrofoam to-go boxes. There were about thirty of them nested together on the floor by the desk, large ones on the bottom, medium in the middle, small on top. They were dirty, but stacked neatly—like a load of dishes ready to be washed.

And the boxes being so tidy made me think that maybe Buck's brother had messed the place up.

Maybe he'd torn through everything looking for something.

Something that fit easily inside a grocery sack.

But what?

And maybe I should have felt creepy, snooping around the room of a man I'd scared to death, but I didn't feel creepy.

I felt curious.

What was a man with so much money on him doing living in a place like this?

Maybe he really *had* robbed someone.

Maybe that someone lived in the Senior Highrise.

But . . . nobody I knew kept stacks of cash lying around waiting to get stolen.

Especially at the Senior Highrise!

And the bills were all twenties. It was more like he'd robbed a *bank*.

So I was feeling more curious than grossed out or guilty, and I found myself snooping around a little desk near the window, looking for something that might explain what he'd been doing on the Highrise fire escape late at night with a boatload of cash in his pockets.

All I found on the desk, though, was an ancient black phone—one with no punch pad, let alone a redial function—a rusted lamp, a small notepad, and a gnawed-on pencil.

Inside the single drawer, I found a Bible, a small stack of sketches, and about a hundred years of grime.

The sketches were done on the same paper as the notepad that was on top of the desk. Three of them were of birds—one in flight, one on a branch, and one that was just the head. The other two were human faces, but just the eyes, nose, mouth, and eyebrows. Like faces floating free from their skulls.

The sketches were all really lifelike, which was amazing because they were actually made of really fine lines that *weren't* actually lines.

They were lines that were made up of gazillions of tiny dots.

The more I looked at the pictures, the more mind-boggling they seemed. How could you make a bird look that real out of *dots*?

But still. Mind-boggling or not, what did pictures made out of gazillions of dots tell me?

Not a doggone thing.

So I laid them on the desk and was just deciding to do what André had asked me to when the phone rang.

"Aaargh!" I cried, jumping back.

Then I just stood there like an idiot, staring at the

phone as it clanged away on the desk, wondering who could be calling.

Well, duh, I finally told myself. It's someone who knows Buck Ritter from Omaha, Nebraska! And then I had the brainy idea that maybe I'd be able to figure out something from *them*.

"Hello?" I said in a deep, rich Buck-Ritter-from-Omaha-Nebraska kind of voice.

"Sammy?" came the whispered response.

"André?" I asked in my normal voice.

"Get out of there," he said. "Get out of there fast!"

SEVEN

I was starting to slam down the phone when I heard André
say, "And don't . . ."

I put the phone back up to my ear. "Don't what?"

"Don't take anything! Dump whatever's in the bags!"
Then he added, "But take the bags!"

"What? Why?"

"Just do it!"

Dumping what I'd put in the bags was easy—which
goes to prove that it sometimes pays to get sidetracked. I
grabbed the box of garbage bags and slipped out of the
room, locking it behind me.

The trouble was, I didn't know where to go or why I
was supposed to get out of there so fast. But I hurried
away from the room, and when I heard the elevator clanging open down the hallway, I ducked into the stairwell.

The Heavenly's stairwell is like a house of horrors. It's
lined with mirrors that bounce your reflection back and
forth to infinity. And since the people who stay at the
Heavenly are usually kinda deranged-looking to begin
with, running into them on the stairs can be very scary.
Most people would rather risk their lives on the elevator.

So I tried to ignore my reflections as I hung around the corner, waiting to see who had just come out of the elevator. I was dying to know what could possibly have made André so jittery. I mean, when I first met André, he scared me with his tough looks, growly "Scat, kid," and menacing cigar. Now I get that he acts like that because of the people he has to deal with every day. Some may be down on their luck, but most of the people who stay at the Heavenly seem to spend their days walking a shaky line between freedom and jail.

Anyway, there I am, hanging back, waiting for some ghoulish monster, or maybe the *police,* to come clomping down the hall, when what do I see?

Two roly-poly middle-aged ladies.

"There it is, right there," one of them says. She's wearing a red-and-white checkered blouse that's really just a big rectangle with a hole for the head. And with her broad shoulders and the way the blouse is kinda flowing out behind her, this lady looks like a picnic table that's decided to get up and go for a stroll.

The other one's got on dark red pants and a bright yellow top and has a speckled green scarf swooped around her neck. "I cannot believe he spent his final days here," she says, keeping her voice low. "What was he *doing* here?"

As I watch them pass by the stairwell, it hits me that if the one lady's a picnic table, the other's the picnic condiments. And instead of the dish running away with the spoon, the ketchup, mustard, and relish are running away with the table!

Something about that totally cracks me up. Dumb, I

know, but the more I watch them hurry down the hall, the goofier I get about it.

Then all of a sudden there's a growl in my ear. "What are you snickerin' about?"

I jump, and there's André, eyebrow arched, cigar clamped between his teeth. "Nothing! Sorry!" I tell him, then try to act cool. "What's going on, anyway?"

"I let the wrong person in last night." He spies around the corner and adds, "Mr. Ritter had no brothers. Not livin', anyways."

"So wait. The guy you let into his room last night told you he was his brother but wasn't?"

"Uh-huh."

I wrap an eye around the corner, too, and whisper, "So those are his . . ."

"Daughters," he growls, and shows me a Sew Superior business card with the name Sandra Ritter-Boswell on it. *Specializing in Alterations, Curtains, and Quilts.* "I feel like a moron. I have no idea who that guy was last night or what he made off with."

"But it couldn't have been much, right? You said it all looked like garbage."

"Yeah, but who knows? And why'd he do that if it wasn't something important?"

I think about this a minute. "What did he look like?"

"Old. Old and bereaved." He snorts. "I even refunded Buck's unused days. Man, I got suckered."

I tisk and say, "Ouch," 'cause at the Heavenly it's cash up front *only,* so for André, refunding money to a guy who'd duped him was like adding injury to insult.

As we watch the Picnic Sisters fumble open the door to room 311, André mutters, "What if he did have something valuable? What if they're here to get it? What if they find out I let some joker in last night without checkin' ID or anything? I don't need the heat. I don't need another investigation!" He curses, then growls, "And I hate bein' duped." He eases back and says, "I've got to get back to the desk." He eyes me as he grabs the box of trash bags. "You know nothing, right?"

I nod. "Not a thing."

He heads back down the stairs, and his mutant reflections make the mad dash to infinity as he whispers, "Keep an eye on them. I'm willing to pay for useful information!"

Now, I find it hard to keep an eye on anyone I can't see. And since the Picnic Sisters have disappeared into room 311, I mosey over and stick my nose inside. "Excuse me," I say, trying hard to block the thought that I had, in fact, scared their father to death. "The manager sent me up to see if I could help you in any way."

They blink at me, and finally Condiments mutters to the Table, "This is a mighty strange place."

"You're right about that," I say with a laugh. Then I step inside the room and tell them, "I just help around here part-time." I shrug. "It's summer vacation. It's a job."

"Well, we appreciate the offer," Picnic Table says to me, "but we're fine."

"You're Buck's daughters?" I ask, not taking the hint to leave. "I'm sorry about . . . I'm sorry he . . . died."

"You knew our daddy?" Condiments asks.

I hesitate, then give a nod. "A little. He seemed nice." Then I add, "And he was an amazing artist."

Both ladies smile real big and say, "Yes, he was!" and that's when I notice that the Picnic Sisters are wearing some serious bling—rings, earrings, necklaces. . . . The stuff looks real, too.

Obviously, they didn't need the cash.

"We had no idea he'd taken a trip. Do you know what he was *doing* here?" Picnic Table asks me.

I shake my head. "They're kinda in the business of not asking questions around here . . . if you know what I mean."

She turns to her sister. "His trailer may have been small, but it was always clean and tidy. This place is just . . . awful." Then she sees the notepad sketches sitting on the desk. "Oh, look, Marabelle. Here's some of Daddy's doodles right here!"

They admire them for a minute, and then Condiments gives a little shudder. "Let's just collect his things and go, okay? I don't want to remember this. I want to get out of here."

So they move around, piling things up, but after collecting everything on the bed and checking the place over, Picnic Table shakes her head and says, "None of this is worth taking. There's nothing even sentimental here. What do you say, Marabelle? Should we just leave it?"

Condiments nods. "There's plenty of sentiment back in his trailer."

"David's going to want his uniform, you know that."

"Well, then you and I will divide his medals."

"David'll have a fit."

"He can't expect to get everything! He couldn't even be bothered leavin' work to help with the arrangements."

"He's probably at Daddy's now, pickin' over things for what he wants."

"Oh!" Condiments gasps. "You think so?"

A storm cloud has suddenly gathered over the Picnic Sisters. "Yes, I do," the Table says. "I'm a fool not to have thought of it sooner."

Now, what my brain picks out of this inside conversation is that Buck Ritter from Omaha, Nebraska, *was* a war vet. "He was in the army?" I ask.

"That's right," Condiments says.

"He was a war *hero*," her sister huffs. She shakes her head. "And he wound up here."

I follow them down the hall. "But . . . he didn't *move* here, right? He was just visiting, right?"

Picnic Table turns on me. "Look, honey, what's it matter? This ain't the Four Seasons like he deserved."

And with that, they marched for the elevator.

The instant they're a safe distance away, I race down the Stairway of Ill Re-Puke, passing by a rickety man who's taking each step carefully. He seems confused. Like he's not sure if he's himself or one of his mutant reflections.

"Huh?" he says as I dart by, and then I hear him breathe in and out in a real choppy way.

So I glance back, and what I see is him and all his mutant reflections clutching his chest with both hands, eyes peeled back in terror.

"Oh no!" I say, screeching to a halt. But when I go

zipping back up the stairs, his warbly voice says, "I'm fine, I'm fine." He gives me a shaky smile. "But you just about scared me to death!"

"I seem to be good at that," I mutter, then call, "I'm sorry!" and hurry down to the lobby.

Even with that little detour, I beat the Picnic Sisters by a mile. "Everything's cool," I tell André. "They're upset that he was staying here, but they weren't searching for anything. They're leaving everything behind."

"You talked to them?"

I nod. "You don't have a thing to worry about."

André takes a big, relieved breath, so I slip in a question I'd been wondering about all morning. "How long did he stay here?"

"Six weeks? Maybe seven?" He frowns. "Who was that cat from last night? What did he take? Bugs me."

Just then the elevator bangs and clangs and dings, so André whips out two green bills, shoves them toward me, and wags his cigar stub at the front door. "Scat."

I grab the cash and tell him, "I'm gone," then zip out of there before the Picnic Sisters can spot me.

Once I'm outside, I look at the money and gasp, "Forty bucks! Forty *bucks*?" 'Cause come on. I snoop all the time. I don't expect to be paid for it!

But as I'm jaywalking across Broadway, my brain starts racing faster than my feet, replaying everything that had happened. Running into Buck, scaring him to death, creeping out in the middle of the night to find his money . . . everything.

Which totally bugged me. I mean, why couldn't I just

be jazzed about adding the forty bucks to my jackpot of cash? Why did I have to think about Buck Ritter at all? Unless I found out that he'd *robbed* someone, it was over. Done with. Buck and his daughters would be winging back to Omaha, Nebraska, Buck's stuff would be donated to the Salvation Army, and someone new would move into room 311.

Why couldn't my stupid brain just let it go?

But the more I thought about it, the more puzzling the whole thing seemed.

Why would a guy who lived in a trailer in Omaha, Nebraska, come clear out to Santa Martina to stay at the Heavenly Hotel?

Was he doing business with someone at the Senior Highrise? But what kind of business? If it was legit, why take the fire escape? The fire escape was a total shortcut from the Heavenly, but you'd really only use it if you didn't want to be seen.

And he sure had acted like he didn't want to be seen— taking his time coming out . . . wearing a hat and dark clothes. . . .

And then there was the fact that him seeing me seeing *him* gave him a heart attack!

But what sort of sneaky business would an old guy be involved in?

Insurance fraud?

Tax evasion?

Blackmail?

Or wait! Maybe he was an old-guy drug dealer. Not for cocaine or meth or heroin or . . . you know, junkie drugs.

Maybe he sold medical marijuana or pain pills or . . . I don't know . . . miracle joint juice!

And maybe he'd collected the money but hadn't delivered the goods to some guy he'd been doing business with. So maybe that guy went to the Heavenly pretending to be Buck's brother so he could get his . . . stuff.

But who was he? And what could possibly cost three thousand dollars? And why pay three thousand dollars for something that wasn't *already* delivered?

I thought about it awhile, and since I couldn't seem to get past that roadblock of questions, I started thinking about other possibilities.

What if the three thousand dollars was a down payment on something Buck had been working on?

Like . . . a piece of art?

Or maybe Buck had won a bunch of money gambling?

But . . . the only gambling you can do in town is bingo night at St. Mary's Church, and you sure wouldn't make off with three thousand dollars.

So . . . maybe he *had* robbed someone? Maybe he had pulled off some sort of old-guy heist!

Or maybe it really was blackmail.

But . . . who was getting blackmailed, and why?

Thinking about it was making me crazy. I wanted to just let it go, but I couldn't.

Where *had* that jackpot of cash come from?

Whose money was stashed at the bottom of my backpack?

Whose money had I been spending?

EIGHT

Before I'd gone over to the Heavenly, I'd explained to Grams that André was letting me earn some money for cleaning the hotel lobby.

It had gone over like a bad joke.

Badda-boom.

And after fifteen minutes of arguing, she'd finally taken off the kid gloves and hit me with: "You are being so stubborn—just like your mother."

It was a low blow, but I didn't let it knock the wind out of me. And eventually she gave in, saying, "You'd better stick to cleaning the lobby—no going in anyone's room!"

"They don't do the maid thing there, Grams. Everyone's on their own."

"And don't come crying to me when he cheats you! The man obviously doesn't put much value in cleanliness."

So slipping back into the apartment after my little "cleaning" adventure, I couldn't help but wag André's twenties in the air. "Hellooo, Grams. Check out how badly I've been cheated!"

She looked up from the kitchen table, where she was paying bills. "Forty dollars?" she gasped. "Why . . . you've only been gone a couple of hours!" She glanced at the kitchen clock. "At most!"

I sat down across from her. "I guess André thinks I'm a hardworking, valuable employee."

She blinked at the money in my hand and shook her head. "When I was your age—"

"Yeah, yeah," I said, heading off her train of thought. "But back then bread was thirty-five cents a loaf, and girls wore dresses."

She hesitated. "Yes, of course." Then her eyes popped a little and she said, "Oh! Marissa called. She was very worked up about something. She wants you to call her right away."

I headed for the phone. "Did you tell her where I was?"

"Yes." She glanced over at me. "I hope you don't mind."

"Not a bit," I said, doing a mental arm pump. Now Marissa knew it was true—I had a job at the Heavenly.

"Hey, what's up?" I asked when Marissa answered the phone.

"You are not going to believe this! You are not *even* going to believe this!"

"What?"

"I've got no credit card, I've got no cell phone, I've got no cash!"

"Welcome to my world," I laughed. Then I said, "What did you *do?*" because at no time in Marissa's life has her mother cut her off from cash.

"I didn't do anything! It must be the stock market or

some bad investment or . . . I don't know! They won't tell me, but they're both losing it like I've never seen. It's been like a war zone here! Can you come over? Can you please come over?"

"Uh . . . how about we meet somewhere? A war zone sounds . . . you know . . . *dangerous*."

"They left, but *I* can't go anywhere because they fired Simone and put *me* in charge of Mikey!"

"They fired Simone? Wow."

Simone had been a lifesaver. She'd kept Marissa and Mikey from killing each other while their parents were off working all the time. Shoot, she'd kept *me* from killing Mikey. He's a won't-shut-up, won't-leave-you-alone, tattle-taling beast of a little brother.

Only he's a supersized tattletaling beast of a little brother.

Let's just say Mikey McKenze sidled up to the candy bar and never walked away.

Anyway, Simone getting canned meant Marissa's summer was officially a disaster. I did a quick check with Grams, then said, "I'm on my way."

Trouble is, the phone rang right away after I'd hung up, and when I snatched it up thinking it was Marissa calling back about something she'd forgotten, I discovered that it wasn't Marissa at all.

It was Mrs. Wedgewood.

"I've got a list, sugar," she said.

I held back a groan.

"Some shoppin' and a little laundry," she said, and I could practically see her cat-ate-the-canary smile.

"Uh, I'm sorta tied up with helping my grandmother this morning."

"Oh, it's not much. I'm sure you can work it in. Come over now, won't you?"

When I hung up, Grams frowned. "This has happened to you more than once—you've got to stop answering the phone!" Then she sighed and said, "So what does she want?"

"The usual," I grumbled.

"I'll do it," Grams said. "I'll just get her groceries when I get ours." She shook her head at her checkbook. "But I have to reconcile this first! I'm missing a hundred and twenty dollars somehow."

"Wow," I said, because in the checks and balances of Grams' finances, that was a lot of money.

But then it hit me that in the checks and balances of my secret stash, it was nothing, and in the back of my mind a little plan started forming.

"I'll get the laundry and the list," I said, heading for the door.

There was no one in the hallway, so I just scooted next door and let myself into Mrs. Wedgewood's apartment.

"How nice to see you, sugar!" she said.

The sweet-talking blackmailer.

She was sitting on a chair at her kitchen table, but with her size you couldn't even see the chair. It was like she was just levitating there. "Here's the grocery list, and the laundry's in the basket by my bed. If you wouldn't mind strippin' the sheets and addin' them to it?"

"Okay," I said, trying not to show how ticked off I was.

I went into her bedroom, yanked off her sheets, and hurled them at the already overflowing laundry basket, and I was just picking the whole load up when I heard someone knocking at the door.

"Come in!" hollered the Wedge.

Now, I was expecting it to be Grams, and I think Mrs. Wedgewood was, too, but as I was starting to leave the bedroom, I heard a man's voice say, "Hello? May I come in?" He had some kind of an accent. Maybe British?

I ducked back and held my breath.

"Why, hello . . . !" I heard Mrs. Wedgewood reply, and the tone of her voice was extra syrupy.

"Excuse this bold intrusion," the man said. "My name is Rex Randolf, and I'm here to thank you for your valiant efforts Tuesday night."

My mind's going, Valiant efforts? What valiant efforts? Does getting out of a shower qualify as a valiant effort? And I'm also trying to figure out his accent. It's not really British, it's more a *style* of talking. It's like a *sophisticated* accent.

So I take a sneaky peek out the bedroom doorway, and what do I see?

Some old guy wearing a red silk scarf, a beret, and tinted glasses. He's tall, and bald on top but with slicked-back hair on the sides, and has a gray moustache. His shoes are like black mirrors, and he's carrying a big ol' bouquet of flowers.

He moves out of view, so I creep forward and watch as Mrs. Wedgewood accepts the flowers. "My!" she says, beaming away. "How very thoughtful of you."

"Would you like me to put them in a vase?" he asks.

"Yes, thank you!" She points into the kitchen. "I believe there's a pitcher in the cupboard, right there."

After he gets the flowers taken care of, he says, "May I call you Rose?" And that's when it finally hits me why this guy is here. Somehow he'd found out that the 911 call had come from Mrs. Wedgewood's apartment—he thought *she* was the one who'd found Buck Ritter from Omaha, Nebraska, on the fire escape landing.

But . . . who was he? He didn't look like anyone I'd ever seen in the Senior Highrise, and he sure didn't look like a cop.

"Of course," Mrs. Wedgewood was saying. "But . . . how did you hear about me?"

"Why . . . the whole building's talking about you!"

"Really?"

"Of course! You're our Highrise celebrity!" He adjusted the pitcher of flowers on the table. "It must've been awful for you! What do you suppose he was doing there?"

"Uh . . . I have no idea. It's a complete mystery to me."

"The police say he didn't even live in this building! Did you get any clues from him? Did he say anything?"

"I, uh . . . I didn't hear a word."

"Was he carrying anything?"

"*Carrying* anything? Uh . . . not that I saw. . . ."

"What about the police?"

"What about them? Mr. Randolf, honestly, all your questions are exhausting me!"

"Oh, how thoughtless of me. Of course. You've been

through quite an ordeal." He turned the pitcher this way and that. "I know. Why don't you join us for Monte Carlo night tonight? It's quite enjoyable, and I'm sure it would do wonders to lift your spirits."

The wheels are still turning in Mrs. Wedgewood's blackmailing little brain, and even though she has no clue what this Rex Randolf guy is talking about, she's doing a great job of not letting on. "Well," she says, "I'm really not much of a card player."

He chuckles, "Not a problem. We play blackjack. It's not hard. I'll be more than happy to teach you."

"Really?" she says, her eyebrows rising clear up behind her curly black bangs.

"Certainly. Why don't I meet you in the rec room around seven-thirty. I'll save you a seat."

"It's tonight?"

He nods. "That's right."

"Why . . . yes! I'd be delighted."

"Very good. I'll be looking for you."

On his way out, he makes a showy old-world bow, and the minute he's gone, Mrs. Wedgewood calls, "Sugar pie! Ooooh, sugar pie . . . !"

I know she's talking to me, so I come out so she can see me.

"Don't tell me you didn't hear all that, 'cause I know you did." She crosses her arms and drills me with her beady brown eyes. "What is goin' on around here?"

Now, in my head I feel like I'm playing blackmailer chess. And I try to think several moves ahead, but after about four if-I-do-this-and-she-does-thats, I finally say,

"You called 911 the other night, trying to save a man's life."

She blinks at me. "I *did*?"

I shrug and kind of look at the ceiling.

"They think I saved a man's life?"

"Actually . . ." I pull a face. "You tried to, but he died."

"He *died*?" Her face crinkles up. "How did I let *that* happen?"

"Uh . . . he had a massive heart attack? You couldn't do much about it?"

"Oh," she says, eyeing me. "But you're saying I tried my best?"

"You certainly did."

She thinks a minute. "Hmm. And where did I happen upon this dying man?"

I pinch my lips together and take a deep breath. "On the fourth-floor landing."

"Of the *stairs*?"

"Actually . . . it was the fire escape."

She gasps. "They think *I* went out on the fire escape to save a man's life? I can barely get to the elevator!"

I scratch my eyebrow. "Look. Do you want to be the Highrise celebrity or not?"

And now we're at the move where I'm hope-hope-hoping she'll say yes, but really, I'm not sure. But my having any chance of winning this game—or at least not losing it—depends on her saying yes.

She blinks at me a minute, then says, "If *you* don't mind, sugar, *I* don't mind."

I try not to act too relieved. "Actually, it wasn't me. It was Grams."

"Uh-*huh*," she says, like a smarty-pants blackmailer.

"I'm serious. But I'm sure she won't mind you being the Highrise's celebrity." I grin at her and add, "Although that Rex Randolf seems *very* classy."

"He does, doesn't he?" she says, blushing.

"And you know, now that I think about it, Grams might be interested in straightening everything out."

"No, no! This is probably best all around."

"Hmm," I say, like I'm giving it some serious thought, "maybe so."

"Then it's settled."

I take her shopping list. "So I guess I should give this to Grams and get your laundry started so you'll have something to wear to Monte Carlo night, huh?"

She was all for that.

And I was all for finding out about Mr. Rex Randolf.

He was up to something.

But what?

NINE

My doing laundry at the Senior Highrise is ridiculously complicated. I have to sneak down the fire escape, go through the front door, make a big deal of saying hello to the manager, Mr. Garnucci, and letting him know why I'm there, go up the elevator and through the hallways, get the laundry, and haul it down to the basement.

All that so if any nosy old guy reports me, Mr. Garnucci can tell him I've got permission to be there.

And *then*, when I'm all done fluffing and folding and delivering the laundry, I have to make a big deal of leaving the building so Mr. Garnucci knows I'm not staying there.

Now, I wasn't about to wait through the whole wash/dry/fluff-and-fold process. Marissa was waiting for me to save her from Mikey! So I just crammed Mrs. Wedgewood's laundry into some washers and got out of there.

On my way out, I took a quick detour into the Highrise's alcove of mailboxes. And I looked and I looked, but I couldn't find a box for Rex Randolf or R. Randolf or any other kind of Randolf.

"Get that laundry going?" Mr. Garnucci boomed as I approached his desk. Mr. Garnucci is always shouting everything he says, probably from having to deal with old people all day. It's like going past a gale force of words.

"Yeah," I tell him. "I'm doing Mrs. Wedgewood's, too."

"You," he shouts, "are a rare and wonderful child!"

"Well, um, thank you, but um . . . hey . . ." I glance around. "Mrs. Wedgewood asked me to find out how she can get a message to Rex Randolf."

"Who?" he bellows.

"Rex Randolf," I whisper. "And could you please not shout? She doesn't want people to know she's . . . you know . . . *enamored.*"

"Oh," he says. Then he whispers really loud, "Well, I'd like to help her out, but I don't know of any Rex Randolf."

"Mrs. Wedgewood says he lives in the building." I shrug. "Apparently, he brought her flowers and invited her to Monte Carlo night."

Mr. Garnucci's eyes pop. "Someone brought Rose *flowers?*"

"Someone named Rex Randolf."

He leans back and shakes his head. *"Maybe,"* he says, looking from side to side, "he's an *imaginary* friend."

Now, I know Rex Randolf is not imaginary, but I laugh and say, "Maybe! Although she gave a lot of detail—handsome, snazzy dresser, beret, neck scarf, moustache, sophisticated accent. . . ."

"In *this* building?" He laughs. "Definitely imaginary."

So I wave and head for the door, calling, "Oh, well. I'll be back later to switch the laundry over."

"See you then!" he booms.

By the time I got to Marissa's, it was one o'clock and I was starving.

"What *took* you so long!" Marissa said when she threw open the door.

I pushed past her, out of the heat and into the coolness of the McKenze mansion. "Let's see . . . sneaky old men with flowers, sweet-talking blackmailers with mountains of laundry, and . . . and you don't exactly live next door!"

She shook her head like, Whatever, then closed the door behind me. "Well, Mikey's in terror mode. And my mother keeps calling here looking for my dad! She's driving me nuts!"

"So quit answering the phone, lock yourself in your room, and ignore Mikey."

"I don't want to lock myself in my room! I don't want to be stuck in this house with Mikey, but I'm not allowed to leave without him!"

"So let's take him to the mall and park him in front of the fish tanks."

"You have no idea what you're saying. I can't just drag him around like I used to. He doesn't listen to me. And he weighs more than I do!"

"How about—"

"And I'm sorry, but I don't know when I'm going to be able to pay you back for the swimsuits!"

She was biting on a nail, fidgeting all over the place—something I haven't seen her do in a long, long time. "Look, just don't worry about it."

"Don't worry about it? Don't *worry* about it?"

"You've done plenty of stuff for me—just forget it, okay?"

The phone rang and she snatched it off an entry hall table, snapping, "What!" into the receiver. Two seconds later her face looked instantly sunburned. "Uh . . . hold on." She covered the receiver and mouthed, "It's *Danny*."

I pulled a little ooooh face and couldn't help chuckling—it was nice to know I wasn't the only one who did stupid things with a phone.

She composed herself, then said, "Hello?" all cheery and sweet-like. "Huh? Oh . . ." She dropped her voice. "Yeah, that was my mom. She's kinda stressed." She went cheery again. "So, what's up?"

She eyes me like, Was that believable? So I gave her the thumbs-up and listened as she fidgeted around the room, saying, "Uh, yeah . . . I'm sure that's all right . . . you know, as long as you can vouch for them. . . ." She looked at me suddenly and smiled. "Well, Casey's a no-brainer, of course. Billy too." She raised an eyebrow my way. "They're probably already invited."

I cringed and looked away. She'd been telling me to invite Casey to Brandon's pool party, but for some reason I just hadn't done it. Something about mixing the old with the new felt . . . uncomfortable.

Or maybe it was something about having Casey see me in colorful underwear that was making me uncomfortable.

Slightly!

But it was too late now. The deed was done.

And once again I'd come out a Casey-calling coward.

When Marissa hung up, she put her hands on her hips and craned her neck toward me. "I can't believe you never called him!"

"Stop that!" I said, looking away. I eyed her and muttered, "You look like a vulture."

"Yeah? Well, you're a chicken!"

I sighed and toed the floor with my high-top. "Look, I just want to play water hoops. I don't want to worry about—"

"Being with friends? Having a little *fun*?"

"Looking like a dork!" I said, facing her straight on. "Like I want him to see me in a bathing suit? Soaked?"

"You look great in that suit! And you look great soaked!"

I rolled my eyes. "Whatever. Look, can we go *do* something? How about the movies? We could sit Mikey up front . . . ?"

Marissa frowned. "No cash, no credit, remember?"

I spread my arms out and looked around. "In this whole house, you can't scrape together enough money to go to the movies?"

She shook her head. "Isn't that pathetic?" She hesitated. "Maybe I could sell CeCe some knickknacks?"

The McKenzes' "knickknacks" are expensive works of art or, you know, outrageously priced blobs of glass. There's one that Mrs. McKenze calls the Kraval that I'm afraid to even *breathe* near. It just looks like a hollowed-out crystal basketball, but apparently it's worth a fortune.

Anyway, the point is, there was no way Marissa would

ever take any of the McKenzes' knickknacks to CeCe's Thrift Store. It would be, like, a death sentence. So very casually, I said, "I could buy us tickets."

Marissa's eyes bugged. "How much money do you *have*?"

I laughed. "I worked for André this morning, remember?"

"Still!" She cocked her head a bit, then laughed. "Well, sure! Let's get Mikey's leash and go."

"His *leash*?"

Turns out, she wasn't kidding.

TEN

The McKenzes don't have a dog, so why they even had a leash was a mystery to me. But then Marissa explained that it's how Mrs. McKenze used to keep tabs on Mikey at amusement parks and stuff, so he developed a positive association with the leash.

Or something.

Whatever, he really didn't seem to mind. He just let Marissa clip it to a belt loop of his jeans, and off we went.

From Marissa's house to the movie theater was all downhill, so walking Mikey there was no problem. We actually had a good time. Plus, it was nice and cool in the theater, the movie was funny, and we ran into Dot and her brothers, which was fun.

Afterward I made a quick detour to the Senior Highrise to switch Mrs. Wedgewood's laundry into a dryer while Marissa finished wiping out the rest of André's money by bribing Mikey with a Double Dynamo ice cream from Maynard's Market.

But when we finally started the trek back to Marissa's house, Mikey started rattling off complaints. "My feet hurt. I'm tired. I'm thirsty. It's too far. . . ."

"Come *on*," Marissa said, clipping the leash back on.

"But I'm tired."

"How can you be tired? We've barely even started!"

"I'm thirsty!"

"You just had an ice cream!"

"But I *am* thirsty!"

"Maybe if you hadn't hogged all the popcorn at the movies, you wouldn't be thirsty!" Marissa grumbled, dragging him along.

"But I *am*," he said, then pulled a total bulldog face and sat down in the middle of the sidewalk.

"Come on," Marissa said, yanking on the leash. "How else are you going to get home?"

"Call Mom!"

"I don't have a phone anymore, remember? And she won't come anyway. We've got to walk."

He crossed his arms, and his face sort of buried in on itself. "No!"

"Get up!"

"No!"

Marissa yanked again, but the only thing that budged was his belt loop. It gave way, and the leash came flying toward her. "Why am I doing this?" Marissa asked, throwing her hands in the air. "Why am I even doing this?"

I squatted in front of Mikey. "How old are you, Mike? Five?"

"Shut up! I'm nine!"

"Nine?" I said with my eyebrows up. "You're kidding, right? There's no *way* you're nine. Six, maybe. At the most."

"I'm nine!"

I snorted. "You're six. Max."

He turned all red in the face, then stood up and started after me. I darted off, then held back, letting him almost catch me before speeding up again. "See?" I said after I'd yo-yoed him along for a while and he was starting to give up. "You're wimping out, just like a six-year-old."

"I'm NINE!"

He started after me again, but after a while he just couldn't run anymore. So I called, "Hey, I bet I know where we could get you something cold to drink."

"Really?" he said, gasping for air.

"Follow me!" I called, and took off again.

Marissa kept up with me, checking over her shoulder the whole way. "Let me guess—Hudson's?"

I tossed her a grin. "Uh-huh."

"Good ol' Hudson," she said, tossing one back.

Hudson may be seventy-three, but he's one of my best friends. He's got a never-ending supply of patience, iced tea, and good advice, and his porch is where I usually wind up when I've got problems.

And Mikey McKenze was definitely a problem.

"Sammy!" he said, swinging his yellow cowboy boots down from the porch railing when he saw me coming up the walkway. "How are you, stranger?" Then right away he added, "And you've brought Marissa. What a nice surprise!" He cocked his head a bit when he saw the leash in her hand. "If you're here to walk Rommel, I'm afraid he's no longer with us."

"Oh! Hudson, I'm so sorry!" I said, because even though Hudson's dog had gotten old and deaf and hobbly, he'd been Hudson's little buddy forever.

"No tears, now," Hudson said when he saw my face. "He had a really good life. And it was definitely time."

Suddenly Mikey comes blustering up the walkway, ruddy-faced and mad. "I'm telling!" he cries. "I'm tellin' Mom you tried to ditch me, and she's gonna ground you!"

"I'm already grounded," Marissa shouts back, "by *you*."

"Oh my," Hudson says, his bushy white eyebrows raised high.

"Hudson, *this* is Mikey," I say with great, dramatic flair. "Mikey, this is Mr. Graham." I zero in on Mikey. "And you'd better be polite, or you can forget about getting anything cold to drink."

Mikey just glowers as he pants at the base of the porch.

"Ah," Hudson says, heading for his front door. "It's a long walk up to Jasmine Street, isn't it, Mike?"

When Hudson's safely inside, Mikey pulls a squinty little face and says, "He's *old*. And he's wearing *yellow* boots."

"That's his style," I tell him. "He's got boots in all kinds of colors and styles."

"Yellow's weird," he grumbles, then just stands there, his forehead gushing sweat.

Hudson reappears a couple of minutes later with two pitchers, a stack of plastic cups, and a bowl of strawberries. "What's your pleasure, Mike, iced tea or ice water?"

Mikey frowns. "Don't you have any Coke?"

"I'm offering iced tea and water," Hudson says evenly.

Mikey just stands there with rivers of sweat running down his face.

"I'll have tea!" I say. "And those strawberries look

amazing!" They were, too. They were big and a beautiful deep red.

So while Mikey's body's stewing in its own steamy salt bath, the rest of us have a cool drink and delicious strawberries. And when Mikey finally *does* decide that iced tea is better than nothing, he takes one sip and sprays it out into the bushes.

"Mikey!" Marissa scolds.

"It's awful!"

"It's unsweetened," she says between gritted teeth.

"So where's the sugar?" Mikey whines.

I was so embarrassed. And I was ticked off, too. I mean, what a brat! But it didn't seem to faze Hudson a bit. He didn't lecture or scold, and he didn't bring out any sugar. He just sipped tea and watched Mikey and Marissa bicker.

Finally I said, "Well! I think we should be going."

"No!" Mikey whined. He looked at Marissa. "I wanna call Mom!"

Marissa eyed Hudson like, Can we *please* use your phone? But Hudson just gave her a sage smile and said to Mikey, "Sorry, Mike. No phone available."

I really wanted to bail on going back to the McKenzes'. My skateboard was still there, but I figured I'd get it later. I'd had more than enough of Mikey McKenze for one day!

But when I said something about needing to get back to Mrs. Wedgewood's laundry, Marissa latched on to me and said, "You can't abandon me now! You have got to help me get him home!"

"But . . . if the Nightie-Napper takes the Wedge's stuff, I'll never hear the end of it!"

Hudson's eyebrows shot up. "The *Nightie-Napper*?"

"They haven't caught him yet?" Marissa asks.

Now, the truth is, I didn't know if they'd figured out who'd been stealing clothes from the Highrise dryers, and I didn't care. Actually, I suspected that it was all just made up. I mean, what else is there in the way of excitement at the Senior Highrise? But I was so sick of dealing with Mikey that I was desperate for a way out.

Marissa rolled her eyes. "Oh, come on! Who'd want to steal *her* stuff?"

"No, really," I said as she dragged me down the steps, "if you were the Nightie-Napper, she'd be *just* the person you'd want to steal from! You could make curtains for a whole apartment out of just one muumuu!"

"What's a muumuu?" Mikey asked, trailing behind us.

Marissa kept dragging me along.

I ignored Mikey and continued pleading my case. "It took two machines to wash six pairs of her undies!"

Marissa stopped and faced me. "Undies are not nighties. Or even muumuus!"

"What's a muumuu!" Mikey demanded.

"It's a big tent of a dress, all right?" I snapped, then turned to Marissa. "Look, they call him the Nightie-Napper, but he steals all sorts of stuff! Sheets, dresses. . . . Do you have any idea how much trouble I'll be in if her good muumuu gets snatched?"

Marissa kept dragging. "You got me into this, you're getting him home!"

I scowled at her and grumbled, "That's the last time I take you to the movies!" But really, what could I do? I caved. And pretty soon Marissa switched from dragging me to dragging Mikey.

Ordinarily, it would have taken ten or fifteen minutes to walk to the McKenzes', but with Mikey dragging and plopping down every half block and *crying*, it took almost forty-five.

The good thing was that when we got to the McKenzes', Mikey went to his room and totally left us alone.

As Hudson says, a tired dog is a good dog.

The *bad* thing was that even though Mikey was no longer being a pest, Marissa was in the world's worst mood, and I couldn't seem to snap her out of it. "I hate my life!" she kept saying, then moaned about her stupid brother and her stupid parents and the fact that she had no stupid money.

Frankly, being "trapped" in her bedroom *suite* surrounded by all her *stuff*, I was having a little trouble sympathizing. And since I really did need to get back and finish Mrs. Wedgewood's laundry, I finally just took off.

I loved tearing down the hill on my skateboard. My whole focus was on avoiding cracks, dodging rocks, and hopping curbs. It was like a high-speed obstacle course where I could crash and burn at any time. No puzzling thoughts, no worries, no Mikey . . . just the wind in my face and the rush of ball bearings battling it out with gravity.

I made it down the hill in one shaky piece, then cruised

along catching my breath. And as I approached Cypress Street, I decided to make a quick stop at Hudson's to apologize for subjecting him to Mikey-The-Whiner-McKenze.

Hudson was still on the porch, or *back* on the porch—who knows? Shoot, he'd had enough time to mow the yard, wash the windows, *and* take a nap.

Anyway, his yellow boots were propped up on the rail and he was reading the newspaper, but the minute he saw me coming up his walkway, he closed the paper and sat up. "Say! I'm glad you came back."

I grabbed my board and went up the steps. "I just wanted to say I'm sorry for bringing Mikey over. Marissa's parents let their nanny go, so Marissa's stuck with him all day 'cause she's home for summer and her parents are still going off to work. Nobody can handle him. He's just . . . impossible." Then I nodded at the newspaper and tried to be real casual as I said, "What's going on in the news? Robberies? Murders? Burglaries?"

He shook his head. "Not a thing." He smiled at me. "Let's hope the trend continues, right?"

I laughed. "Right!"

He put the paper aside. "Interesting you should come back," he said. "I've been thinking."

I plopped down in the chair next to him. "Yeah?"

"It seems to me that Mike could benefit from some structure. Some discipline." He eyed me. "And some better eating habits." He poured me a glass of tea and handed it over. "From the bits and pieces you've told me, I have the impression that the parents aren't around much. . . . Is that right?"

"They're *never* around. Even when they are, they're not."

"Hmm," he said, and then just sat there for the longest time.

"What?" I finally asked, because I could tell he was thinking *some*thing.

"How do you think they would feel about having Mike come here during the day for the rest of the summer?"

"Come *here*?" I snorted. "Marissa would love that, but you're crazy! You saw him—Mikey's a nightmare!"

Hudson gave a wily smile. "He'd be just fine."

"But . . . I don't get it. *Why?*"

He gave a little shrug. "It's been pretty quiet around here since Rommel passed." He laced his fingers together across his stomach. "And the way I see it, it won't be long before it's too late to help Mike. Now . . . well, I believe I could turn him around."

I blinked at him a minute. "Turn him around? Do you have any idea what that's gonna take? He needs boot camp or something."

Hudson nodded. "Mm-hmm."

I sat up straighter. "Mm-hmm? So it'd be like Hudson's Boot Camp?"

Hudson threw back his head and laughed. "I hadn't thought of it that way, but I like the double entendre. Although it would be more of a day camp than a boot camp." He chuckled. "But maybe I'll buy him a pair of boots at the end of it."

"So . . . you're really serious?"

He took a deep breath, then smoothed back one of his

bushy white eyebrows. "It's probably more up to them than me. They may be insulted, or they may be uncomfortable with the idea. I couldn't blame them on either account, but yes, I think I'll make the offer."

We talked about it some more, and I wound up giving Hudson the McKenzes' phone number. And the whole way home I just kind of shook my head in amazement at Hudson, thinking about what a cool guy he is. What a *good* guy he is. I mean, come on, who in the world voluntarily takes on Mikey McKenze?

And thinking about all that got me thinking how Hudson had been a rock-solid friend to me since day one. He was always helping me out. Always helping me *figure* things out. Maybe it was about time I did something for *him*.

The more I thought about it, the more I liked the idea. But it had to be something totally cool. Something totally unexpected.

And then it hit me that I could actually *buy* him something! I had money! He wouldn't have to know it was from me. I could just deliver it to his porch with an anonymous thank-you card.

Or wait—a secret admirer card!

Yeah, I thought as I clicked along toward the Senior Highrise, a surprise gift from a secret admirer would make Hudson feel really good. Really . . . happy. It wouldn't be some cheap little knickknack, either. Hudson Graham deserved something *nice*.

After all, I had the money—why not spend it?

ELEVEN

"There you are, Sammy-girl!" Mr. Garnucci shouted when I came through the front door. "Mrs. Wedgewood called down here wondering if I knew what had happened to you!"

I headed toward the basement. "Hey, I've got my own chores at home! It's not like I *live* here, you know!"

He chuckled and waved, and off I went, zipping down to the basement to pick up Mrs. Wedgewood's laundry. And when I had everything crammed into the basket, I put my skateboard upside down across the top of it, anchored the whole thing with my chin, and took the elevator up to the fifth floor.

Now, Mrs. Wedgewood does not appreciate getting her laundry back in a big crumpled mess, and I don't appreciate the way she micromanages the folding of her Dumbo-sized drawers. So I did what I always do when I'm stuck with her laundry.

I went home.

And I was actually looking forward to having a nice little folding session with Grams while I told her all about Mikey and the leash and Hudson's Boot Camp, but the minute I walked through the door, I tripped.

I didn't trip *on* anything—it was just the unexpected sight of my mother that sent my skateboard clanking and the laundry and me sprawling.

"Are you all right?" my mother gasped in her overly dramatic soap star way.

I looked around frantically, going, "Where's Dorito?" because the last time my mother visited, she let him out and I almost lost him for good.

"He's fine!" Grams said. Then she added, "He's hiding in the closet."

"Smart cat," I grumbled, standing up.

I eyed my mother suspiciously as I put the clothes back inside the basket. "Why are you here? What happened?"

For such a good actress, she gave a really fake laugh. "Nothing *happened*, I just thought I'd surprise you with a visit."

"It was a double surprise for me," Grams laughed. "I ran into her at the grocery store!"

My face pinched. "At the *grocery* store?" I turned to my mother. "What were you doing at the grocery store?"

She gave me a movie star smile. "I didn't want to show up empty-handed!"

Grams laughed again. "I was doing Mrs. Wedgewood's shopping, and there she was!" She leaned in a little, acting like she was sharing something top-secret. "Jewel has gone into a coma, so your mother has a few days off."

Jewel is my mother's character on *The Lord of Willow Heights,* and even though comas, amnesia, sudden deaths, and resurrections are nothing out of the ordinary for soaps, her being home because her character was out of commission for a few days was.

"What?" my mother said, because my face was still pinched. "Must you always be so suspicious?" She gave me a hug and then sat very daintily on the edge of the couch. "Can't a mother come home to see her daughter once in a while?"

A year ago I would have snipped, Yeah, I've wondered the same thing myself hundreds of times! but now I just gathered the laundry and started folding Mrs. Wedgewood's clothes.

The first thing I picked up was a pair of granny panties. My arms could barely stretch wide enough to hold them straight.

"What are *those*?" my mother gasped.

"Blackmailer briefs," I said, folding one arm in, then the other arm over.

"*What?*" my mom said with a lot of dramatic wind gushing from her mouth.

Grams jumped in, saying, "They're Rose's underwear."

Mom's jaw dropped. "She must be *enormous*."

"Shhhh!" Grams whispered. "She'll hear you!"

I eyed her. "Like her being enormous is a secret or something?" But she was right—the rest of Mrs. Wedgewood might be a disaster, but her hearing is strangely bionic.

So while Grams and my mother lowered their voices and gossiped about the Wedge, I fluffed and folded and sorted and stacked. And when I was all done, I said, "I'll be back," and went next door to deliver the laundry.

The first thing Mrs. Wedgewood said was not Thank you so much! or Nice of you to spend your day doing my laundry, or anything you might expect someone to say after you've washed and dried and folded her clothes. No, she said, "Took your sweet ol' time, didn't you?"

"My friend had an emergency," I said, pushing past her.

"Well, I'm sure my dress is going to need ironing now."

And that's when it hit me—I hadn't folded her dress.

I hadn't seen it since I'd moved it into the dryer.

Inside, I'm going, Oh no! But on the outside, I'm trying to stay cool. "No problem," I tell her as I move toward her bedroom. "You want me to put these away?"

"Why, yes, sugar. That would be most appreciated."

So I put away Mrs. Wedgewood's clothes, and sure enough, there's no dress. "Wow," I tell her as I take a different muumuu out of her closet. "I'll bet this looks great on you!"

She shakes her curly-haired head. "It washes me out. Makes me pale and sickly lookin'. That's the problem with mail order. You just can't tell from a catalog, and it's too much bother to return."

"How about this one?" I ask, taking another dress out. "Ooooh. Now *this* has Rex Randolf written all over it. Subtle, classy . . ."

"Sugar, that is *ugly*."

I wanted to scream, So why's it in your closet? but I'm busted anyway. Her eyes zoom down on me as she hobbles forward with her walker. "What happened to my dress? Did you ruin it in the wash? Did you *bleach* it?"

"Uh . . . your dress?" I say, looking around like it's gotta be there somewhere.

"Yes," she snaps, "my dress! What happened to it?" Then she gasps and her eyes pop wide open. "The Nightie-Napper! The Napper got it, didn't he!" She clanks forward. "This is your fault! This is all your fault! You should never have left my things alone in that basement!"

"Look, Mrs. Wedgewood," I say, scooting for the door. "I probably just accidentally left it in the dryer. I'll be right back."

But it wasn't in the dryer. It wasn't anywhere. And after I tried to negotiate with her about it, Mrs. Wedgewood finally dropped the sweet talk and went straight for blackmail. "Buy me a new one—or else!" She looked at her wristwatch, which was like a mini boa constrictor choking off her wrist. "Monte Carlo night starts in one hour. Go to Large and Lovely in the mall, and don't you *dare* just buy me the cheapest thing you can find! Nothing in peaches or beiges. . . . I want something festive! Blues, greens. . . . The one I had was perfect! I can't believe you let the Nightie-Napper steal it!" She clanked toward me with her walker. "What are you waitin' for, girl? GO!"

"But I don't have any money!" I tried, looking as pathetic as possible.

"Then *find* some!" she snapped, and pushed me out the door.

Now, I guess I could have asked my mother for money.

But my mother would have made a horrible fuss, and knowing her, she would have found some way of ruining everything. I mean, I could just see Mrs. Wedgewood ratting on me because my mom was on her high horse. And moving to Hollywood to live with her instead of Grams was the last thing I wanted. Aside from leaving all my friends behind, I'd be living with a person who played a formerly amnesiac, currently comatose aristocrat on a gag-me soap. Not my idea of fun, especially since my mother "adopts" her character, practically living the role in real life.

And I guess I could have asked Grams, but I knew she was still worried about the hundred and twenty dollars that she'd lost somewhere in her checkbook.

And since I already *had* found some money, I went back to my apartment, grabbed my backpack and skateboard, and said, "I'll be right back."

"Wait!" my mother and Grams both cried. Then Grams said, "Dinner's just about ready!"

Something delicious-smelling was baking in the oven, and I was starving, but I had no time. "I have to go get something for Mrs. Wedgewood. I'll be back in less than an hour. Go ahead and eat without me!" Then I zipped out of there.

I was ticked off, all right. And I really resented spending my hard-found money on the Blackmail Whale, but I did find a "festive" muumuu in quadruple-XL on the sale rack. And then on my way out of the mall I spotted something in the art gallery window that I thought Hudson might really like. It wasn't an Ansel Adams or a Howard Bond or some other black-and-white photographer Hudson admires, but there was something about it that I really liked.

I was in a hurry, though, so I didn't go in and see how much it was. I just jetted back home.

"Here," I said, delivering the muumuu to Mrs. Wedgewood.

"Ooooh," she said, turning on the sugar. "Why . . . it's perfect!" Then she smiled at me and said, "I'm sorry for getting so testy before. It's just that it's been ages since I've been invited out, and then to have nothing to wear? You understand, right, sugar?"

I almost said, No, you blackmailing, slave-driving, ungrateful hippo! but instead, I bit my tongue and made a speedy exit.

Now, normally when I tell Grams I'll be right back, I'm *not* right back. I'm sidetracked somewhere trying to *get* right back. And then a lot of times something *else* happens and I wind up getting sidetracked from my *sidetrack*.

I've been known to be really, *really* late.

But this time I was back *way* within the hour like I'd promised, only instead of getting praised for not being late, I walked in to find Grams fuming.

For once, though, it wasn't at me.

"Where's Mom?" I asked, looking around.

"Apparently," Grams said, tying an apron around her waist, "our apartment is not up to Lady Lana's standards."

"What?"

She gave me a prim look. "Your mother saw a mouse."

"Oh, good grief," I said. "She freaked out?"

"The tail was still twitching in Dorito's mouth, and there was blood." She eyed me. "Need I say more?"

I served myself some leftover casserole. It had broccoli in it, but I didn't even care. I was *starving*. "So where'd she go?"

"Back to Hollywood, for all I care." She ran water into the sink, saying, "She appears without warning, insults me, and disappears. Why'd she even bother to come? I can do without surprises like that!"

"Wow, Grams," I said, taking a big bite. "She doesn't usually get to you this bad. What did she say?"

She frowned at me over her shoulder. "She called our home a flea-infested hovel."

That was a *really* low blow, even for my mother, because Grams takes great pride in keeping the apartment spotless.

Now, you'd think that I'd be happy that for once someone besides me was back-combed by my mother, but I actually just felt bad for Grams. And I didn't really know what to say, so instead of saying anything about the infamous Lady Lana, I wolfed down some more casserole, then asked, "Do you need me to get rid of the mouse?"

"I already took care of it," she said, but her chin was quivering. And before I could say anything else, the phone rang. "That's probably her." She sniffed. "The ungrateful prima donna!" She snatched up the phone and in a very controlled voice said, "Hello?"

Two seconds later I could tell it was not my mother.

Judging by Grams' deep breathing and closed eyes and counting to ten, it could only be one person.

Rose Wedgewood.

"Fine," Grams said. "She'll be right over." And when she hung up the phone, she looked at me and said, "Our neighbor wants your help getting dressed for Monte Carlo night." Her lips pressed together a moment, then she went back to the sink and snapped on yellow dish gloves. "Monte Carlo night! If that woman is mobile enough to meet a date at Monte Carlo night, she's mobile enough to do her own laundry!"

But I was actually glad she'd called.

I was hoping it would give me the chance to figure out what Rex Randolf was really up to.

TWELVE

I really didn't think Rex Randolf was planning to meet Mrs. Wedgewood at Monte Carlo night. If he was, why would he use a fake name?

Or if it was his real name and he didn't live in the building, why was he acting like he did? And how would he know about Monte Carlo night?

No, I was pretty sure he wanted Mrs. Wedgewood out of her apartment so he could get *into* her apartment.

So he could *case* the joint.

I also suspected this had something to do with my hitting pay dirt. If he thought the Wedge had tried to rescue Buck, then he probably also thought she had the money.

And it was looking like he wanted it back.

But if it was his to get back, why would he go through all this Monte Carlo night stuff? I mean, if Buck Ritter from Omaha, Nebraska, had stolen the money from him, ol' Rex would've come right out and said, That dirty rotten son of a gun robbed me! instead of going through this whole stupid "thank you for your valiant effort" rigmarole.

Besides, according to Hudson, no robberies or burglaries or murders had been reported.

And the more I thought about it, the more it seemed that Rex Randolf might be the "old and bereaved" guy who'd been over at the Heavenly taking stuff out of Buck's room. The whole situation was starting to feel bigger than three thousand dollars.

It felt . . . sneaky.

Shady.

Almost desperate.

But . . . maybe I was just feeling guilty. Maybe there was a perfectly reasonable explanation for all of this and I was just jumping to wacko conclusions because I'd been spending the money of a guy I'd scared to death. Maybe Rex Randolf was just a lonely old guy trying to fill his day with a little excitement. A lot of people in the Senior Highrise drive Grams crazy because they let little problems fill their whole day. "Don't they have anything better to do?" she grumbles.

But Rex Randolf sure *looked* like a guy who had a life. A beret? Tinted glasses and a silk scarf? Come on—a guy without a life would not dress like that!

And that's when it hit me.

Maybe he *didn't* dress like that normally.

Maybe it was an old-guy disguise!

The thought totally threw me. I mean, I don't think of old guys as being sneaky, disguise-wearing con artists. I think of them as being either kind or totally ornery, because every one I know seems to be one or the other. There must be a fork in the road of life—I don't know when it comes along or where it is, but I know it's there. And when you get there, there's a big ol' arrow with

CRABBY pointing one way and another big ol' arrow with KIND pointing the other.

That's the picture I had in my mind, anyway. At no time had I ever envisioned a third sign that said SNEAKY. But all of a sudden it was like the Cheshire cat had popped up with his crazy grin, holding a sign that said SNEAKY.

My mind started running down the possibilities of the Sneaky Path. Maybe the reason Mr. Garnucci didn't know anybody by the name of Rex Randolf, or anybody who wore a beret, a scarf, and tinted glasses and spoke with a sophisticated accent, was because "Rex Randolf" was trying to conceal who he really was. And if this guy did live in the building and was actually planning to meet Mrs. Wedgewood at Monte Carlo night, why didn't he give his real name?

So the Sneaky Path led me right back to the place I'd started—the only thing that made sense to me was that Rex was hoping to case the Wedge's apartment and this was his way of getting her out of the way.

The *problem* was, if ol' Rexy-boy was going to be searching Mrs. Wedgewood's apartment for Buck's missing money, it's not like I could spy on him. I mean, even if I could get inside her apartment, where would I hide? He'd definitely look under the bed and in the closet and under the kitchen sink—my usual dive-for-cover hiding places.

So as I was helping Mrs. Wedgewood get ready, I was racking my brain for a way I could sorta keep tabs on him—or at least know if he was in the apartment—without being caught.

And then I had a brainstorm.

Except that the brainstorm required me to get back inside the Wedge's apartment after she was gone.

Mrs. Wedgewood was in the bathroom, all decked out in her new muumuu and plastic pearls, doing a last-minute sweat-blot. I figured it was now or never, so real quick I grabbed a napkin off the kitchen table, tore off a piece, folded it tight, and crammed it in the hole part of her front door latch.

I tested it quick, but the paper wasn't fat enough, so I crammed in a little more.

"Sugar?"

Now it was too big. And really obvious!

I pried it out and ripped off a little of the napkin, then tried again.

Clank, clank came the walker.

"Sugar?"

I closed the door quick.

"What are you up to, sugar?"

"Just checking the hallway," I said, but I sounded jumpy.

Guilty.

Lucky for me, I was also guilty of something else. She gave me a cagey smile. "Makin' sure the coast is clear?"

"Uh . . . hey," I said, moving toward her as I slipped the rest of the napkin in my back pocket. "Would you like me to get Grams to help you down to the rec room?"

"Why . . . that would be so nice!"

"Do you have everything you need?"

"My purse is on the bed, and my key is on that little hook, right there."

So I grabbed both, and when she was through the door, I closed it behind us.

"Test it now, sugar," she said.

So I rattled the knob while I *pulled* on it, showing her how locked up tight her apartment was. Then I guided her away from the door and said, "I'll go get Grams."

Grams had a book in her hand and was just about to sit down on the couch when I barged in. I made an exasperated face and rolled my eyes. "She wants you to walk her down to Monte Carlo night and stay with her until her date shows up."

"This is unbelievable!" Grams fumed. But when the Wedge appeared in the open doorway, she got up and grabbed a sweater.

And since I'd never actually checked out with Mr. Garnucci, I grabbed my skateboard and said, "Well, I'd better get home! Bye!"

Mrs. Wedgewood snorted like, Oh, right, but Grams just played along. "Thanks so much for all your help today, sweetheart. I know Rose appreciates it no end!"

And since they were going to be moving at a snail's pace and the elevator can take a while to show up, off I flew down the hall, down the regular stairs, and through the lobby, calling, "See ya later, Mr. G.!" as I breezed out the front door. And that's when it hit me—if Rex Randolf did show at Mrs. Wedgewood's while she was at Monte Carlo night and I could somehow get a *picture* of him, I could show it to André and ask him if he recognized him as the guy who'd been inside Buck's hotel room. I could also show it to Mr. Garnucci and see if *he* recognized him.

Now, I was banking on Mrs. Wedgewood taking at least fifteen minutes to get down to the rec room.

She's that kind of slow.

And I figured Rexy-pooh wouldn't dare case the apartment until he was sure she was down there. Which meant that I had time to put my plan into motion, but not much.

So I made a beeline over to the Pup Parlor, and when Vera answered the door, I panted, "Hey! I have a *huge* favor to ask."

"Ask away," she said, showing off the gaps where teeth used to be.

"I need to borrow your digital camera for an hour. Maybe two."

The yellow polka-dotted bows on the sides of her hair seemed to quiver in horror. But after a second she said, "I take it it's an emergency?" and led me upstairs. "Holly's out with Meg fetching ice cream," she said. "You want me to tell her to give you a call?"

"Uh . . . how about I just talk to her when I return the camera."

"Sounds good."

So I got the camera and a very quick set-point-and-shoot lesson, then bolted out of there and over to the fire escape.

Luckily, I didn't scare anybody else to death on my way up.

I stashed the skateboard and the camera in Grams' apartment, then zipped back down the hallway to finally test Mrs. Wedgewood's door.

I pushed and . . . "Yes!" I whispered as the door gave way.

I slipped in quick, then went straight to the kitchen.

Our apartment's phone is corded and anchored to the kitchen wall. And I know when our old neighbor Mrs. Graybill lived next door, she had a phone just like ours. But Mrs. Wedgewood must've done some sweet-talking to Mr. Garnucci, because she now has a portable jobbie.

It was on its back, charging in the base on the kitchen table, but after I checked out the recharge contacts, I realized that I didn't really understand how it worked. And after another minute I started to get nervous—I was wasting time!

So I ran back home, called Mrs. Wedgewood's number, let our phone dangle from the cord, ran *back* to the Wedge's apartment, and answered her phone.

The red light on the base was flashing.

Shoot!

That would totally give it away!

So without turning it off, I rested the phone on the table and started opening kitchen drawers until I found her junk drawer.

Thank God for junk drawers.

I found scissors and a small roll of thin white double-stick foam.

Perfect!

I cut a piece, peeled off the back, and put it on the flashing light, but since you could still see it flashing, I put on another layer, which pretty much concealed it.

Then I cut another couple of pieces, stuck them

together for thickness, and put them over the metal contacts on the base. Then I laid the phone back in the cradle.

The handset still said PHONE ON, but really, you wouldn't notice it unless you actually *looked*.

I pushed the phone and base toward the back of the table, trying to make it look casual behind the pitcher of flowers ol' Rex had brought. Then I shoved the scissors, the roll of foam, and all the scraps into the junk drawer and dashed for the door.

The hallway was clear, so I took the wadded-up napkin out of the jamb, pulled the door closed behind me, and darted home.

The minute I was inside my own apartment, I kinda fell apart. I started shaking and sweating, and my hands were suddenly all clammy. I went over to our phone, held it to my ear, and heard a whole lot of nothing.

So I let it dangle again and got busy practicing with Vera's camera, figuring out how to zoom in and turn the flash off, and when I was comfortable enough with it, I draped it over my neck and went back to the phone.

I listened hard.

Not a rustle, not a crackle, not a clank, not a sound.

I kept on listening for what seemed like forever. And I was just starting to doubt myself—just starting to think that maybe Rex Randolf wouldn't be casing the Wedge's apartment after all—when I heard something.

A *clink*.

A *whoosh*.

And then footsteps!

I crammed the phone up hard against my ear.

I heard fast footsteps with hard soles.

And definitely no clunking walker.

A shiver shimmied through me. How had he broken in? Was he some sort of professional burglar? Had he managed to make a mold of Mrs. Wedgewood's key while she wasn't looking? Or were our rinky-dink locks that easy to jimmy?

Then I heard static, and for a second I thought my little eavesdropping setup had quit working.

But all of a sudden there was a voice.

A man's voice.

And what he said made me feel like spiders were racing up my spine.

THIRTEEN

"This is the Jackal. Do you read me, Sandman?"

"Loud and clear," came the crackled response.

"I'm inside."

"I don't know how long she's going to last. I'll shadow her, but get busy!"

"Roger that."

Their voices were echoey but intense. And neither voice had any kind of sophisticated accent. So who were these people? Was one of them Rex Randolf? Or were these two *other* men? Whoever was down in the rec room had to be someone who lived in the building, and if he was shadowing Mrs. Wedgewood, he couldn't be Rex Randolf.

So was the Jackal Rex Randolf?

My head was swimming as I stood there listening to the Jackal rummage around Mrs. Wedgewood's apartment. I couldn't quite believe that any of this was real. It was like some weird espionage movie where the operatives were the Jackal and Sandman.

Only they weren't ripped or dashing or even, you know, *smooth.*

They sounded like old guys!

And they were shaking down a fat lady!

The sounds got fainter, then louder; fainter, then louder again. I listened to this until *finally* there was a crackle and then, "Mayday. Jackal, do you read me? Mayday."

"Roger that. Target not acquired. Time frame?"

"Ten, max."

"Could she be carrying?"

"Negative. Baggage not suitable."

The Jackal cursed, then said, "I *know* she was lying—it was obvious! It's got to be here someplace."

"Don't push your luck."

"The trapdoor gives me an extra five."

Their voices were getting louder and louder, but I didn't notice right away because I was so busy trying to decipher their little code words and I was excited that the Jackal had said "*I* know she was lying"—now I was sure that he *was* Rex Randolf!

In the back of my mind, I realized that their voices were also becoming less echoey, but I was listening so hard that it hadn't even dawned on me that maybe I should be worried.

"Should I tail and report?" came the crackling voice of Sandman, which all of a sudden seemed *loud*.

"Stand by," the Jackal said, and although I could hear him loud and clear, it sounded like he was *whispering*.

Then all of a sudden it was quiet.

Not silent.

Quiet.

My heart started slamming around, and I almost

panicked and hung up the phone. But at the last second it hit me that if he *hadn't* seen the PHONE ON display and I hung up, the phone would start making little *bee-boo-beep*s and prerecorded off-the-hook announcements and then he'd notice the phone for sure!

So I held on, my heart hammering and my hands shaking.

Then all of a sudden I could tell he'd picked up the phone. He didn't make a sound and I sure couldn't *see* anything, but I could *feel* him through the wall, holding the phone up to his ear, listening.

Just like me.

His end clicked off.

So very carefully, very *quietly*, I hung up our phone and just stood there, shaking.

BRINGGGGGGG!

I jumped through the ceiling, then spun around in a circle with my eyes cranked and my whole body feeling like it was about to explode.

I was busted! He'd hit star-69!

Or . . . had he?

Maybe it was another case of me thinking it was someone it wasn't.

Maybe it was just Marissa or Holly or . . .

I felt like tearing out my hair. Why couldn't we have a phone with caller ID like the rest of the world?

My mind was spinning like crazy, but with zero traction. I felt like a mouse on a wheel racing to escape a cat standing patiently by. What if it *was* the Jackal and he could hear the ringing right through the wall?

The wheel suddenly opened and I hit the ground running. I snatched the phone off the hook, and in the deepest, most casual voice I could muster, I said, "Domino's Pizza."

There was a slight hesitation, then *click*.

I hung up, too, and just stood there, shaking.

It *had* been him!

It's okay, I told myself. The Domino's bit threw him off. It's okaaaay.

Only I knew that it wasn't okay.

In the pit of my stomach, I knew it wasn't anywhere *near* okay.

I was too shaken up to even try to take a picture of the Jackal leaving Mrs. Wedgewood's apartment. Instead, I just sort of hid in our apartment until Grams and Mrs. Wedgewood returned from Monte Carlo night. I helped Grams deliver Mrs. Wedgewood home so I could undo everything I'd done to her phone.

I was quick enough so Grams didn't notice, and Mrs. Wedgewood didn't even look up. She just clomped into her bedroom without a word.

When Grams and I were safely home, she immediately launched into a play-by-play of her "torturous ordeal" with the Wedge. From knocking over a man to scarfing up everything in sight, Mrs. Wedgewood apparently made quite an impression.

"And people thought she was *my* friend because that date of hers never showed up!" Grams moaned, "I am positively mortified!"

Then around nine o'clock we started getting phone calls.

I jumped when the first call came in.

It was just Hudson.

He and Grams exchanged some pleasantries, then she turned the phone over to me.

"Hey, Hudson. What's up?"

"I thought I should let you know that the McKenzes turned down my offer."

"Lucky you," I laughed. But then I realized that he was calling because he was bummed about it. So I added, "Look, it was really nice of you to even *think* about doing it."

"Thinking about helping isn't actually helping."

I didn't know what to say to that, and after a few seconds he said, "Just thought you'd like to know," and got off the phone.

"What was that about?" Grams asked after I'd hung up.

"Hudson offered to have Mikey do kind of a boot camp at his house, but—"

The phone rang again.

I jumped again.

"He did *what*?" Grams asked, hurrying over to answer the phone. Her brow was knitted funny and her eyes looked almost scared.

Obviously, she understood how crazy an offer it was.

She put up a finger, answered the phone, and with barely a "Hold on a moment" handed it over to me.

It was Marissa.

"You should be so proud of me!" she whispered.

"Yeah?"

"I totally put my foot down! I told my mom that you and I were going to throw the softball around at the ball-park tomorrow and—"

"We are?"

"Don't you want to?"

"Sure. But . . . when?"

"Ten? Or are you working?"

I almost said, Working? but then I remembered—I had a job at the Heavenly.

"No, that's okay. Ten's good." Then I added, "But how is that putting your foot down?"

"I told my mom I'm not Mikey's parent and he's not my responsibility."

"And?"

"And she said she *had* to be gone and I *had* to take Mikey with me to the park."

"So?"

"So I told her fine, but if he threw another tantrum, I was just leaving him behind."

"You told her *fine*? Aw, Marissa, I am not up for another episode of Mikey Monster."

"Wait! I'm not done." She was whispering really fast now. And it sounded like she was jumping up and down behind racks of clothes in a closet or something. "You should have seen me. I was being totally calm and mature, but *Mikey* started storming around, throwing an absolute tantrum about having to go with *me*, and—you're not going to believe this—he knocked over the Kraval!"

"He knocked over the—no! Did it break?"

"It shattered into a million pieces!"

I absorbed this crystal-crushing news for a minute, then said, "Your mom must be freaking out."

"That is the understatement of the century!"

All of a sudden I could hear Mrs. McKenze screaming in the background.

"Uh-oh," Marissa whispered. "She's looking for me. Gotta go." And with that, she clicked off.

"What was *that* about?" Grams asked when I hung up.

"Mikey broke the Kraval!" I gasped.

"The Kraval? What's the Kraval?"

But then the phone rang *again*.

And I totally jumped.

Again.

Grams shook her head as she moved to answer the phone. "What a night!"

This time it was Vera wanting to know when I would be returning her camera. I looked at the clock—it was almost ten. My big plan of snapping a picture of Rexy-boy hadn't even come *close* to happening. "Uh . . . can I bring it back tomorrow?"

"Did you break it?" she asked suspiciously, and the truth is, I knew why—no matter how careful I try to be, stuff I borrow from people tends to get bashed or crashed or broken.

But not this time!

"No!" I said, trying to sound hurt that she would think such a thing. "I haven't even used it."

"I'd feel a lot better if you'd bring it back tonight." Then she added, "I know it's late, but a deal is a deal."

"You're right. I'm sorry. I'm on my way."

When I was off the phone, Grams eyed me and said, "What have you borrowed and not used?"

"Her camera," I grumbled, scrambling around for a reason I might borrow a camera when I was stuck in an apartment building with nowhere to take pictures.

"And why exactly did you borrow her camera?"

"You're going to think I'm really childish," I said.

"Go on."

"Well . . . Holly's never been here, right? So she's never seen Mrs. Wedgewood, right?"

"Ah," Grams said, tilting her head back a little. "And she doesn't believe there's such a thing as a waddling whale?"

"Grams!"

She gave me a disgusted scowl, then whispered, "That woman is a *nightmare*. A blubbery, blackmailing nightmare!"

"Grams!"

It was weird to have her acting just like me. And weird for me to be going "Grams!" instead of her going "Samantha!"

She went back to prim and proper. "I'm sorry. I know I'm not setting a good example. And if she were that large because of some medical problem, I'd be sympathetic, but that's not the case." She eyed me. "Did I tell you how she inhaled the entire spread at Monte Carlo night?"

"Yes, Grams," I said, because I didn't want to hear the disgusting details all over again. I grabbed the camera and said, "And I've really gotta go. I'll be right back."

"Be careful. And don't you dare get sidetracked. Come *right* back." And then—I couldn't believe it—she muttered, "And try not to scare anyone to death, would you?"

"Grams!"

She laughed. "Not funny yet, huh?"

"No!"

I zipped down the fire escape, flew across the grass, and jaywalked across Broadway. And when Holly answered the Pup Parlor door and asked me if I could come up for a while, I said, "I told Grams I'd be right back. But I'm meeting Marissa at the ballpark tomorrow at ten—wanna come?"

"Sure." Then she asked, "Why'd you need the camera, anyway?"

"I'll explain later. But tell Vera I'd like to borrow it again, okay? I didn't get a chance to use it."

So I was staying on track. I went straight for the fire escape, zigzagged up, passed by the Landing of Death, and was almost to the fifth floor when a word suddenly smacked forward in my brain.

Trapdoor.

Had Rex-the-Jackal-Randolf meant the fire escape door?

And since the Wedge's apartment was even closer to the fire escape than ours, it sure *would* save him time getting down from the fifth floor.

But the only way he could go *in* the fourth floor's fire escape door would be if the latch was jammed.

Just like what I'd done to the *fifth*-floor door.

And the only reason you'd want to do *that* is if you wanted to come and go a lot without being seen.

Just like me.

Then I remembered how Grams had told me she'd slipped away from the police through the fourth-floor door. How had she been able to do that? Maybe somebody else had opened it from inside the building . . . or maybe the door didn't latch.

I looked all around, then eased back to the Landing of Death.

I pulled on the door.

There was no *clunk*.

No *thunk*.

No catch.

Just the smooth release of a trapdoor opening.

FOURTEEN

They hadn't used bubble gum like I had on our door.

They'd used some kind of weird gray putty.

I pried out just enough so the door would latch. If the Jackal and Sandman were using the fire escape regularly, they'd just think it was worn down or compressed or something and put more in.

If it was *gone*, they'd know someone was onto them.

And if they didn't put more in, then that would mean that it had been the regular way in for Buck Ritter from Omaha, Nebraska, not them. Which would mean that the Jackal and Sandman probably both lived in the Senior Highrise.

Something about that made me feel very uneasy.

I closed the door tight, then jetted up to my bubble-gummed jamb and zipped down to our apartment. "That was fast," Grams said. She had her nose back in her checkbook, but she glanced up and whispered, "It's a good thing you were gone, because Rose called demanding you come over, and I could honestly say that you were not here."

"What did she want this time?"

"Something about you being her witness."

"Her witness? To what?"

"I have no idea." She sighed and slapped closed her checkbook. "And I have no idea what happened to that hundred and twenty dollars. I just cannot seem to find my mistake!"

"You think I should go over?"

"At this hour? No! She has become far too demanding!" She wobbled her head a little. "Whatever new emergency she's having can just wait."

I went to bed feeling very clouded. Like all the marbles in my head were separated from each other with little pieces of cotton. I didn't feel the sharp clicking of clear thoughts—just the quiet thudding of all the things that had happened since I'd run into Buck on the fire escape.

Maybe I was just tired.

Or maybe I didn't really *want* to make the connections.

Sure, I'd been snooping around, trying to piece things together, but maybe I was slipping the cotton between the marbles on purpose.

Maybe, for once in my life, I didn't really *want* to figure things out.

That night I had a weird dream about the money. At the beginning of the dream the money was safe and sound, stashed in my backpack. I could *see* it down there, bound and beautiful. But when I reached in to pull it out, it disintegrated into a weird, gritty green sand that ran right between my fingers. The next stack of money did the same thing, and so did the third, and all I could find in my backpack was sand.

Cold, gritty green sand.

I tried to shove the sand back together, tried to pat it into money again, but it kept falling apart. It was just . . . gone.

The first thing I did in the morning was dive into my backpack.

No green sand.

Just cold hard cash!

But in the back of my mind I was worried—there was obviously something underhanded or sneaky or . . . I don't know . . . *illegal* about this money. Why was Buck sneaking around with so much cash on him? And why had he begged me to get rid of it?

After brooding about it for a while, I decided that I could (a) go to the cops or (b) figure it out myself.

But really, why would I do either?

Why would I risk giving up the money?

So if I didn't want to go to the cops or figure things out myself, I could (a) hide the money forever and hope that Sandman and the Jackal didn't track me down or (b) . . . spend it!

All of it!

And quick!

That way if Sandman and the Jackal *did* figure things out, they still couldn't *prove* it. There'd be no evidence!

The more I thought about it, the more I liked the spend-it option.

I liked it a lot!

I'd already burned through some of the money, but

now I felt like I could *really* spend it! I mean, why would I do stuff like borrow Vera's camera when I could buy one of my own?

I could get my own cell phone!

My own . . . anything!

The first thing I did, though, was count out a hundred and twenty dollars and slip it into the secret-stash section of Grams' purse. She thinks she's so sly when she goes to the bank and hides cash there. I think she puts it there in case she gets robbed. That way she'll be able to give up her wallet but not lose all her money. Not that some robber wouldn't take her whole purse, but I think it makes Grams feel safer somehow.

Anyway, then when she was in the bathroom, I stashed a couple of bills in the back of her underwear drawer and jabbed another sixty bucks inside a pocket of her favorite coat.

When I heard the toilet flush, I zipped back to the couch and pretended like I was still asleep. I was really bubbling with excitement, though—leaving presents around for Grams was fun!

I waited until after she'd made her morning cup of tea to do a pretend stumble to the bathroom. "Morning," I mumbled.

"Good morning, sweetheart," she said, and when I came back out, she was at the kitchen table, poring over her checkbook and bank statement again.

"Can't you just ask the bank?" I asked, plopping down across from her.

"It's my mistake," she grumbled. "It's my job to figure

it out." Then she looked up and said, "Did your mother call last night while I was tied up with Rose?"

I shook my head, thinking that if she had, she got a busy signal.

"Unbelievable," she grumbled.

I snorted. "What's unbelievable about it? Her character's comatose, remember?"

Grams blinked at me through her glasses. "What does that have to do with anything?"

I shrugged and laughed. "I don't know!"

Grams shook her head. "Where did she go? One does not come all the way from Hollywood to be scared off by a little mouse!"

"One does if one is Lady Lana."

"So you really think she's gone back home?"

I nodded. "Yup."

Grams shook her head some more, and I swear there was steam coming out of her ears. "Why did she even bother to visit?"

I shrugged and laughed again. "Her character's comatose?"

Grams rolled her eyes and got back to her checkbook. "How about making some oatmeal?"

"I'm on it," I said, standing up.

I don't know what it is about the way Grams makes oatmeal, but hers always turns out better than mine. I think it's patience. I can never seem to put in enough of that ingredient. I just crank up the heat and go. And I don't mean for just the twenty-minute, good-for-your-cholesterol multigrain oatmeal that we have almost every day. I can't even really handle the instant kind. Either it's runny or pasty or I accidentally boil it over in the microwave because I'm in a hurry.

But whatever. I was in charge, so I did the best I could, then added brown sugar, maple syrup, almonds, and dried cranberries.

Enough of that and even *my* oatmeal tastes great.

Anyway, I sat down to eat and was just starting to be scolded by Grams for pouring on so much syrup when the phone rang.

"There she is," I said, nodding at the phone.

"Hrmph!" Grams said, in the way only my grams can. "She can just stay comatose."

I laughed. But as the phone continued to ring, I finally asked, "You're really not going to get it?"

"Why would I?" She wagged her spoon in the general direction of the ringing phone. "You go ahead if you want."

I eyed her. "That can be dangerous, you know."

"Hrmph!"

"Fine." I scooted away from the table. "I'll just pretend I'm you." So I went over, picked up the phone, and in my most granny-like voice said, "Hello, dearie?"

Grams shot me a look, and I was just about to crack up when a voice said, "Is Samantha there?"

It was not my mother.

It was a deep voice.

A *male* voice.

I felt a flush of panic as I remembered the Jackal pressing star-69.

I warbled, "Nobody here by that name, dearie."

"Uh, is this 922-8846?"

As the numbers tumbled over the line, the voice sounded more normal, and I realized who it was. *"Casey?"* I whispered.

"Sammy?" he whispered back.

"Why'd you call me Samantha?"

"Why'd you say you weren't there?"

Now, Casey hadn't had my phone number very long, so it wasn't like I was used to him calling. And the fact that he *was* calling, and so early, was kinda weird. But before I could say anything, he said, "Sorry. I guess I should have said who I was, huh?"

I laughed. "Would have helped."

He laughed, too. "You do a pretty good old-granny imitation."

I eyed Grams. "My grandmother does not agree." Then I said, "So what's up?"

"My dad banished me to my mom's for a few days. I've gotta get out of here."

"No kidding," I laughed, picturing him having to live with Heather and their sharp-clawed mother. "Why'd he do that?"

"He had to go out of town, and he had some sudden revelation that I needed to be closer to my mother and sister." He snorted. "This is definitely not doing it." Then he added, "What are you up to today?"

"Throwing the softball around with Marissa and Holly."

"Hey, how about I call Billy and maybe Danny? Boys against girls?"

"Really?"

"Sure!"

So I told him where and when we were meeting, and by the time I was off the phone I'd forgotten all about Mrs. Wedgewood and the Jackal and Sandman and having scared Mr. Buck Ritter from Omaha, Nebraska, to death.

I was going to play softball with my friends.

It'd be what summers were supposed to be—fun!

Unfortunately, we weren't the only ones who showed up at the park.

FIFTEEN

Softball's a year-round sport in Santa Martina. Everyone plays. There's even a seniors league, which is for anyone over sixty. I've never actually watched a seniors league game, but I hear the women's division is intense. Bunch of old-geezer gals spittin' and squawkin' at each other, hobbling around trying to make the play.

Go, Granny, go!

Anyway, Marissa and I arrived at the ballpark at almost the exact same time. She was beaming as she swung off her bike. "Guess what?"

"Uh . . ." I looked around. "Does it have to do with Mikey?"

"He's at Hudson's Boot Camp!"

"Seriously?" I asked, picking up my skateboard.

"I can't believe Hudson actually *wants* him there. The guy's crazy . . . but I'm FREE!" She leaned her bike against the dugout and twirled around. "I'm FREEEEEE!"

"Did your parents send him to Hudson's because he broke the Kraval?"

"That and a hundred million other things. Which I don't *even* want to talk about. I want to pitch!"

She took her glove off the handlebars, and as we headed into the dugout, I said, "Well, guess what?"

"What?"

"Holly's coming, and Casey called this morning. He's gonna meet us here, too."

"Really?"

I shrugged and acted all casual-like. "Yeah. And he's gonna see about bringing some friends."

She grabbed me by the arm. "Danny?"

I grinned. "Uh-huh. And Billy."

"This is, like, the best day ever! Come on! Let's warm up!"

So I parked my board and backpack in the dugout, got my catcher's mitt, and took my position behind home plate.

Holly arrived next, and then Casey showed up with Billy and Danny, and before you knew it phones were getting passed around and more people got invited. Dot and her brothers came, and *Brandon* appeared and summoned a posse of girls—something that's apparently easy to do when you're a high school swim star. Pretty soon Marissa's idea of throwing me a few pitches had become a full-on game of girls against guys, with innings and outs and base steals and *dust*.

Big glorious clouds of dust.

It was a blast, too. Especially with Billy "Class Clown" Pratt playing. He runs bases like he's doing an obstacle course, high-stepping through imaginary tires or ducking under invisible limbo bars or zigzagging around nonexistent cones. He's just a maniac!

And usually, an easy out.

Anyway, we'd been playing for over two hours and the girls were *wiping* the guys 9–2. And I'm squatting behind home plate, getting ready for Marissa's next pitch, when out of the corner of my eye I catch a glimpse of something red moving on the sidelines. So after the ball smacks into my mitt, I glance over, and what do I see creeping into the dugout?

The Fire Ant of Summertime Fun.

The Wicked Wasp of the West.

The stinging, fighting, sneaking, biting, one and only Heather Acosta.

Now, I've learned that the best way of dealing with that nasty redhead is to ignore her. And since she was wearing gold flip-flops and blinding white supertight hot pants, she was not exactly dressed to play. So if she was just going to stand around and watch, what did I care?

But as she disappeared into the dugout, I remembered— my backpack was in there.

And in my backpack was money.

Lots and lots of money!

Now, you may think I'm being paranoid, but Heather has a history of stealing my stuff, and I was not about to let it happen again. So I called, "Time out!" and headed for the dugout.

"Forget her!" Marissa called.

I shook my head.

"Come *on*," Marissa said, stamping her foot. "Who cares?"

I hurried over anyway, and out of the shadowy coolness

of the dugout came, "Wassa matter, loser? Afraid I'm gonna steal all your money?"

Now, okay. Heather was making fun of me because she knows I have no money. Look up "perennially broke" in the dictionary and there'll be a picture of me. But her saying that sent a jolt through me 'cause yes, that's exactly what I was worried about.

I tried to act all cool and nonchalant as I swept through the dugout, grabbed my backpack, and said, "No, I just don't want you *planting* stuff that'll get me in trouble," 'cause she's been known to do *that,* too.

But when I reappeared from the dugout, Brandon was abandoning the steal he'd made to second base, saying, "It's one o'clock already? I've gotta go! I'm going to be late for work!" He pointed around the field as he back-pedaled away. "Don't forget! Pool party at my house tomorrow! Starts at noon! Everyone's invited!"

He hadn't even completely left the diamond when the posse of girls he'd summoned suddenly had places they needed to be.

Then Billy shouted, "I need food!" and Dot's brothers said, "Yeah, we're done, too," and since the DeVrieses live clear out in Sisquane, Dot had to go with them. Then Holly said, "I need to get home, too. I've got to be at the Humane Society at two," and that was it—the game fell apart as fast as it had been put together.

And maybe Casey and Danny and Marissa and I could have gone out for burgers or something, but Heather had emerged from the dugout and was fire-anting around. "Mom wants you home," she said to Casey, but she said it all saccharine sweet, with a so-sorry-to-break-it-to-you shrug. "Something about you leaving a disaster where her kitchen used to be?"

Then she batted her lashes at Danny. "You're welcome to come over, too. I made fresh-squeezed lemonade . . . ?"

Without so much as a glance at Marissa, Danny said, "Sounds great!"

Heather didn't invite us, of course, and Casey was obviously embarrassed about the whole situation. So Marissa eased back and started collecting her stuff, and I followed because I knew she was fighting back tears. And when I glanced over my shoulder, Casey gave me the I'll-call-you signal as he headed out, so I nodded and waved and tried to act like everything was cool.

I sat in the shade of the dugout with Marissa until she was all cried out. I didn't bother to tell her that Danny Urbanski was a weasel and totally not worth it—she already knew that's what I thought. Instead, in an effort to get her to see the bright side of *her* life, I said, "So what do you suppose Hudson's got Mikey doing?"

She finished drying her eyes and snorted. "I'll bet he's already run away!"

"Run?" I laughed. "I doubt it." Then I grinned at her. "So you wanna go spy?"

She took a deep breath, held it a minute, then grabbed her stuff and said, "Sure," which sorta surprised me. But as she marched up the dugout steps, she grumbled, "And when we're through there, there's someone *else* we're gonna spy on."

That got my eyes popping. "You're not thinking . . . ?" I chased after her. "You're not *serious*, right?"

She grabbed her bike and turned it around. "Oh yes I am!"

"This is a bad idea," I muttered. "This is a very bad idea!"

Spying on Mikey was strange because I was also spying on Hudson, which did not feel right at all. They were outside, painting Hudson's back fence. Mikey had a pail. Hudson had a pail. They were both just brushing away, and I could tell Hudson was talking, but I couldn't hear what he was saying.

It wasn't a lecture, though. It was a story. I could tell from the way Mikey was stroking paint that he was listening. Really listening. And every once in a while, Hudson would reach over and help Mikey stroke out some paint that was put on too thick, then get back to painting his own board and back to the story.

Hudson tells the best stories, and I was kinda itching to grab a brush and help so I could hear, but obviously Marissa wasn't. "Doesn't seem like boot camp to me," she grumbled.

"He's painting a fence," I whispered.

"They're in the shade. He's obviously not suffering."

"But that's Mikey. Painting a fence!"

"Whatever. Let's go."

Now, I knew she meant, Let's go to Heather's, but I really did think it was a bad idea. Plus, I couldn't help worrying that if we got caught, people would think I'd been spying on *Casey*. So as we walked along, I tried to talk her out of it. Finally she spun on me and said, "How many times have you dragged me someplace I haven't wanted to go? How many *spying* operations have I done with you? This is the *least* you can do for me!"

It was so true.

But I still didn't want to go.

"Fine!" she finally said. "I'll go by myself!"

Well, I couldn't let her do *that,* so I said, "Look. Can we at least leave all our stuff at Hudson's?"

She stopped, thought, then turned around. "It *would* be kind of hard to spy with all this, huh?"

So we parked her bike and my skateboard and her softball stuff by Hudson's side gate, but I left my backpack on, acting like it wasn't even there. No way I was leaving nearly three thousand dollars by the side of the gate!

Luckily, Marissa had her mind more on Danny and Heather than on what I was hauling around on my back, so she didn't even notice.

Now, I was actually pretty familiar with Heather's house. Not because I'd ever been *invited* there. No, because I'd crashed a party there once. A costume party where Heather had no idea I was me.

Until later.

But *anyway,* Mrs. Acosta's little red sports car was not in the driveway, which was a good thing. A run-in with Candi Acosta is like facing off with a chainsaw killer in high heels—you're not sure whether you should run or laugh.

But since she wasn't home, we didn't have to worry about *her,* so we just snuck across the yard and peeked through the kitchen window.

Didn't see a soul.

The kitchen looked pretty tidy, too—nowhere near disastrous.

We eased over to the family room.

Not a soul.

We spied over the back fence.

No one there, either.

So we crept along from one window to the next, looking inside, seeing a whole lot of nothing. And when we got to the end of the house, we turned the corner and made our way along a small aisle of dirt between a row of oleander bushes and the house, over to where we knew Heather's bedroom was.

The oleander was great cover because it ran from the back of the house clear out to the sidewalk, but still, I was feeling really, I don't know . . . *voyeurish*.

"Maybe we shouldn't look," I whispered.

"Maybe we *should*," Marissa whispered back, and she sounded very ticked off.

But as she moved in closer and inched up to the window, I decided to just hang back. The last thing I wanted was to be caught spying through Heather Acosta's bedroom window!

So while I knelt in the dirt, Marissa eeeeased up to the wall.

Her eyeball inched up over the windowsill.

And all of a sudden she choked back a gasp.

"What?" I whispered.

Her eyes were enormous as she waved me over.

And really, how could I not?

I went over and looked!

SIXTEEN

It was Danny and Heather, all right.

Kissing.

I turned around and slumped down the wall, saying, "Oh boy," then dragged Marissa away from the window.

Tears were rolling from her eyes. "Ohmygod. Ohmygod-ohmygod-ohmygod!"

"He's a jerk, Marissa. There's your proof."

"*She's* the jerk!" She flung back her tears. "I officially hate her more than you do!"

I let out a puffy-cheeked sigh. "Let's get out of here, all right?"

"Where's her mother?!" she asked, creeping along behind me. "Where's *Casey?*"

I'd been wondering the "where's Casey" part myself, but as we got to the corner of the house, it was the "where's her mother" part that got answered.

A little red sports car was now parked in the driveway.

I grabbed Marissa's arm and pointed. "Heather is so busted!" But all of a sudden Heather's bedroom window scrapes open and we realize that *we're* the ones about to be busted!

We dive into the bushes as Danny comes tumbling out

the window headfirst. He lands on his hands and thumps to the ground, then just stays there a minute, cursing as he shakes out a wrist.

Now, Marissa and I are both holding our breath and trying to stay stock-still, but then there's this *sound*. A sputtering, hissing, *crackling* sound.

Our eyes peel back as we look at each other like, What's *that?* and all of a sudden water comes shooting out of little pipes sticking up from the ground. I get hit from the side, but Marissa's practically sitting on one of the pipes and gets sprayed right across her butt.

She chokes back a scream and sort of penguins to the side as I try to cap the sprinkler with my hand. We're not the only ones getting doused, though. Danny's acting like a wet firecracker, sputtering curses as he shoots past us and escapes to the sidewalk.

I just want to bolt out of there, but Marissa's scared to death of being seen by Danny. So we have to wait in the spurting sprinklers and mounting mud until she's sure the coast must be clear. And then, when I go to make a break for it, she yanks me back and says, "What if Heather's looking out a window?"

So instead of cutting across the yard, we stay behind the bushes and go over the sprinklers and through the dirt. By the time we're on the sidewalk, we're soaked, and caked with mud.

Marissa's so upset about Danny, though, that she doesn't even seem to care. She just marches along, her shoes squooshing like mad. "I can't believe it! How can he possibly like her? Doesn't he know how manipulative and conniving and *evil* she is? She spins a sticky little *lemonade* web and he jumps right in!"

Sometimes when you're upset, you just need to get it out of your system. People giving you reasons why you shouldn't be feeling the way you do won't actually change the way you feel. It just makes you feel like people don't really *understand* the way you feel.

So even though I thought Heather snagging Danny might be a good thing in the long run, in the short run Marissa needed to vent, and as a friend it was my job to help her. So I nod and say, "Heather's like one of those brown recluse spiders."

"She *is*," Marissa says, looking at me with big eyes. "Small, sneaky, deadly. . . . Only she's a *red* recluse!" But then her eyes suddenly brim with tears. "He *kissed* her! He seriously kissed her!"

I shake my head. "How could anyone even *think* about kissing a red recluse?"

"Exactly!"

"And then she dumped him out the window!"

"Well," Marissa says, taking a deep, stuttery breath, "maybe this is all good."

I suddenly felt very clever. By letting her vent, she'd figured it out on her own! She was *finally* getting over Danny Urbanski. "Exactly," I said, trying not to sound like I was gloating.

She nodded. "It was probably going to take something like this for him to see her for what she is."

I stopped short. "What? No! No, no, no! Danny is not that . . . mature. Danny is . . . an opportunist."

"An opportunist?"

I shrugged and started walking again. "That's what Grams calls people like him. They look for opportunities without really *caring*."

She fell in step beside me. "Danny is not an opportunist. *Heather's* the opportunist!"

I groaned. "Marissa, wake up. He was kissing Heather! What more proof do you need? He's either an opportunist or an idiot!"

"He is not! He's . . . he's . . ." She started crying again. "I thought he liked me. I really did."

I stopped her and let out a puffy-cheeked sigh as I gave her a hug. "I think part of him does, okay? But he would make a lousy boyfriend, and there's no way he's good enough for you."

She shook her head. "My life's a disaster. Everything is going wrong all at once. Danny, my family, no money, no *phone* . . ." She looked down at her shorts. "And I look like I peed my pants!"

I laughed because that's exactly what it looked like.

"It's not funny!"

"Yes, it is!"

She laughed a little. "No, it's not!" Then she took a deep breath and said, "I'm going to go home."

"Me too," I said, 'cause even though my jeans didn't look nearly as bad as her shorts, they were sticking to my legs and were all dirty from playing softball and I just wanted *out* of them.

When we got to Hudson's, Marissa's mom was on the porch with Hudson, deep in conversation. So rather than getting tangled up in any of that, I decided to be smart—I just waved hello, grabbed my board, and headed home.

On the way up the fire escape, I tried the door on the Landing of Death. It was still locked up tight, which actually made me feel relieved. Safer. The thought of people going up and down the fire escape, going in and out without being seen . . . it gave me the heebie-jeebies.

Especially since the fifth-floor door is always "unlocked."

Anyway, I got in fine, survived Grams' "Good heavens, what happened to *you*?" fine, and was going into the bathroom to take a shower when all of a sudden an *earthquake* hits the building.

The walls shake.

The floor ripples.

The windows practically bust out of their frames.

I look over at Grams, and she just calmly shakes her head and says, "It must've been a doozy this time," because it *wasn't* actually an earthquake. That's just what it *feels* like when Mrs. Wedgewood falls off the toilet.

Like an aftershock, the Wedge starts sledging the wall.

"This cannot go on," Grams mutters as she checks the hallway. And when she sees that the coast is clear, she waves me along. "Come on."

Now, really. I didn't think anything could top the sight of Mrs. Wedgewood in all her bald, blubbery glory on the shower floor.

Boy, was I wrong.

We found her stuck between the toilet and the wall like we usually do, but this time she was face*down* instead of facing us. A corner of her muumuu was dipping in the toilet bowl, but the rest of it was flipped up over her body. You couldn't see much of the top half of her—just a puff of her big black wig and her hand clutching a toilet plunger.

But the *bottom* half of her was sticking straight up in the air, and her underwear had somehow snagged on the toilet paper roller, twisted, and stretched *way* up her crack.

It was, without a doubt, the biggest wedgie the world had ever seen.

"Don't just stare!" Mrs. Wedgewood cries from behind the toilet. "Help me!"

Grams gasps, "How on *earth* . . . ?" Then we sort of flutter around, trying to figure out how to tackle the problem. I mean, normally, we grab Mrs. Wedgewood under her armpits and heave-ho, but this time she's facing the wrong way and we can't even *reach* her armpits. All we've got to work with is a big ol' butt.

"This is going to take a licensed engineer and a crane," Grams mutters.

Apparently, Grams forgot that Mrs. Wedgewood has supersonic hearing. "That was not nice!" Wedgie Woman snaps.

"I'm sorry, Rose, but honestly—I don't see a way to help you. We're going to have to call the fire department."

"No!" she cries. "*Please*. Think of something!"

Grams studies her a minute, then asks, "Do you have any rope?"

"Rope?" the Wedginator cries from behind the toilet. "What would you do with rope?!"

"Perhaps we could loop it around you and pull."

Mrs. Wedgewood's back end starts quivering in fear. It's like big rolling hills of lard about to avalanche. "No! No rope!"

But talking about rope gives me an idea. "How about a sheet?"

Grams looks at me and nods. "That might work."

So I jet off to Mrs. Wedgewood's bedroom and rip the top sheet off her mattress, but on my way back I hear, "Knock-knock! Hello? Rose?"

I dive for cover inside the kitchen and hold my breath, thinking, This is not good.

Not good at all.

SEVENTEEN

In our hurry, we hadn't closed Mrs. Wedgewood's door all the way, and now we had company.

And it's not someone who's come to help.

Oh no. This someone has a phony sophisticated accent.

"Knock-knock!" the voice calls again. "Hello? Rose?" So I get down on my stomach and peek around the kick space of the cupboard, and sure enough, it's Rex-the-Jackal-Randolf and he's now standing inside. He's wearing the exact same getup as before, only this time he's holding a large box of chocolates instead of a bouquet of flowers.

"May I help you?" Grams asks, and she's sounding pretty flustered.

"Why, hello there," the Jackal says, cranking up the charm. "I'm Rex Randolf. And you are . . . ?"

My brain's shouting, Don't say it, don't say it, don't say it! But my grams believes in good manners and all that stuff, so she says, "Rita Keyes," and shakes his hand. Then she starts easing him toward the door. "But I'm afraid you've come at a very bad time. Rose is . . . uh . . . not available."

"I see," he says. "Well, perhaps you can give her these and a message?"

Grams tells him, "Certainly," then takes the box of chocolates and steers him toward the door.

"Tell her that I feel awful about last night. I was taken ill and just couldn't make it." He turns and sort of looks around when he reaches the door. "I hope she isn't suffering the same misfortune!"

Grams eases him out without letting on about anything. "I'll be sure to give her the message. And the chocolates."

"Would it be all right to come back later today? I really should apologize in person."

Grams starts to close the door. "I'm sure it would be." Then she adds, "But I would suggest calling first."

He steps back in. "Exactly what I would have done, but I didn't have her number."

Grams hesitates, then says, "Wait right here," and practically trips on me as she comes into the kitchen. She catches herself, then scribbles down Mrs. Wedgewood's number on a scrap of paper and goes back to where the Jackal's waiting. "Here you are, Mr. Randolf."

"It was very nice to make your acquaintance," he says, tossing her a final smile as he leaves.

"Likewise," she tells him, then shuts the door tight and locks it.

Now, this whole time Wedgie Woman hasn't made a peep. And that would have been amazing except for the fact that she's got bionic hearing, which is what was keeping her quiet. But the minute the door's shut and locked, she cries, "He walked right in? I am mortified! Which one of you left the door open?" Then she wails, "Help me! I'm in pain!"

I could feel Grams thinking, You *are* a pain! but she just led the way to the bathroom, saying, "Rose, if this doesn't work, I'm calling the fire department."

"No!" the Wedge cries. "It'll work, it'll work!"

But as I stand there looking at those two big bumpy moons, I don't know how in the world I'm ever going to get the sheet around her. I'm dealing with a complete roadblock of blubber on one side and a gaping toilet bowl with part of a muumuu soaking in it on the other.

"We've got to close the toilet," Grams says, shaking her head. "Then you can stand on the lid and work the sheet around her."

The first step in doing that was to take the muumuu out of the toilet. I tried not to think about what I was touching as I squeezed it dry with a towel.

"Maybe you could cover her up?" Grams whispers.

So I start to drape the muumuu over her behind, only just as I'm reaching over, she cuts the cheese.

I'm not talking a silent stink bomb, either.

This thing goes *pttttttttuuuuuuuuupppppppp, pttttttt-tup*, blasting past her wedgie like a hurricane.

"Aaaaaah!" I cry as I get blown back.

"Sorry!" the Wedge-o-Matic says. "I couldn't help it!"

After I recover from the shock of the blast, Grams and I try to wave the air clear, but really, it's hopeless. And since the key to us getting *out* of there is getting the Big

Wedge *un*wedged, I lower the toilet lid, climb aboard, and get to work.

It took about five minutes, but I did finally get the sheet around her. And when Grams had one end and I had the other, I said, "Okay, Mrs. Wedgewood. We're going to try to pull you up. Help us any way you can."

"Okay!" she cries.

So we grunt and groan, and just when I'm starting to think it's hopeless, she suddenly pops free.

Grams collapses on the floor, panting for breath, and Mrs. Wedgewood leans on the toilet for a minute before untangling her undies. When she turns to face us, her wig's half off, her face is practically purple, and her whole body's shaking. So I grab her walker and hand it to her. "Oh, thank you, sugar," she pants. "Thank you so much!"

She leans heavily on her walker, and when she's caught her breath a little, she says, "I'll have you know, that was no ordinary fall!" She turns to Grams, who is washing her hands at the sink. "This building still has mice, Rita! I almost cornered one, but he got away!"

"*That's* how you wound up in that position?" Grams asks, looking over her shoulder. "Chasing a *mouse*?"

"I was chasing it down with the plunger when . . . when I stumbled and twisted wrong and lost my balance." She pulls her wig into place. "Mice are dreadful creatures! Full of disease! And so destructive!"

I washed up, too, but Mrs. Wedgewood clickity-clacked straight out the door with her walker, saying, "I'm going to call Vince Garnucci right now! That little monster's still on the loose in here, and I won't be able to sleep a wink tonight!"

But as Grams and I leave the bathroom and Mrs. Wedgewood clacks toward the kitchen, I hear something. Something that I'd never heard before at the Wedge's apartment.

A phone ringing.

Our phone ringing.

Right through the wall.

It didn't matter who was calling or why. What mattered was I could hear it, because if *I* could hear it now, the Jackal had heard it the night before.

Suddenly it felt like all the blood in my head just whooshed away.

Escaped.

Went somewhere safer.

The Domino's Pizza bit was a big mistake.

What was I going to do?

The biggest messes I've gotten into seem to happen because of the *little* things I do wrong. Actually, they seem to happen because of the things I do to *cover up* the little things I do wrong.

Somehow the covering up becomes its own, even bigger mistake.

Which then needs covering up.

Anyway, I really do try to learn from my mistakes. I try not to make the same one twice. But mistakes are *tricky*. They're sneaky little masters of disguise. They dress up in so many different ways that you don't recognize them, and then all of a sudden they pull off their mask and say, *Ha-ha*, and there you are, face to face with a mistake you swore you'd never make again.

But as Mrs. Wedgewood called Mr. Garnucci and Grams peeked down the hallway to make sure the coast was clear for us to go back home, my brain was still trying to remember who knew what and who *didn't* know what. I needed to remember so I could figure out what to do about Rex Randolf. The Sandman had seen Grams with Mrs. Wedgewood at Monte Carlo night, but did Rex-the-Jackal-Randolf know that Grams was Grams? I mean, had *he* seen them together on their way down or something?

No, I told myself. He wouldn't have risked *being* seen.

But . . . what if the Sandman had taken a picture?

Like I'd wanted to do with Rex Randolf?

What if the Sandman had shown the picture to the Jackal and now the Jackal was lurking outside, waiting for Grams to come out of Mrs. Wedgewood's apartment so he could find out where she lived?

It didn't feel too likely, but still. Picture or no picture, he now knew Grams' name. He could just look up "Keyes" on the mailboxes and know which apartment was hers!

And if he'd heard the phone ringing when he'd called from the Wedgie's apartment, *and* he knew that Grams lived in the apartment next door, *and* he figured out that Grams had been down to Monte Carlo night with Mrs. Wedgewood, then the obvious question was, Who had answered, "Domino's Pizza"?

Plus, he had to have figured out by now that Rose Wedgewood was not someone who would be on the fire escape or someone who could run for help in an emergency.

So what was his next step?

Break into *our* apartment so he could search for the money there?

The money *had* to be what he was after.

Right?

The more I tried to figure it out, the more panicked I felt. All of this was heading in a very bad direction.

And then, right when Grams gave me the coast-is-clear nod, that sneaky little master of disguise finally pulled off its mask, and there I was, face to face with the same mistake I'd made over and over again.

I'd kept the truth from Grams.

Scratch that.

I'd *lied* to Grams.

But *still* I told myself that this was different. This was . . . fixable. There had to be some way to smooth things out, to fix things *and* keep the cash.

I pulled Grams back into the Wedgie's apartment and whispered, "What if that Rex Randolf guy is waiting out there?"

"No one's out there," Grams said. "I just checked."

"But . . . what if he's *hiding* somewhere?"

She cocked her head. "Why would he be doing that?"

I shrugged. "I just get a creepy vibe from him."

She studied me a minute. "Why?"

"It's . . . it's . . . it's the way he acts. There's something . . . not right about him."

She studied me some more, and then rather than just

saying, Oh, pshaw! and dragging me home, she patted my forearm and said, "You wait right here."

So while Mrs. Wedgewood complained to Mr. Garnucci about the building being infested with mice, Grams walked up and down the hallway, checking for sneaky creaky old guys. And when she finally returned and said, "There's no one," well, I sure wasn't going to hang out with the World's Biggest Wedgie for the rest of the day. I took a deep breath and followed Grams home.

I couldn't help looking over my shoulder, though.

I did it three times.

It sure *felt* like someone was watching.

Watching and waiting for the right time to pounce.

EIGHTEEN

There was no doubt in my mind—Rex Randolf would be back. And when he showed his sneaky little face again, I wanted to be ready. So after I finally took a shower, I told Grams I was going over to see Holly, then escaped the apartment and went to the mall.

I was really backsliding, but I couldn't seem to stop myself.

I did *not* want to give up the money.

I didn't mind *spending* it, though. I mean, what else was I going to do with it?

Save up for college?

Please.

I'm thirteen!

And since having the money in the apartment made me feel nervous—like somehow I might be putting Grams in danger—I went to the mall and started doling out dough.

The first thing I bought was a new pair of jeans. They were the kind Marissa swears by, with a little bit of stretch in the denim. They looked old, so I knew Grams wouldn't notice, and the minute I tried a squat in them, I was sold.

Com-fy!

I also bought a sweatshirt 'cause the zipper on my old one is about toast and the sleeves are way too short.

Then I went back to that art store and found out that the photograph I thought Hudson would like was five hundred and fifty bucks! Plus tax! I almost fell over, but after thinking about it for a while, I bought it anyway.

Hudson Graham really is the coolest old guy ever.

When I mentioned that it was a present, they wrapped it for free and threw in a gift card. So I filled out the card in really swirly handwriting:

For Hudson—
Thank you for making this world a better place.
Your Secret Admirer

I checked it over and couldn't help smiling.

This was fun!

After that I bought some other random stuff. Like a pretzel and a corn dog and a strawberry-orange Juicers and a couple of See's candies.

I was having a blast!

But the main thing I bought was a digital camera. It took me forever, too. I checked out all the display models and finally chose a supercompact one that could zoom way in. It was smaller than a deck of cards and could fit in my pocket easy. The owner's manual was three times as big as the camera!

The camera needed to be charged, and I needed to figure out how to work it, so I parked myself in a sort of secluded corner of the food court near a power outlet, plugged in the camera, and started reading the manual.

It was already after six when it finally hit me that maybe I should be getting home. I packed everything up quick, threw out the box and wrappers, and then realized I still had Hudson's gift to deliver.

So I found a pay phone, called Grams, and said, "Hey. Thought I'd check in. I'm over at the mall."

"Oh!" There was a little pause and then, "Well, thank you! I was wondering. Holly called here looking for you."

Uh-oh. I took a deep breath and forced a laugh. "Yeah. You know me. Little Miss Sidetrack."

She laughed. "Casey also called."

"Really?" I said with embarrassing enthusiasm.

"He said he'd try back later." Then I could practically see her scowl. "And *Rose* called right before you did." She dropped her voice to a whisper. "I've been summoned to attend to her royal highney."

I busted up. "Grams!"

She hrmphed, then said, "Excuse me, but I've seen a little too much of that woman's backside lately."

"So . . . is she . . . stuck?"

"No. That Rex fella is stopping by."

"Oh?" I took it down a notch and tried to act casual. "When?"

"He's coming over at seven-thirty." She gave a little snort and whispered, "Heaven only knows what he sees in her." Then real matter-of-factly she says, "He's quite a handsome man. Very dapper. I wonder if he's new to the building. I certainly would remember if I'd seen *him* before."

Well, *that* sent all my quills flying. "Don't *even* say that, Grams. He's a smooth-talking snake!"

She tisked. "Oh, Samantha."

"Grams! Promise me you won't let him into the apartment if he decides to 'swing by.' "

"Why would he swing by? He doesn't even know where I live."

My brain was screaming, *Maybe he does!* but I couldn't say it. I didn't even want to *think* it. "Look. Just don't let him in, okay?"

But now what? I had to come up with a plan. A plan to get Rex-the-Jackal-Randolf digitized so I could find out who he really was. For that, I needed to buy myself some time. So I said, "I won't be home for . . . probably another hour, okay?"

"Are you with Marissa?"

"No . . . but I might go see her. She was in a real frump earlier."

"About her family again? Say! You never finished telling me about Hudson offering to help out with Mikey."

"I'll, uh, I'll catch you up when I'm home, okay? Or hey! You know what? You should give Hudson a call and ask him about it—it's quite a story. And he'd probably really like to hear from you. Did you know Rommel died?"

"No!"

"So call him."

There was a short pause and then, "Okay. I will. And thank *you* for calling, sweetheart. I really do appreciate it."

So I got off the phone and went straight over to

143

Hudson's to deliver the present. I was hoping that Grams had just picked up the phone and called him right away, because Hudson is almost always hanging out on his porch and I sure didn't want to be spotted leaving the present. The whole fun was in him *not* knowing who the present was from. Plus, if he knew it was from me, there was no way he would accept it.

He knows I can't afford five-hundred-and-fifty-dollar photographs!

Luckily, he was not on the porch. But I still wanted to be careful, so I practically *crawled* up to his front door, then eeeeeased the package between the screen door and the door frame, and scurried back to the street.

My heart was totally pounding by the time I was in the clear. I don't know why I was so excited about leaving the present, but I really, really was.

I tried to put it out of my mind, though. I had to figure out how in the world I was going to get a picture of the Jackal without him seeing me. The Senior Highrise hallways aren't very wide, and they don't have a lot of, you know, *architectural* features. There are some dusty plastic plants in big plastic pots, but not many, and no pillars or, you know, *fanciness*.

It crossed my mind that there were trash chutes, but I nixed that right away. I mean, who would hide in a trash chute? It's a *chute*. A big metal shaft for garbage. And even though they're plugged up half the time, if you climb in one, you're gonna gain a whole new definition of Dumpster diving.

It'd actually be more like *dumbster* diving.

Anyway, I'm walking along, racking my brain for how I'm going to conceal myself so I can take a picture, when it hits me—I'm going about this all wrong!

I don't have to hide some*place*.

I just have to hide my *age*.

How do you hide in a building full of old people?

Be old!

I skidded to a halt and did a quick U-turn. I knew the perfect place to pick up an old-guy disguise—or actually, an old-*lady* disguise—but I didn't have my skateboard, and I didn't have much time.

So I raced over to the SMAT bus pickup area and checked the schedule that was posted by the benches where people were waiting, and almost right away the bus I needed drove up.

I got on board, paid the fare, and sat down, thinking that I should have gotten an old-lady disguise *ages* ago. Cruising around the Senior Highrise would be fun!

When we got to the Stowell Center shops, I got off the bus and hurried over to CeCe's Thrift Store. I love CeCe's—it's got the best funky old stuff you've ever seen—it's just CeCe herself that kinda scares me. She's a bag lady turned entrepreneur, and she's tough.

Sharp.

And let's just say she and I have had a couple of little, uh, *clashes*.

But if you're going to CeCe's Thrift Store, you're gonna have to deal with CeCe. She's always there. So I took a deep breath and went inside, and the instant she spotted me, she said, "Up here with that backpack."

She's got signs all over the place telling you to check backpacks and "big bags and purses" and that shoplifters will be "thrown in jail."

I knew this going in, and really, in all the times I've been to CeCe's with my backpack, I've never had a problem with her stealing stuff out of it. And since the money was on the bottom under all the other stuff I'd bought at the mall, and since the camera was inside a pouch that was inside *another* pouch, I just tried to act like I didn't give a hoot as I passed her my pack.

She put it down behind the counter and said, "It's been a while."

I hesitated 'cause it almost sounded like she missed me. "Yeah," I said, then went about my business. I didn't have time to chitchat with a thrift store shark! I had to put a disguise together.

And I had to do it quick.

NINETEEN

On my way back to the Highrise, I swung by Thrifty. I needed an Ace bandage, and I needed some makeup.

Some old-lady makeup.

I'm not talking about the kind old ladies use to cover up their pale, spotty skin and dark circles. No, I needed something that would *give* me pale, spotty skin and dark circles!

Now, both Billy Pratt and Casey were in plays for drama class last year, and Billy, especially, isn't afraid to paint his face up weird. He can actually make himself look old or all bruised up or just ghoulish with a simple pencil. I've watched him do this *shading* thing that's really kind of amazing.

So I bought a pencil.

And a sharpener.

And some pale pancake makeup.

And an ugly orange lipstick.

Maybe once you're old, you don't see colors right anymore, I don't know. But you're definitely old when you start thinking bright orange or gag-me pink lipstick looks good. You're also old when you forget how to color inside the lip line. Old ladies go *way* over the top line. Or they go lopsided. Or usually, they do both.

Anyway, I also bought some clip-on earrings and a mirror, and by the time I got back to the Senior Highrise, it was after seven o'clock and I was not *even* ready to go inside the building. I still looked like a teenager! And it wasn't like there was a phone booth nearby where I could jump inside and magically transform into Old Lady Superspy. I had to do this piece by piece, in a secluded little area next to the trash chute Dumpster.

I sat on the ground, set up my mirror, and got to work covering up my tan with the pale makeup. Then I shaded on bags under my eyes, and spots, and penciled on lines like I'd seen Billy do. I sort of smoothed them over with some more makeup, and then did the same thing to my hands.

That chewed up about fifteen minutes.

Then I went to town with the orange lipstick. I just pictured the way our old neighbor Mrs. Graybill used to put on her lips, and when I was done, I looked ridiculous!

Just like Mrs. Graybill used to.

Next I clipped on the earrings, took off my high-tops, stripped out of my jeans, and shoved the flat, worn-out pillow that I'd gotten at CeCe's under my T-shirt, wrapping it on around my stomach with the Ace bandage.

Instant tummy bulge!

Then I pulled a big flowery dress over my head, layered a sweater over it, and put on some cloudy beige knee-high hose and a pair of thick, rubbery shoes that were a little too small and an amazingly ugly tan. I took off my ball cap and my softball wristwatch, redid my ponytail up higher, pulled on a gray wig, perched little spectacles on my nose, and checked myself out in the mirror.

It was kinda scary! And if you didn't look too close, pretty convincing.

And since most people in the building had bad eyesight, I told myself that if I kept my distance and *acted* old, I might really be able to pull this off.

"Hello, dearie!" I said to myself. "Eh? What was that?"

I checked my watch. It was already seven-thirty!

I turned the camera on, shut off the flash feature, and put it inside a pea green handbag, then stuffed all my regular clothes in my backpack and stashed the backpack behind some bushes.

Old Lady Superspy was ready to rock!

Or at least snap a few pictures.

I thought about going in the front door but decided that it was too risky. If Mr. Garnucci was at his desk, he'd call hello like he always does, then want to know who I'd come to visit and all of that.

Besides, I was running late. The Jackal was probably already at Mrs. Wedgewood's. So I charged up the fire escape, checking the fourth-floor door on the way.

Still locked.

Once I got up to the fifth-floor landing and saw that the coast was clear, I hurried down to Mrs. Wedgewood's and put my ear up to her door. I held my breath and listened hard.

I could hear voices!

So I took a deep breath, hunched a little, and reminded myself to be, you know, *creaky*. Then I rang the bell.

"Who is it?" Mrs. Wedgewood sang out.

"Mabel Florentine!" I said in a quivery voice. "I'm

here to see Rose Wedgewood. Mr. Garnucci sent me to document a *mouse* problem."

She called, "Come in!" like she almost always does because, well, getting to the door herself can take a while.

So I stepped inside, and there was the Jackal, sitting in the living room with a cup of coffee and a plate of cookies, dressed exactly the same as before.

"Excuse the intrusion," I said, using my best granny vocabulary. "Mr. Garnucci sent me up. He said you were upset about a mouse. If there are still mice, we certainly want to know!"

"Oh, there are mice!" the Wedge crowed. "And Vince had better get rid of them!"

I nodded and took the camera out of the purse. "Mr. Garnucci says we need to build a case so we can get the exterminator back. Where exactly did you see the mouse?"

"Back there!" Mrs. Wedgewood says, motioning toward the bathroom. "But he could be anywhere. And I don't see how you'll ever get a *picture* of him!"

Now, Rex-the-Faker-Randolf seems to be looking at everything but me—the coffee, the cookies, the armrest—it's like he's afraid *I'm* going to recognize *him* or something.

"Oh," I say, "this is for *solid* evidence." I hold it up to my eye and move it around like I have no idea what I'm doing. "Like droppings. . . ." I look down at my feet. "Or mouse holes. . . ." I look over at Rexy-baby and click, then look up at the ceiling and back down at my feet. "This fandangled thing is so hard to see through! I think I'll just take a quick look-see around and get out of your hair."

Now, the Senior Highrise is definitely not a deluxe

building. The trash chute's usually plugged, the plumbing backs up, we've got mice and, of course, a Nightie-Napper. And in an ordinary building, sending an old lady to take pictures of mouse droppings would be crazy.

At the Senior Highrise, it was barely odd.

And lucky for me, Mrs. Wedgewood was putting on a show of politeness and Rex Randolf was obviously just wishing I would leave. So I did a sort of stiff-legged waddle over to the bathroom and slammed some cupboard doors around with one hand while I checked the picture of Rexy-baby with the other.

It was a three-quarters shot and plenty good enough.

"Find anything?" a voice behind me said.

The voice was low and calm.

And it shot me right out of my skin!

The trouble with jumping out of your skin is that you do it before you can stop yourself. And then trying to crawl back *inside* your skin as you pretend you never jumped out in the first place can be very tricky.

Especially if you're thirteen trying to crawl back inside old-lady skin.

"I'm just tryin' to bang him out!" I say, slamming the cupboard door some more with one hand as I hide the camera in between the folds of my skirt with the other. "He's in here someplace, Rose!" I call in a warbly voice. "There's droppings behind your toilet!"

"That's exactly where he was!" she cries from her sunken spot on the sofa. "You tell Vince you found evidence! You tell him to get rid of this infestation once and for all!"

I ease my way past the Jackal, keeping my face down and

turned away, then I slip the camera back in the purse and force myself to move slow and creaky as I go toward the front door. "There's obviously still a problem," I call over to Mrs. Wedgewood. "I'll tell him what I found, dear. Don't you worry!"

I half expected the Jackal to grab me by the scruff of my neck and rip off my wig, but he didn't. He just let me out and closed the door.

So there I am, in the clear, about to dart down to the fire escape, when all of a sudden I notice something.

Our apartment door is cracked open.

And there's an eyeball behind glasses peeking out.

I'm being spied on by my own grandmother!

Grams backs away when she realizes she may have been spotted, and I just stand there for a second not knowing what to do. Part of me wants to just go home and tell her it's me, but then I'd have to explain why I'm dressed up as an old lady.

Another part of me wants to make a mad dash for the fire escape, but if she saw that, she'd *know* it was me.

What I do *not* want to do is creak my way over to the elevator or the regular stairs. It's the long way, for one thing, and my ugly tan granny shoes are starting to kill me. But also, I don't know how long the Jackal will stay at the Wedge's apartment, and I sure don't want to come face to face with him again.

Once was scary enough!

And it sure didn't seem like he'd be at the Wedge's apartment for very long. I mean, why was he there at all? How long would it take for him to realize he'd hit the big dead end of information?

But really, I had no choice—our apartment door was still cracked open, and I could feel Grams watching.

So off I go, hobbling past our apartment, looking straight ahead, feeling like a really sneaky, *creepy* granddaughter.

By the time I made it to the elevator, my feet were in pain, and as I'm punching the elevator's call button, I'm thinking that I can't *wait* to get back into my high-tops. But after a couple of minutes go by, I decide, Forget the stupid elevator! Like everything else in the Senior Highrise, it's old and slow and might pick this very moment to break down for good. So I abandon that route out and limp on over to the inside stairs. My shoes are *chomping* on me, and my fakey stomach's starting to sag, but I keep on limping on until I'm down on the fourth floor.

At this point, my foot is bleeding, and really, walking all the way along the fourth-floor hallway and down the fire escape in crabby shoes is going to be pure torture. So I take a minute and rip off those petrified toe-chompers, then check the hallway and head for the fire escape, rubbery shoes in one hand, pea green purse in the other.

But just as I get near the elevator, it dings.

I come skidding to a halt 'cause in a flash it hits me—it might be the Jackal!

I'd called the elevator to the fifth floor.

What if it had arrived in time to give *him* a quick ride down?

I start backpedaling like mad, but it's too late.

The elevator door's already sliding open.

TWENTY

There was nowhere to duck, nowhere to hide. So I did the same thing I did the night I scared Buck Ritter to death.

I sucked up against the wall.

Only this time I'm in a flowered dress.

Carrying ugly tan shoes.

And I'm in a lighted hallway!

Sure enough, it's the Jackal who steps out of the elevator. And maybe I should have made a mad dash back to the inside stairs, but for some reason I just stood there like a great big granny splat against the wall, my heart machine-gunning in my chest.

And then the weirdest thing happens.

The Jackal steps out and turns his head a little to the left, then turns right and walks down the hall away from me.

I just stand there, splatted against the wall.

How could he *not* have seen me?

I mean, old-guy eyes are one thing—this was like he was *blind*.

Whatever. I tiptoed out of there, keeping one eye on him as he walked in the opposite direction, and when I was safely around the corner, I watched him stop and knock on an apartment door. He knuckled it four times, then two, and a few seconds later the door whooshed open and he disappeared inside.

I waited another minute, then tiptoed over to the apartment the Jackal had gone into.

It was number 427.

Four-two-seven, I told myself. Four knocks, two knocks, lucky number seven.

Now, I'm not about to stand there with my ear to the door or anything. My nerves are totally fried and I just want to get *out* of there! So before something else happens, I race down the hallway, slip out the fire escape door, and fly down the stairs.

The cool air feels great, and before I've even reached my backpack, I've got my wig and glasses ripped off. And as soon as I've got my backpack out of the bushes and I'm safe and sound in my little hiding place by the Dumpster, I pull on my jeans and tear off my disguise, stuffing it all in CeCe's plastic shopping bag.

Then I hide the bag in the bushes where my backpack had been and hurry up the stairs. But halfway up I happen to notice my hand.

It's still covered in spots.

Which means my face is, too!

Holy smokes!

So I flip a U-turn, race back down the stairs, find a spigot, and use one of my socks to scrub my face and hands the best I can and *then* go up to the fifth floor.

"*There* you are!" Grams says when I come through the

door, and before I can even say I'm sorry for being late, she closes the door and whispers, "Strange things have been going on around here!"

"Really?" I ask, plopping my backpack down like it's just my same old backpack instead of something that's got a couple thousand dollars, a digital camera, and some cool new clothes in it.

"*Very* strange."

"Like what? Objects moving through space?" I ask all nonchalantly as I head for the bathroom to check myself out in the mirror.

"No!"

"Hang on," I tell her, closing the door, 'cause I really need to use soap to clean my fake old-lady spots all the way off.

When I come out, Grams starts in about everything she was able to overhear and over*see* with Mrs. Wedgewood and "that handsome Mr. Randolf" and "a strange woman with the ugliest shoes you've ever seen," and she's in the middle of telling me about "an awful, banging, clanging racket" when all of a sudden the phone rings.

She interrupts herself to pick it up, and after a minute she says, "Just a moment," then hands me the phone, whispering, "It's Marissa. She sounds *very* upset." Then she adds, "Oh! And Casey's called four times looking for you!"

My eyebrows shoot up, but she just shrugs. So I turn to the phone and say, "What's up?"

"Ohmygodyou'renotgoingtobelievewhat'shappened! Mylife'sadisaster!" And even though I could kinda decipher that part, pretty soon she's bawling her eyes out and talking at the same time, which just sounds like, "Brawthwo breeeth a boosta neeeeeee!"

"Marissa! Marissa! Calm down! Are you all right?"

"No! My life's a . . . a—*hic*—disaster!"

"Is anybody dead?"

"No! But almost!"

"What? What do you mean, almost?"

"My parents got into a—*hic*—awful fight! My mom was—*hic*—*screaming* at my dad! It was even worse than when Mikey—*hic*—broke the Kraval!"

"Do you know why?"

"It has to do with money, but—*hic*—she won't tell me!"

"Did you ask your dad?"

"He's *gone*. He tore out of here so fast he—*hic*—totaled my bike!" She starts bawling again. "Please come over! Please! I feel like my whole world is falling apart!"

Grams is looking at me like, *What is going ON?* So I pull a face and cover the phone. "Can I go spend the night at Marissa's? She's having a meltdown."

She nods. "Just call me when you get there so I know you're safe."

So I get off the phone, grab my backpack, my skateboard, and my toothbrush, give Dorito a quick kiss on the nose, and head for the fire escape.

Again.

On my way over to Marissa's, my head felt like a bubbling, steaming kettle of soup.

Scratch that.

It felt like a whole *cauldron* of stew.

Yeah, that's it. My head was full to the brim of Problem Stew. I'd been adding stuff to the mix so fast, and things were heating up so fast, it felt like the whole mess would just boil over if one more little thing got put in.

At least for once it wasn't all *my* problems. But I think that's what was making my head feel like it was about to boil over. Besides giving Buck Ritter from Omaha, Nebraska, a heart attack and hiding the money from . . . well, *everybody,* Marissa and her problems with Mikey and Danny and Heather and now her *parents* were also swimming around in my brain, and I couldn't seem to keep the lid on *any* thought. I felt all mushy-headed. Like I couldn't keep one thought from splattering into another.

Normally when I'm in a stew, I wind up at Hudson's. He's really good at giving advice without you knowing he's giving advice. He's kinda tricky that way. He listens, says a few things, and somehow makes you feel like *you're* the one who's figured it all out.

But I didn't really have time to stop by Hudson's about my poor stewed-up, splattering head. It was late and I had to get to Marissa.

When I arrived at the McKenzes', the first thing I saw was Marissa's bike at the side of the house, totally demolished. And before I was even at the front door, Marissa came flying out of the house and threw her arms around me. "I'm so glad you're here!" she sobbed. "I don't know what to *do.*"

I eyed the bike. "About your parents?"

"About anything! My life's a disaster!"

"Hey," I said, holding her out a little and looking her in her bloodshot eyes. "Your parents have gotten into fights before, right? They'll get over it."

"Not like this! *Nothing* like this!"

"But it's about money, right? Not about something, you know . . . *irreversible*?"

"Yeah," she whimpered. "Yeah, I *think* so."

"So they'll fix it. They're money wizards! Everything'll be fine!"

Her chin started quivering. "But it doesn't *feel* like it's going to be fine. It feels . . . horrible!" Her chin quivered and twitched faster and faster until it looked like it was full of Mexican jumping beans. Finally she blurted, "And Danny kissed Heather!"

She lunged at me and bawled into my shoulder. "How could he have kissed *Heather*?"

I sighed. "He's a jerk, that's how."

"*She's* the jerk!"

I rolled my eyes and took a deep breath. I felt like we'd already covered this ground, but obviously we were back at square one.

"How would you feel," she sniffed, "if you saw Casey kissing . . . I don't know who! Anyone! Tenille! Amber! Anybody."

I tried, but I couldn't really picture it.

"Never *mind*," she said with a great big pout. "Casey would never do that." She turned and marched for the house. "You're right. Danny's a jerk. I should hate him."

"There you go!" I said, chasing after her. "Say that again."

"He's a jerk and I should hate him!"

"Louder!"

"He's a jerk and I should hate him!"

"Louder!"

"HE'S A JERK AND I HATE HIM!"

"LOUDER!"

"HE'S A JERK AND I TOTALLY AND COMPLETELY HATE HIM!"

"Okay!"

But we were now at the front door, and Mrs. McKenze was coming out. "Stop that!" she hissed. "He's your father and you are *not* to shout things like that! This is our business, not the whole neighborhood's!" She pointed at me. "Stop egging her on!"

"But—" Marissa said, but her mother had already stormed back inside. And really, what could she say? There's no way she was going to tell her mother about Danny and Heather!

"See?" Marissa said, throwing her hands into the air. "See what I'm having to deal with?"

"See?" I said with a grin. "She's sticking up for your dad—they're gonna be fine."

When we were inside the house, we headed straight to Marissa's bedroom.

Well, as straight as you can go in the McKenzes' house.

We passed by their "casual" living room, which is full of highly polished everything, turned a corner, and passed by the kitchen hallway and the big double doors that lead to the room where the Kraval used to reign supreme. And we were just going around another corner to head upstairs to Marissa's bedroom when we heard the phone ringing.

It was snatched up, and two seconds later Mrs. McKenze's office door flew open. She seemed startled to see us there, but right away she drilled me with her eyes and said, "Do *not* give out our number as your place of contact!"

"I didn't!" I said, all defensive-like.

"So why are *boys* calling here?"

My brain went, Casey?

My mouth went, "I have no idea!"

She stared at me a second, then without a word she pulled back into her office and slammed the door.

And as we're heading up to Marissa's bedroom, I'm thinking, So . . . was that Casey? I mean, who else could it be? But why *was* he calling the McKenzes'? Him calling the apartment was a new thing. Him calling the McKenzes'? He'd never done *that* before.

Once we were safely in Marissa's bedroom, I said, "I promised Grams I'd call and let her know I was okay."

So Marissa got me a phone, and when I called home, Grams informed me that Casey had called *again*. "I don't know what's going on, but he seemed almost frantic. You really need to call him back."

"Okay. I will."

So I got off the phone and punched in Casey's cell phone number.

He answered the phone with, "Sammy?"

"Sorry I didn't call you back sooner. My life's been crazy."

"Can you get down to the Landmark Broiler? Like, *now*?"

"The Landmark Broiler? Why?"

There was no answer.

"Casey?"

No answer.

"Hello? Hello, Casey?"

I punched off and redialed his number.

Right away it switched over to voice mail.

"What's wrong?" Marissa asked.

"Come on," I said, grabbing her by the wrist.

I had to get to the Landmark Broiler.

Like, *now*.

TWENTY-ONE

"The Landmark Broiler? But it's dark out!" Marissa said as I dragged her through the house.

And that's when I remembered—her bike was totaled.

Now, even if there was a skateboard somewhere in the house, Marissa would never be able to use it. She'd be a bag of broken bones *way* before we reached downtown.

But since the Landmark Broiler was miles from Marissa's house, I needed her on *something* with wheels 'cause I sure wasn't going to leave her behind.

"Do your parents have bikes?"

Her face scrunched up. "Are you kidding?"

"Does Mikey?"

"No."

"There's got to be something with wheels. Anything with wheels!"

"What is going *on*?"

"I have no idea, okay? But something is. Something big."

"How big could it be?"

"I don't know," I said, looking around the garage. "But Casey sounded really spun up. And the phone went dead!" Then, just to get her to help me look, I kinda slyly said, "Maybe it has to do with Heather."

She totally perked up. "Heather?"

And that's when I spotted a bike tire peeking out from behind big collapsible party tables that were leaning against the wall. "Hey!" I said, pointing. "That's a bike!"

But when I pulled it out, I discovered that it was a small bright yellow banana-seat bike with high handlebars that had yellow and blue plastic streamers sticking out of them.

It also had *training* wheels.

"I can't ride that!" Marissa cried. "Mikey got it when he turned five. He rode it, like, once!"

I studied it for a second, and after doing a quick search of the garage for other choices, I said, "It's better than nothing." I pulled it forward. "I'm not leaving you here to mope, okay? Just get on the bike and let's go."

She grumbled a minute, then tested the tires with her thumb. They were low, so she grumbled some more as she pumped them up, and off we went.

Now, it's kind of a long story, but let's just say that before I got my skateboard back from the jerk who stole it, I used to get rides on the handlebars of Marissa's bike.

She'd crash every time.

Or come close to it, anyway.

And watching her ride Mikey's banana bike into town made me really, *really* glad I had my skateboard back. There's no way I would've survived on those handlebars! Just watching her was scary. She had to scrunch way up to pedal, and with the little plastic fringe flapping in the wind and the way she was concentrating so hard because the training wheels didn't let her lean and the handlebars were hard to steer with, she looked like some wild child escaping the circus.

"This better be important!" she said when we got to the restaurant. "And he'd better be here. I'm not riding this thing another foot!"

I picked up my skateboard and started walking through the parking lot, muttering, "I sure hope he's okay," as I looked around for Casey.

"Casey's probably *fine*." She pushed the banana bike along. "*I'm* the one you're supposed to be worried about." Then, before I could say anything, she muttered, "And if anyone saw me on this stupid bike, I'm gonna die. Hello, morgue—I'm dead."

"No one saw you," I said, searching for Casey.

"What are you *talking* about? How could they miss?" She sighed. "I just hope Danny wasn't one of them."

I snapped to. "Hey! He's a jerk and you hate him, remember?"

"Oh yeah," she said with a pout.

So there we are, walking through the parking lot of the Landmark Broiler, me holding my skateboard, Marissa pushing along a clown bike with training wheels, when all of a sudden Marissa grabs my arm and points. "Look!"

So I look, expecting to see Casey in . . . I have no idea what kind of crisis. But instead I see a dressed-up couple coming out of the restaurant, walking along the awning-covered walkway.

At first I don't understand why Marissa's gasping and grasping and carrying on like the world's exploding. I mean, my head's wrapped around finding Casey, and the couple she's pointing to is not a teenage guy in jeans and a T-shirt.

But then the world does seem to go *ka-blam* as I realize that Marissa's not pointing at just some *random* couple leaving the restaurant.

"That *is* your mother, isn't it?" Marissa whispers.

I nod, but really, that's about all I can manage.

"And the guy with his arm around her?" She pulls a face at me. "Is that . . . ?"

I take a deep, deep breath and nod. "Casey's dad."

"That's it," I said, watching them move along the walkway under the awning. "I officially hate her."

"Wow," Marissa gasped. "I thought *I* had problems." Then she added, "Look how cozy they are!" and *then* she started musing over all the things I didn't want to think about. "Maaaaan. If they get married, that would make Casey your stepbrother, Heather your stepsister, and Candi your step*mother.*"

"It would not! To be my stepmother, that witch would have to marry my *father.*"

"Good point," Marissa said with a very calm nod. "But Casey and Heather—"

"Stop! What are you trying to do? Torture me?"

"Hey!" came a voice behind me.

I spun around. "Casey!"

He nodded out at our wonderful parents strolling toward his dad's car. "Nice, huh? How do you want to deal?"

"By never talking to them again?"

Casey shook his head. "That's not an option for me. On the outs with him means I'm stuck at my mom's." He grabbed my hand and said, "Come on," and as he pulled me toward the little lying lovebirds, he eyed Marissa's bike and said, "Can't wait to hear the story behind *that*."

Mr. Acosta was just opening the passenger door for my mother when Casey and I sort of appeared beside them. My mom gasped, then immediately tried to make it seem like we were the ones who'd done something wrong. "How dare you follow us like this!"

"What?" I sputtered. "I didn't follow you! Grams and I thought you went back to Hollywood! But I get it now—you didn't come home to see *us* at all. You came to see *him*. It was just bad luck that Grams saw you at the store!" I could feel a cold hard knot tying in my heart. "Grams is gonna love this."

"This is none of her or your or . . . or anybody else's business!" Then she threw in her two cents' worth of parenting. "And what are you doing out so late? You should *not* be out this late!"

Casey had his eyes locked on his dad the whole time, but his dad could only seem to look at his shiny-shoed feet. Very quietly, Casey said, "You told me the two things that mattered to you were *trust* and *truth*. If you wanted to go out with Sammy's mom, why didn't you just say so? I know how to make myself scarce. You didn't have to lie and say you were going out of town or banish me to Mom's with some stupid excuse about me needing to bond with her and Heather."

Mr. Acosta glanced at him. "Can we discuss this at home?" His voice was low, and it was easy to see he felt awful.

Casey snorted. "So I'm allowed to come home?" But then he started to back away. "You know what? Forget it."

Mr. Acosta seemed torn and really embarrassed, looking at my mom, then Casey, at my mom, then Casey. Finally he said to Casey, "Why don't you stay right here. I'll take Lana to her hotel, then give you a lift home."

Casey tossed him a disgusted look. "I can get home fine without you."

My mother got in the car, still acting like *I* was the one who'd done something wrong. So I said, "Should I tell Grams you'll be stopping by the flea-ridden hovel before you leave town?"

She glanced at me and whispered, "Insolence is very unattractive."

"So is being comatose," I whispered back. "Wake up, would you? You're not the only one with feelings!"

She blinked at me twice, then shut the door.

So I caught up to Casey and Marissa as Casey's dad called, "I'll see you at home, son!"

"Wow," Marissa said when we were a safe distance away. "That was freaky!"

"Freaky?" I asked.

"Yeah," she said, pushing the bike along. "It's like you guys are the adults and they're the children."

I looked at Casey, who muttered, "Freaky is right." He shook his head. "Why'd he have to lie to me? Why didn't he just *tell* me?"

Marissa was right, though—it was all kinda backward and freaky. "You know what?" I said to Casey. "I think you need to have a serious talk with your dad. You need to tell him that my mother is a bad influence and that getting tangled up with her could have seriously negative consequences."

"She didn't *make* him lie. He didn't have to!"

"But see? That's her influence. That's how she deals with things she doesn't want to face—she lies. And if she's already got him lying, too, what's next?"

He shook his head. "Man. He must really like her."

"Which is freaky enough right there," I grumbled.

We walked along for a minute, then he eyed me and said, "I'm glad you made it out here."

"Well, you sounded really stressed, and then the phone went dead—"

"My battery died. It was already low this morning, and I've been trying to get you all day. First after I found out that Heather was totally lying about Mom being ticked about the kitchen—I went back to the ballpark, but you guys were gone. Then when I spotted my dad and your mom driving through town—I thought I was hallucinating."

"Did you follow them to the Landmark Broiler?"

"I couldn't keep up, but the Landmark Broiler is my dad's favorite place, so I came down here on a hunch, and sure enough, his car was in the lot." He looked at me. "Glad I finally caught you."

I looked down. "Yeah, I'm sorry I was so, you know, *crazed* today."

He raised an eyebrow at the banana bike. "Did it have something to do with transportation issues?"

I sure didn't want to explain what I'd *really* been doing, so I said, "Yeah, Marissa's kind of in crisis mode."

"Kind of?" Marissa said. *"Kind of?"*

Casey laughed. "Yeah, what do you mean, kind of? To ride around on that thing, you've got to be in *serious* crisis mode. What happened?"

And see, that's the great thing about Casey. He can make you laugh and still let you know that he cares. And boy! Did Marissa ever use the opportunity to tell him what was wrong with her life. From having no money to her dad storming off and backing over her bike, she told him about everything . . . except Danny.

When we got to the corner where we had to turn to go up the hill to Marissa's house and he had to go straight to start the long ride out to his dad's house, Casey kinda stood facing me a minute. Finally he said, "Well, I guess I'd better go. I'll see you at the pool party tomorrow, huh?"

I nodded. And I felt like I wanted him *not* to go, but there we all were on the street corner feeling kinda, you know, *awkward*. So I just gave a dumb little wave and said, "Yeah."

"See ya, Casey!" Marissa called as he took off on his skateboard, and the minute he was a little ways down the road, she turned to me and said, "He would *so* have kissed you if I wasn't here!"

I heaved a sigh and started up the hill. "I don't think so. Things feel weird now." I kicked a rock. "Good ol' Lady Lana's ruining everything."

I mean, come on.

What guy in his right mind wants to kiss his future stepsister?

TWENTY-TWO

Casey *has* tried to kiss me before.

A couple of times.

Or at least I *think* he was planning to. What do I know? I've never been kissed by a guy.

Well, okay. So there was that one time Billy Pratt kissed me, but that was done on a dare. It was just another one of Heather's stupid schemes to mess up my life, so it doesn't count.

Anyway, the problem with the times Casey's tried to kiss me was that I wasn't ready. Either I was still freaked out about him being Heather's brother, or I was too self-conscious about . . . well, stuff like my lips being dry and chapped and *cracked* from camping in the wilderness.

You do not want your first kiss to be on dry, chapped, cracked lips.

You just don't.

But in the short window between getting over the fact that Casey was genetically linked to Heather and the fear that he might become *my* brother, I'd sort of shied away from kissing him.

Maybe I was a kissing coward.

Or maybe I still couldn't believe that a guy as amazing as Casey actually *wanted* to kiss me.

Whatever. As we trudged up the hill to Marissa's house, I felt really heavyhearted. For months Marissa and Holly and Dot had told me how terrific Casey was and how lucky I was that he liked me, and for months I'd come up with excuses about how come he and I could never work out.

Hudson had once said something about a "self-fulfilling prophecy," and when I'd asked him what that was, he'd said, "It's getting what you expect. If you expect the worst, that's exactly what you'll get. Instead, you should expect great things—you'll get *them* instead."

At the time it all sounded like a bunch of mumbo jumbo, but now it seemed like the situation with Casey was a self-fulfilling prophecy—I'd believed for so long that it couldn't work out that now, just as I was finally admitting to myself that I wanted it to work out, it was too late. The whole thing was just blowing up—lit fuse courtesy of my self-centered mother.

Fortunately, Marissa's mother distracted me from getting terminally ticked off at my own. We could hear Mrs. McKenze's voice through her office door as we tiptoed down the hallway. "Bob, please. Walk away. Just walk away. . . . Yes, I know you're on a roll, but . . . Bob, *listen* to me. You can't win it all back. You'll lose what you've won. Just walk away! . . . It's okay, we'll work it out. Just come home! . . . Bob! Bob, no! *Listen* to me! Red may *seem* lucky, but you've been drinking, and . . . Bob? . . . Bob? . . . Bob!"

From the cursing that followed, it was obvious he'd hung up on her. Marissa looked at me with wide eyes and whispered, "He went back to Vegas?" She knocked twice on the door and walked in. "Mom?"

"Not now," Mrs. McKenze said, frantically stuffing things into a briefcase. "I've got to go." She saw me standing in the hallway. "Sammy's still here? Well, that's good." She eyed me. "Just stay out of trouble, all right?" She slid her laptop into the briefcase and turned to Marissa. "Can you check on Michael tomorrow? Tell him I love him?"

"Check on him? Where is he?"

"He's . . . he's staying at Hudson's tonight." Marissa's eyes bugged out, so real fast Mrs. McKenze added, "It's fine. Everything's fine. He wanted to stay there, and under the circumstances . . . I just can't handle dealing with him right now."

"Are you going to Vegas?" Marissa asked, her voice small.

All Mrs. McKenze's frantic motion stopped for a second, then she shut the briefcase lid. "*If* I can catch the eleven-thirty flight."

"How much has he lost?"

Mrs. McKenze snapped the latches closed. "More than I care to think about." She came around from behind her desk, gave Marissa a quick hug and kiss, and said, "I'll get him home and we'll straighten this all out. Don't worry. We'll recover. Everything will be fine." She hurried down the hallway, calling, "If there's an emergency, contact Aunt Nola and Uncle Bruce. But *please* don't tell them we've got problems, all right? We don't need the whole family to know!" She was out of sight now, but right before the door to the garage slammed, she shouted, "And feed Michael's fish!"

Marissa and I decided the fish could wait.

We were starving!

So we fed ourselves first, snacking on chips, Oreos, and ice cream. And even though we'd eaten a lot, I was still hungry. It had been a long, incredibly intense day, and I needed something *real* to eat. But that's the problem with the McKenzes'—there's *never* anything real to eat. It's all prepackaged, microwavable, man-on-the-run stuff.

And then Marissa, who'd just finished putting two Pop-Tarts in the toaster, suddenly gasped and punched the bright blue eject button on the toaster. "What am I *thinking*?" she said, snatching the Pop-Tarts out of the slots. "I'm wearing a *two*-piece tomorrow!"

"Oh, good grief." I took a Pop-Tart out of her hand and chomped down. "Forget the stupid two-piece. We're playing water hoops!"

She punched open the trash compactor with her foot and chucked the other Pop-Tart inside it. "Not the whole time. . . ."

One look at her pathetic pout and I understood. "Aw, Marissa, come *on*."

"It looks really good on me," she said, her eyes doing a total puppy-dog plead.

"Yeah, it does."

"And he *is* going to be there."

I sighed. "We really need to find you a new crush."

But then she said, "And *she'll* be there, too."

I choked on a chunk of Pop-Tart. And after a coughing fit, I said, "Who? Heather?"

"Of course Heather."

"Why would *she* be there?" But suddenly I realized that of course she would be. Heather had been at the ballpark when Brandon had called out that everyone was invited. "Oh, maaaaan!" I chucked the rest of my Pop-Tart into the compactor. "Talk about ruining a party."

Marissa pulled a face and shook her head. "I can't believe you hadn't thought of that."

To me this was like visiting Disneyland with a sniper on your tail. Heather wouldn't actually get in the pool and *play* water hoops. Oh no, she'd act all cool and superior and snipe from the sidelines. She wouldn't just sun herself or enjoy the food or hang out and be *normal,* she'd find some way to make us miserable. Anything to make us miserable.

"Look, Marissa," I said once I was over the shock of it, "you do not want to compete for Danny's affections like that. Your best bet is to ignore him and ignore her."

"Oh, I'm going to ignore him, all right!" she said. "And I'm going to make sure I look good doing it."

I groaned, but I knew there was no talking her out of it.

The phone rang, and after Marissa picked it up, she said, "Okay . . . okay . . . okay . . . I will. . . . Okay . . . okay . . . okay, bye," and hung up.

"Your mother?" I asked.

Marissa nodded. "She made the flight. She says I shouldn't worry, not to eat junk food, and to feed the fish." She eyed me. "She also wants me to keep you away from matches."

"Matches? Why matches?"

She laughed. "Some vision about you burning down the house."

"I do *not* deserve that."

She laughed again and said, "Come on. Let's go feed the fish."

Now, since we were both wiped-out tired, no one had to tell us to go to bed. We just wound up in Marissa's room and dived for the covers. "What a day," Marissa said with a yawn. "Softball . . . spying on Heather . . . riding Mikey's bike downtown . . . my parents . . . your mother. . . . Holy smokes."

I propped up on an elbow and looked at her. "That softball game was this morning?"

She laughed. "Yeah."

I plopped back down. "Holy smokes is right!" Because between all the things Marissa had listed, I'd also run around town *buying* stuff and infiltrated the Highrise as Old Lady Superspy.

No wonder I was wiped out!

"G'night," Marissa mumbled after a minute.

"Good night," I said back.

"My family is such a mess," she said, the words all slurring together.

"Mine too," I chuckled.

"Yours has *always* been a mess. Except for your grandmother. She's a rock."

I nodded in the darkness. Grams was definitely a rock.

"Wish I had a rock," she mumbled. "My parents have always been more into work than spending time with me or Mikey. And now my dad's got a gambling problem?" Her voice was totally drifting off now. "Money makes you do weird stuff. It controls you. Once you have it, it's hard to let it go."

She may have been talking herself to sleep, but I was now wide-awake.

Money *did* make you do weird stuff.

Since I'd hit the dead-guy jackpot, I'd done some *really* weird stuff.

Desperate, almost.

Besides being paranoid about my backpack, I'd lied to Grams, lied to Marissa, kinda lied to Casey, lied to Mrs. Wedgewood, lied to André. . . . Who *hadn't* I lied to since I'd found the money?

And talk about money making you do weird stuff—how much weirder can you get than sneaking around dressed up as an old lady?

But, I told myself, I wasn't *addicted* to the money. I didn't have a *problem* with money. It's not like I *needed* it.

I just . . . liked it.

I liked being able to slip money in Grams' wallet or leave a present for Hudson on his porch.

I liked being able to buy my own big salty pretzel at the mall or spring for the movies or Juicers.

Was that so wrong?

Marissa let out a deep, quiet breath. "*You're* my rock, Sammy." She rolled over. "I don't know what I'd do without you."

A minute later I could tell she'd fallen asleep. And I should have felt great about what she'd said, but I didn't. How could I be her rock when I was keeping secrets from her and lying?

I was, like, a *fake* rock.

One of those phony movie boulders.

And that's when it hit me that I was living a double life. There was my secret life with money, and the normal one without.

The awful thing being, I couldn't see giving either of them up.

TWENTY-THREE

I might have drifted off thinking about life with money versus life with no money, only a thought flashed through my mind that jolted me totally awake.

The Jackal's picture!

I'd been so detoured by Marissa's call and Casey's call and my mother with his father and all of that, that there'd been no place in my mental stew for what I was going to do with the Picture.

But now here I was, wide-awake in the dark, wondering what I *should* do with it.

And after a good fifteen minutes of thinking out different scenarios in my head, I finally decided that what I needed wasn't some little image on a screen—what I needed was a real hold-in-my-hands picture.

Now, I could have asked Marissa to print it for me in the morning, but I didn't want to have to explain who the Jackal was or why I had a camera.

Same thing with Hudson.

Or anyone else I knew with a computer.

And after spending about ten seconds running through all my printing choices, I snuck out of bed, picked up my backpack, and tiptoed down to Mrs. McKenze's office.

Five minutes later I discovered that her office computer required a password. So I tiptoed into Mikey's room, told his fish, "Shhhh!" and booted up his computer.

No password required!

It took me about half an hour to figure out how to get the image of Rex-the-Jackal-Randolf from the camera to the computer and then crop it so it was mostly face and hardly any background. But when his sneaky mug was finally coming through the printer, I pumped my fist and whispered, "Yes!"

When I was done, I shut everything off, hid all my stuff inside my backpack, and eased back into bed. I was awake for quite a while, though, thinking about ways I could use the picture to find out what was going on with the Jackal and the Sandman. And the plan I finally settled on involved freaking them out a little. Nothing major—just enough to get them to quit trying to track down the money.

Anyway, the next morning when the phone rang, it felt like I'd just fallen asleep. Only there was light coming through the window. And Marissa was already up, her hair wet from a shower.

"Hello?" she whispered into the phone.

"I'm awake," I mumbled, wrapping a pillow over my head.

"Everything's fine," Marissa said into the phone. "Uh-huh . . . Uh-huh . . . Why? . . . That's not very nice! . . . Fine. Whatever. . . . Okay! Fine!"

After she hung up, I unwrapped the pillow and eyed her. "Let me guess. She's on her way home with your dad and she wants me out of here."

Her jaw dropped. "How'd you know that?"

I snorted and sat up. "Educated guess."

"I'm sorry, Sammy."

"No big deal. I've got a bunch of stuff to do before the pool party, anyway."

"Like what?"

I laughed. "Like go home and sleep."

"I'm *really* sorry, Sammy!"

So we made a quick breakfast of scrambled eggs and toast, and I took off. And I must've been on autopilot, because I was planning to go straight to the Heavenly Hotel to enact my little freak-out plan, only I wound up at Hudson's.

"Sammy!" Hudson called from the porch as I clicked along the sidewalk. And since I couldn't exactly say, Uh, sorry, I wasn't really planning to visit, I turned up his walkway and said, "Hey, Hudson!" like I was totally glad he was out on his porch, stopping me from getting where I wanted to go.

I plopped down in a chair next to him and eyed his hot tea and muffin. Maybe it was residual hunger from the day before, I don't know, but even though I'd just eaten, my stomach was totally growling at the sight of Hudson's blueberry muffin.

"Where are my manners?" he asked, getting up and disappearing inside.

"Where are *mine*?" I said with a laugh as I scooched his tea and muffin over to my side of the table.

He was back outside a minute later. "Do you know anything about a gift that was left on my porch?"

"A gift?" I asked all nonchalantly. "What kind of a gift?"

"It's a wonderful framed photograph."

I bit into what was now my muffin. "No card on it?"

He laughed, "Yes, but it was from a 'secret admirer.' "

"Oh, Grams is gonna love that!" I said, 'cause Grams and Hudson have been on-again, off-again for almost a year.

Hudson raised a bushy eyebrow my way. "Michael seemed to think it was from you. He said the *e*'s were just like your *e*'s but I told him you certainly didn't have the means to buy a gift like that." He took a bite of his muffin and grinned at me. "He suggested that maybe you stole it."

I snorted. "Oh, right," I said, trying to act cool, even though the thing with the *e*'s had me in total shock. "Like I'd give you a stolen present?" I sat up a little. "Besides, I don't steal stuff! Or play with matches!"

"Matches?"

"Never mind," I grumbled, slouching back into my seat.

He took a sip of tea. "I think it was probably the McKenzes. I wish they wouldn't feel that they have to do something to thank me for having Mike here."

Now, it was one thing for him not to know who the present was from, but it kinda bugged me that he thought the *McKenzes* might have given it to him.

They seem to think I steal, egg people on, and play with matches.

So I said, "I kinda doubt it was the McKenzes. They're in total crisis mode."

"Hmm," he said. "I could tell there was something going on when I spoke with Mrs. McKenze last evening." He dropped his voice a little. "While Mike's still sleeping, could you give me a few details about their situation?" He looked over his shoulder toward the door. "That poor *boy* is the one in crisis mode."

I almost said, Why? 'Cause you won't let him have Twinkies? But at the last minute I bit my tongue and whispered, "Because he doesn't want to be here?"

Hudson shook his head, but it wasn't the usual calm wag back and forth. His head quivered, his eyes twitched, and thoughts just seemed to be sputtering around inside his head. "He told me some things last night—I just can't imagine."

"Things?" I sat up a little straighter. "Like what things?"

"Like how badly he's teased at school."

I wanted to snort and say, For what? Being a whiny, tattling, annoying monster? but I could tell that Hudson really was upset. And even though I'd known Mikey for years and Hudson had only known him a couple of *days*, I didn't want to come across as a know-it-all jerk. So I just said, "For . . . ?"

"For being overweight! He broke down and cried last night, Sammy. He is terrified of school starting up again. It was heart-wrenching."

I kinda shrugged and nodded. "Kids can be really mean." I pulled a little face. "Especially when someone's a whiny tattletale."

"But . . . what came first? The name-calling or the

whining? Nobody should be called Chunky Monkey, or Fatty McWide, or Chubby Cheese, or Blubber Butt, or the Flab-o-Matic, or Tub-o-Chub, or Lardo. . . ." His voice trailed off as he shook his head.

I just sat there a minute, blinking. "He told you all that?" But then I decided that Mikey was making stuff up for sympathy. You know, pulling an old guy's chain.

Mikey McKenze is the *master* of pulling people's chains.

Hudson let out a puffy-cheeked sigh. "What bothered me most was Jab-the-Flab."

"Jab-the-Flab? What's that?"

"At recess, kids poke him and run." He shook his head. "And of course he can't catch them. Recess must be a nightmare."

For the first time in my entire life, I felt a strange wash of sympathy for Mikey.

Jab-the-Flab?

Not even *he* would make that up.

"So," Hudson was saying, "any insight would be very much appreciated."

I took a deep breath. "This is top-secret, okay? Mrs. McKenze doesn't like other people knowing their business."

He nodded, so I gave a quick rundown of the situation, and when I was done, he just sat there, quiet. No philosophical thoughts, no musings; he just sat there, quiet.

So I finally got up and said, "Sorry, Hudson, but I've got to go. I've got a million things to do before Brandon's pool party this afternoon."

He snapped to. "A pool party? Well, enjoy yourself!"

"Thanks!" And as I hit the sidewalk, I called, "Say hi to Mikey for me!"

Which was weird.

Never in my life had I wanted anyone to say hi to Mikey for me.

Never.

TWENTY-FOUR

When I finally made it to the Heavenly Hotel, I plomped my backpack on the counter and got right to the point. "Hey, André. I have something that may interest you. The only catch is, you can't ask me any questions." I looked right at him. "Deal?"

He pushed his cigar stub forward with his lips, then reeled it back in and clamped it between his front teeth. "Deal," he said, looking a lot like a laughing camel.

I pulled the picture of the Jackal from my backpack and slid it across the counter. "Look familiar?"

"That's him!" he said, and for the first time in the whole time I've known André, the cigar fell out of his mouth. He snatched it up and jabbed a finger at the picture. "That is definitely him!" He looked at me. "Where'd you get this? How'd you know? Who is he?"

I pinched my lips, raised my eyebrows, and waited.

"Oh yeah," he said, looking totally dejected. "But how can you expect me not to ask questions?"

I gave him a little smile. "That's also a question."

He rolled his eyes, then said, "So now what? Which is also a question, I know, but you gotta be willing to answer that one . . . !"

I laughed. "Now you call the police department and ask for Officer . . . make that *Sergeant* Borsch."

His forehead was suddenly all knotted up. "Wait a sec—isn't he that jerk cop who gives you trouble everywhere you go?"

I sort of shrugged and nodded. "Yeaaaaah . . . used to be."

"Whaddaya mean, *used* to be? I remember that cat. He's one royal pain in the . . . uh, *backside*."

I nodded again. "Let's just say we understand each other better now. He's really not as incompetent, vindictive, and obnoxious as he comes across." I gave a lopsided little smile. "He's actually all right."

André shook his head. "Well, this is big news to me." He chomped down on the cigar again and gave me the camel look. "And I'm not sure I believe it."

"The *point* is," I said, tapping the picture, "you were duped by this guy, and you seemed pretty tweaked about it. I don't know his name, but I'm pretty sure I know where he lives. If you don't *care* who he is or what he took out of Buck Ritter's room, that's fine." I started to pull the picture back. "I mean, what do *I* care?"

André slapped the picture down. "No, okay. I just don't really get how you got his picture or why you're doing this."

I looked him in the eye. "You don't treat me like a little kid, André. You've always been, you know, *decent* to me. Even nice. I mean, come on. You gave me a job, right?"

"Are you saying this is costing me?"

"No!"

He just stood there, blinking across the counter at me, his cigar completely still.

I just stood on the other side, looking straight at him, not twitching an eyelid.

Finally his cheeks crinkled up a little and he said, "But why that Borsch guy? Why not—"

"Who? Squeaky and the Chick? Look, I'll give you the picture. All I'm asking is that Sergeant Borsch is the *only* person you talk to about it and that you don't mention my name or how you got the picture." I started to pull it back again. "If you don't care, that's fine. I'll stay out of it."

André scratched his neck and muttered, "I haven't quit kicking myself since it happened. I do not get duped. Ever."

I shoved the picture toward him. "So do something about it. I've also got information on someone he's working with—"

"He's *working* with someone? Who? What are they up to?"

I frowned. "André, those are questions." Then I grumbled, "I don't know what they're up to, okay?" I took a deep breath. "Look, I'll tell you what I know, but you have to promise to leave me out of it. You talk only to Sergeant Borsch, and you never mention me." I leveled a look at him. "Do we have a deal or not?"

He frowned at me a minute, then muttered, "Deal."

For insurance, I stuck my hand out.

He hesitated, then shook it.

"Okay," I said, lowering my voice—not that anyone else was around, I just automatically lowered my voice. "I'm pretty sure they both live across the street in the Senior Highrise. The manager there knows everybody. His name's Vince Garnucci. Get Sergeant Borsch to show him this picture and he should be able to tell who he is."

André gave a short, quick nod. "Vince Garnucci. Got it."

I pointed to the picture. "This guy's *friend* lives in apartment four-two-seven. Tell Sergeant Borsch that he should knock four times, then two times."

"What's that? Some kinda secret knock?"

I leveled a look at him. "Just make sure you tell him to do it."

"But—"

"André! We have a deal."

"Right," he said, but from the look in his eye, I could tell he wasn't sure if he'd made a deal with *me* or some shifty stranger.

After I left the Heavenly, I went up the street to the Pup Parlor. Meg and Vera were already busy sudsing up a Boston terrier when I jangled through the door.

"Sammy!" they both called. Then Meg said, "Holly'll be glad to see you." She shut off the spray nozzle and lowered her voice. "I think she's nervous about that pool party today. I'm afraid she'll decide not to go."

I headed for the stairs. "Don't worry—she's going!"

So I jetted up to the apartment, calling, "Hey, Hollister!" as I looked around for her.

She stuck her nose out of her bedroom. "Hollister? What's that about?"

I chuckled. "I don't know—it just came out." I headed over to her room. "I thought we should come up with a game plan for today."

"Uh . . ."

"You're going," I said, 'cause I could see she was wavering with doubt.

"But I don't really know any—"

"You're going!" I edged past her and into her bedroom. "Let's see your suit."

Holly's room is like a little cottage getaway. There are quilts hanging on the wall, little stuffed bunnies and bears arranged like cheerful friends on her cute white dresser, a dish of potpourri next to a little white alarm clock on her nightstand. . . . Her room always looks perfect. No socks kicking around, no magazines tossed on the floor, no pinned-up posters. . . . Maybe it's because Holly used to be homeless and now really *values* her room. Or maybe she's just tidy. I mean, I don't have my own room, but I know if I did, it would be a complete disaster. That's how it was back when I lived with good ol' Lady Lana, and if I ever get let loose in another room of my own, I'm sure that's how it'll be again.

So maybe Holly's tidy and I'm a slob.

Or *maybe* I've just never had it bad enough.

Whatever. The point is, for a girl who used to get her dinners from trash cans, Holly keeps her room incredibly neat. And when I asked to see her suit, she went to her closet and there it was, on a *hanger*.

"Cool!" I said, 'cause it was this sparkly blue with just a hint of green—like the ocean—and it was a one-piece. "I really like that!" The tags were still on it, though, which seemed to me like she was leaving her options open to return it. So before she could stop me, I snapped them off and said, "No backing out—I'll come get you a little before noon, okay?"

"Are you changing there?"

"Nah. I just wear my suit under my clothes, bring a towel and sunblock, and go for it."

"We're riding skateboards, right?"

I nodded.

"So . . . do you bring a backpack?"

"Uh, yeah." But all of a sudden I was wondering what exactly I *was* going to do about my backpack.

Or more precisely, about the money.

I sure didn't want to leave it in my backpack and worry about it while I was playing water hoops!

That would totally ruin the fun.

And I sure didn't want to leave it somewhere Grams could find it.

That would totally ruin everything!

So . . . what was I going to do about the money?

"Sammy?" Holly was asking.

"Huh?"

"Man, you just totally spaced."

"Oh. Uh . . . sorry." I headed for the bedroom door. "I've got tons to do before the party." I smiled and said, "I'll be back—you be ready!"

She laughed and waved. "All right!"

I gave Meg and Vera the thumbs-up on the way out, then hurried home to Grams.

"Good news!" she said from over in the kitchen, where she was unpacking a sack of groceries. "I found that hundred and twenty dollars!"

"Really?" I asked, all surprised-like.

"I don't remember doing this, but I must have withdrawn it as cash. It's hard to find a subtraction error when one doesn't enter the transaction!" She laughed. "I hope I'm not losing my mind!"

"You're not losing your mind," I said, feeling great that she was so happy. I checked inside the grocery sack and discovered something that I couldn't believe. "A Double Dynamo?" I asked, pulling up the yummiest ice cream drumstick known to man. "Are you losing your mind?"

She laughed again. "I always tell you no, so I decided to surprise you."

"Wow."

"But you know, I really should stop shopping at Maynard's. It may be convenient, but T.J. has become a complete boor."

"What do you mean, has become? He's been that forever."

"But how long have I been shopping there? He's always curt, but today he checked my money!"

"What do you mean, he checked your money?"

"He held it up to the light, he marked it with one of those pens they use to see if it's real . . . he was just boorish. After all the shopping I've done there, he treats me like a criminal!"

My stomach suddenly bottomed out.

Not real?

I forced a laugh. "So I take it your money passed muster."

She hrmphed. "Of course it did! Like I would pass off bad bills?"

I watched her shelve a package of shortbread cookies and tried to act all nonchalant as I asked, "Did you pay with that hundred and twenty dollars?"

She gave me a curious look. "I didn't spend all of it, if that's what you're asking."

I did my best to cover up, adding real quick, " 'Cause I really do think Maynard's is a rip-off."

So there I am, recovering from one scare, when all of a sudden there's a knock at the door.

Grams looks at me.

I look at her.

And just as she's signaling me to head for the closet—which is where I always hide when something like this happens—the person knocks again.

Only this time there's a voice along with it.

A commanding voice.

One I recognize.

One that has me wanting to hide somewhere much safer than the closet.

TWENTY-FIVE

Dorito hears the voice and goes flying past us toward Grams' bedroom.

Smart cat.

But as I'm shooting off in the same direction, Grams grabs me by the arm and says, "Samantha! You don't have to hide from him anymore, remember?"

"Oh yeah," I say with a choppy laugh. "Right."

But it doesn't feel right. Nothing about this feels right.

Why is he *here*? He's supposed to be checking on the Jackal, not *me*.

Did something tip him off?

Did he figure it all out?

Why else would he be knocking on *our* door?

"It's okay," Grams whispers. "You're here 'helping' me."

So I stand there like an idiot while she whooshes open the door and says, "Sergeant Borsch, how nice to see you! Come in, come in!"

So in he steps. He's in uniform, all right, and he's got a piece of paper in his hands. A piece of paper folded in half, which he's recreasing over and over between his finger and thumbnail.

My brain runs off in a panic.

Is it a search warrant?

An order to arrest?

Why's he standing there looking at me so funny?

It's like *he's* nervous.

"Glad you're here," he says to me with an awkward smile. "I need to ask you something." He looks to the living room. "Can we all sit down?"

By now my knees are like jelly, but I try to make my voice steady as I say, "Sounds serious."

He sits in a chair and says, "Well, actually, it is." He's still creasing that paper, over and over. And I'm a total basket case, wondering how in the world things fell apart so fast. I'd spent the whole night thinking up the perfect plan, and now *poof*, I'm busted.

He's looking right at me, and he's twitching here and there like a little boy who's being forced to tattle on a good friend. I'm actually almost feeling sorry for *him* having to break the news to me that I'm busted. I mean, we'd come such a long way since the day he'd tried to arrest me for jaywalking. Since the time I'd called him the Borschman.

Finally he takes a deep breath and says, "Sorry to hit you with this out of the blue, but, you know Debra?"

I blink at him, and the first thing that zips through my mind is, Huh? followed immediately by, Debra the *Dodo*?

"Our receptionist at the station?" he asks.

That's Debra the Dodo, all right. And it's not that she's *dumb*, it's that she has a really big nose that she piles high with makeup, and she wears her hair in a huge *nest* on the top of her head.

So I nod, and I know *I'm* looking like a complete

195

dodo, but I have no idea what Debra has to do with me being busted.

He gives that search warrant or order to arrest or whatever it is one final crease and takes a deep breath. "Well. Debra and I are getting married next month, and we'd like you to be in the wedding."

I blink at him.

And blink some more.

And finally I blurt out, "You and Debra are getting *married*?"

Grams scolds, "Samantha!"

"I didn't mean it like that—I'm just . . . I guess . . ." I shake my head. "I had no idea."

He chuckles. "Let's hope third time's the charm."

Grams leans forward a little and says, "Are you saying you'd like Samantha to *come* to the wedding or you'd like her to be *in* the wedding?"

"Well . . ." He looks at her, then me, then laughs and says, "Debra wanted you to be a bridesmaid, but I convinced her that would be . . . uh . . ."

I cringe. "A disaster?"

He laughs and says, "Besides, I can't see you in a frilly dress and shiny shoes. But Deb and I would like for you to be in charge of the guest book and maybe do a reading?"

"Really?" I ask, still not quite believing what I'm hearing. "You want *me* to be in your wedding?"

"Unbelievable, isn't it?" he says with a chuckle. "But it was arguments about you that got Debra and me talking to each other, and we're both . . . how do I say this . . . *fond* of you."

"Wow."

He looks at me. "So . . . ?"

"So she'd be honored to," Grams says, giving me a little scolding look. "And congratulations. You certainly deserve to be happy."

"Thank you, ma'am," he says, then lets out a deep breath and slaps the paper with the back of his hand. "Now back to business."

And that's when I make a *huge* mistake. My big mouth shoots off with, "What *is* that?" and when he unfolds it, what do I see?

The picture I'd given André.

How dense did I want to be?

Of course that's what it was!

But I'd been so paranoid about him busting *me,* and then so shocked about him asking me to be in his *wedding,* that my brain was all muddled up.

"Why, that's Rex Randolf," Grams says. "Has he done something wrong?"

Now, I'm giving Grams the fingertip-slice-at-the-neck signal, but when Officer Borsch cocks his head at her and says, "You know this man?" does she zip her lips?

No!

She says, "Yes! He's visited our neighbor a few times. Actually, he knocked on *my* door last night."

I stop midslice. "He did?"

Grams nods and tisks and rolls her eyes. "I don't know what he wanted, really. I refused to let him in, and later Rose accused me of trying to steal her man, if you can believe that!"

"Rex Randolf, huh?" Officer Borsch says. "Your

manager says he's never seen this man before." He slaps the picture with the back of his hand. "And this is not someone you'd overlook. Very flashy dresser."

So since it was too late to keep Officer Borsch from knowing we knew the guy, I toss in, "Maybe it's a disguise . . . ?"

Grams' eyebrows shoot up at me, and Officer Borsch nods at the picture like, Hmm . . . maybe so. Then he says, "We do have another lead that I'll follow up on—see if it gets us anywhere."

"But . . . ," Grams says. "Lead for what? What's he done? Should we be concerned?" She turns to me. "A *disguise*?"

Officer Borsch sucks air through his teeth, thinking. Finally he says, "It would probably be wise not to have any more interaction with him until we know more about him. I'll do some investigating and let you know."

"But . . . what's he *suspected* of having done?" Grams asks.

"That's a good question," he tells her. "Unfortunately, I don't have a good answer."

So off he goes, and the minute he's gone, Grams turns to me and says, "Why were you trying to hush me up? You obviously don't trust him!"

"Who?"

"Rex!"

"Well, we used to not trust the Borschman!"

"But we do now!"

"Mostly!"

"How can you say 'mostly'? He asked you to be in his wedding!"

"His *third* wedding."

"Samantha!"

I was heading for the bathroom.

I couldn't even remember who knew what anymore. My big mushy stew brain was totally bubbling over. I needed a minute to put on the lid. To turn down the heat. To *think*.

"Why are you going in there? Are you avoiding me?"

"What? No! I need to go!"

So I ditched her and went inside the bathroom and locked the door. But as I paced around trying to sort things out, I just got more and more confused. Grams didn't even know that Rex Randolf had come to Mrs. Wedgewood's apartment supposedly to thank her for her valiant efforts in saving Buck Ritter. Grams basically knew *nothing*, except that I'd scared a man to death.

But she had dozens of questions lining up—that was obvious. And if I tried to weasel out of answering them, she'd know I was lying. And then the question would be *why* I was lying.

How was I ever going to get out of this?

So there I am, pacing back and forth in the bathroom, *panicking*, while Grams is outside, saying, "Samantha, why are you hiding in the bathroom? What is going on with you?" My brain is spurting and spattering and totally boiling over, and really, I just can't take it anymore—I'm ready to bust out of the bathroom and spill everything to her.

But then, just as I'm reaching for the doorknob, I have a brainstorm.

A wonderful, stew-busting, *brilliant* brainstorm.

TWENTY-SIX

"There's something I have to tell you," I said as I stepped out of the bathroom.

Grams heaved a big sigh. "Well, hooray. I was worried you were back to keeping secrets."

I swatted back my fluttering conscience and said, "I actually think you'd better sit down."

She studied me as she sidestepped toward the living room. "What on earth have you gotten into now . . . ?"

"It's not me," I said, coaxing her along.

"Then who? Marissa?"

"Marissa's fine." Then I muttered, "As fine as you can be when your father's got a gambling problem, anyway."

She gasped. "Is that what's going on there?"

I nodded. "But never mind about that. This isn't about her."

She'd done an over-the-shoulder glancy sidestep the whole way to the living room, and now she was just standing there. "Why do you look so serious?"

"Because you're going to be upset." I pointed to the sofa. "Sit."

"Samantha! What's this about?"

"Sit."

So she sat down and clasped her hands in her lap. "Tell me."

"It's Lady Lana."

Her eyes went wide, and she sat up straighter and gasped. "Is she all right?"

I rolled my eyes and plopped into the easy chair. "Oh, she's *fine*."

Grams let out a breath and relaxed a little. "So?"

"So she's still in town."

Grams just sat there, her hands clasped, quiet.

Waiting.

So I took a deep breath and said, "She's dating Casey and Heather's dad."

I could see the wheels start to turn in her head. First slowly, and then as what I'd said sank in, really, really fast. And when she'd built up a nice head of angry steam, I filled in the details about what had happened at the Landmark Broiler. By the time I was done, she'd completely forgotten about Officer Borsch and Rex-the-Jackal-Randolf and was storming around the apartment calling my mother a "duplicitous diva" and swearing that she was done with her.

I just sat back and watched, feeling hugely relieved.

I was off the hook!

And the money was still mine.

Grams went to her room to lie down, and I putzed around the apartment feeling very clever. Only after a while my cleverness high kinda wore off and I started feeling a little bad.

Actually, I started feeling *really* bad.

I had totally played my grandmother.

And I'd used my own mother to do it.

I found myself sitting on the couch staring at the wall.

My head started to feel like it was going to boil over again.

And now I also had an awful, icky feeling brewing in my gut.

When I finally stopped staring at the wall, I decided that I had to hide the money before I went to the pool party. I needed my backpack, and there was no way I was going to risk having it stolen at the pool party. After all, *Heather* was sure to be there.

So with Grams safely in the bedroom, I unzipped a sofa cushion and lined up the stacks of cash along the back side of the foam. When I was all done, I tested it, and you could totally not tell anything was there.

I did the same thing with the camera.

And when I was ready to leave for the pool party, I took the sweatshirt and jeans I'd bought out of the backpack and peeked into Grams' room. She was lying on the bed, but her eyes were open. "I'm going to get going," I said, easing inside and casually slipping the new clothes inside my drawer of Grams' dresser.

"Where are you going again?" she asked, like she was in a complete daze.

"To the pool party, remember?"

"Oh, right."

"I'm picking up Holly and we're riding over together."

"Yes, yes, of course."

I went over and kissed her on the top of her head. "Forget about her, Grams."

She shook her head. "Where did she get her selfish streak?"

I snorted. "It's not a streak, Grams. She's covered in it." I rubbed her shoulder. "And not from you, that's for sure."

"Well, I am tired of being treated like a doormat." She looked up at me and patted my hand. "You go and have fun. I'll see you . . . When do you think you'll be home?"

"I don't know. . . . It'll be a while." I started for the door, saying, "Why don't you call Hudson? Why don't you go *talk* to Hudson? He gives really good advice, you know."

She nodded absently. "Maybe I will. It was nice to talk to him yesterday." Then she added, "He's a good man, taking Mikey under his wing."

So I got out of there and crossed the street, but before I went over to Holly's, I ducked into the Heavenly Hotel. "Any news?" I called out to André.

There were people hanging around the lobby, so he waved me over. "Your Sergeant Borsch left here very skeptical," he said, leaning across the counter, "but returned with a whole new attitude."

"Yeah? What did he tell you?"

One eyebrow arched way up and the other scrunched waaaay down while his cigar went for a little stroll to the far corner of his mouth. "The manager couldn't ID the guy in the picture, but your secret knock worked like a charm."

"And?"

"And the man in four-two-seven says he's never seen the guy in the picture before in his life, doesn't know any Buck Ritter, and has never been over to the Heavenly . . . but your Sergeant Borsch doesn't believe him."

"Really."

André shook his head. "Said the man was nervous, uncooperative, and definitely hiding something."

"So what's he going to do now?"

"Well, he was very curious about some things."

"Like . . . ?"

"Like how I knew about the knock, where I got the picture, and what I think was taken out of Buck's room." His eyebrows evened out while his cigar shot to the middle of his mouth, where it stuck out at me like a cannon.

"So what did you tell him?"

"I told him a whole lot of nothing." One eyebrow started reaching for the sky again. "But your Sergeant Borsch won't get a search warrant unless he knows what he's searching for."

"Hmm. That does make sense," I said with a shrug.

He did his camel-lip curl. "So now what?"

I gave a big shrug this time. "*I* don't know. Whatever you want. You were the one duped. . . ."

His lips stayed curled back for the longest time, and I was actually starting to get a little nervous over the way he was staring at me. Finally he rolled the cigar to one side and said, "There's something fishy about this whole situation."

"Yeah, I agree," I said. But since I was feeling like it

was *me* he was starting to get suspicious of, I said, "I don't know how else I can help you, André. Maybe you should go over there and, you know, confront the guy in four-two-seven yourself? Or maybe you should just let it go. Whatever that guy took wasn't yours, right?"

"I *had* let it go," he grumbled, "until you came in here and started stirring things up."

"*Me?* Look, I'm sorry. I was just trying to help." I started moving toward the door. "And now I'm late getting to a pool party, so . . . whatever."

"Hey!" he called after me. "I do appreciate it!"

I nodded and waved and clanged out the door.

I hit the sidewalk, and I should have been relieved, but my stomach was suddenly squooshy again. André had been a hard-won ally. Someone who'd gone from distrusting me to being my friend.

And here I had totally played him, too.

Just like I had my grams.

I tried to shove the thought from my mind as I jangled through the Pup Parlor door. "Hey, Vera! Hi, Meg!" They were busy shaping pouf balls on the ankles of a large poodle.

"Sammy!" they both cried.

I laughed. "It's always so nice to come here."

"Always so nice to see you!" they said in unison. Then Meg added, "Holly's upstairs. Thanks for dragging her out to this. She's still a bundle of nerves."

She was, too. I found her sitting on the edge of her bed with her backpack on her lap and a kind of wide-eyed fear on her face. I plopped down next to her and laughed. "I can't believe you!" I shook my head and said, "You've survived so much—this pool party is not gonna kill you!" I stood up and grabbed her arm. "Come on, it'll be fun."

She pulled back. "You know how mean they can be."

"Who? Girls?" I sat down again. And something about Holly's battle with nerves calmed the squooshies of my own stomach. "Look, it's not a beauty pageant. We're playing water hoops! To the death!"

"But Marissa told me Heather's going to be there." She looked at me. "Heather calls me Trash Digger. Still. Did you know that?"

I didn't, but I wasn't about to let Heather ruin the day. "She calls everybody something. I'm Loser, remember? Who cares? Just stay in the pool—I'm sure she won't even get in. She'll be afraid to get her hair wet." I pulled a hideous face and screeched, "I'm melllllting!"

Holly laughed and then smiled at me. "Thanks."

"So let's go!" I jumped up. "Water hoops—to the death!"

TWENTY-SEVEN

Brandon McKenze's mother is a stay-at-home mom. And, according to Marissa, since she's only got Brandon to stay at home for, she's made a career out of being involved in his life. She's PTO president, coordinates school book fairs and fund-raisers, and helps out at swim meets.

Brandon's father is an eye surgeon. Or more like a *vision* surgeon. He does those laser treatments on people's eyes so they can get rid of their glasses, and he's kind of a celebrity in Santa Martina because television ads for his "world-renowned vision center" run all the time.

Personally, I think the ads are kinda cheesy, but judging by Dr. McKenze's gorgeous brick castle of a house, with its fairy-tale climbing ivy and acre of circular driveway, they're effective.

"I had no idea," Holly gasped as we took in the house from the street. She let out a low whistle. "And I thought *Marissa's* house was over the top."

"It is," I laughed.

"Are they in competition?"

I didn't get the question at all. "Competition? Who?"

"Marissa's family and these guys."

"I don't know," I said as I grabbed my skateboard. "I never thought about it before."

She picked up her skateboard, too, and walked with me up toward the house. "Well, have they always been rich?"

"Marissa's family made a ton of money on the stock market." I nodded up at the house. "These guys moved here when Marissa and I were in fifth grade."

"So only a few years."

I shrugged. I didn't think the subject was very interesting. Who cared? Both families were obviously really rich.

Then we heard, "Hey, wait up!" from behind us, and when we turned around, there was the DeVries Nursery truck, making a teen girl delivery. Marissa scrambled out first, followed by Dot.

"Call ven you vant a ride home, *ja*?" Mr. DeVries said out the passenger window.

"I will!" Dot said back, and we all waved goodbye as he pulled away.

Marissa was wearing sparkly green flip-flops, green shorts that were kinda, well, *short,* and a white halter top. She was also wearing a sun hat and oversized sunglasses, and was lugging along a big duffel full of who knows what that was totally throwing off her balance.

"Stop scrutinizing me," she said, flip-flopping toward us.

"Am I scrutinizing you?" I asked, all innocent-like.

"Duh," she said, and I know her eyes rolled behind her movie-star glasses, even though I couldn't see them.

"How are your parents?" I whispered when we were walking side by side.

"I don't want to talk about it," she said under her breath.

So I dropped it and just tagged along as she led the way, following pool-party-thataway signs around the house to the backyard.

Brandon's backyard is definitely over the top. Besides the pool, which has loungers, patio tables, and chairs all around it, there's an enormous covered patio, plus a row of cabanas for changing clothes and a *bathroom* cabana. All that makes sense, especially if you're going to invite a bunch of teenagers over and you don't want them dripping through the house or peeing in the pool, but just because it makes sense doesn't mean that most people *have* those things.

Shoot, most people don't even have a pool.

And as if that's not enough luxury for one backyard, there's also a *putting green* on the far end of the property.

"Wow," Holly and Dot whispered as we wound around the walkway that led to the pool area.

"Yeah," I said. "Can you believe people live like this?"

I spotted Brandon with a group of his high school friends, and saw his mother, who was directing some girls I recognized from the softball game as they brought platters of food out to a long table on the patio.

Marissa suddenly skidded to a stop. "She's here *already*?"

My focus instantly switched to the direction Marissa was looking, and there she was, the Bummer of Summer herself, laying an oversized hot-pink towel over one of the lounge chairs.

"I *hate* that she's here!" Marissa seethed. "And look at her, acting like she owns the place. This is *my* cousin's house!" Marissa's feet were planted, but the rest of her was shooting forward. She looked like a fancy-schmancy poodle yanking on an invisible leash.

"Eeeeasy," I said, putting a hand on her arm. "The best thing you can do is act like you don't care, remember?"

"There's Danny!" Dot whispered. "On the patio!"

People suddenly seemed to be coming from everywhere. From inside the house, from behind us, from a flagstone walkway winding through shrubs and palm trees on the *other* side of the pool. . . . I felt like a boulder in the middle of Teen River.

"Can we park somewhere?" I asked.

Marissa snapped to. "Yeah. Let's stake out *our* territory." Then she marched straight for a lounger on the opposite side of the pool from Heather, laid out *her* towel, and got her bag all . . . *situated*. You know, first she had it on one side of the lounger, then she moved it to the foot of the lounger, then she put it on the *other* side of the lounger, and finally she pushed it halfway *under* the lounger.

Holly, Dot, and I just stood by, watching.

"What are you staring at?" Marissa huffed. "Grab a seat before they're all gone!"

I shoved my skateboard under her lounger and dumped my backpack next to her bag. "Done."

Holly did the same.

Dot looked around uncomfortably. "There aren't that many loungers. . . ."

Marissa was not happy with our junk everywhere but didn't actually *say* anything. She just sat down and swung her legs around. "Which is why you need to grab one before somebody else does!"

I took Dot's bag out of her hand and put it next to the backpacks. "We're not here to *lounge*, Marissa. We're here to play water hoops." I sorta frowned at her. "This is no way to compete with Heather."

Her jaw seemed set in cement.

"You don't *want* to compete with her this way. This isn't you!"

She crossed her arms and tilted up her nose. So after a minute of just standing there, I shook my head and said, "Come on," to the other two and took off.

While I led Holly and Dot over to the patio area, Marissa stayed put, glaring through her movie-star glasses at Heather, who was casually rubbing herself down with sunscreen.

"Sam-my!" Brandon called when he spotted me, and when we were closer, he said, "Holly and Dot, right?" They nodded and smiled, and he slung his arm around my shoulders and called out to the world at large, "Everyone! This is Sammy, Holly, and Dot!" Then he turned to me and dropped his voice. "Where's Marissa?"

I pointed across the pool.

"That's *Marissa*?" he said.

Brandon's mother was suddenly right beside us. Her eyes twinkled at her son. "She's a teenager now, you know." She smiled at me and said, "So nice to see you again, Samantha," then turned to Holly and Dot. "Welcome!"

She was off again before we could say anything back, and Brandon wasn't shy about putting us to work. "We're kinda behind on everything. Can you bring out the hoop and divide the skullcaps?" He pointed toward a flagstone walkway. "It's all in the storage shed back there."

"We're on it," I said, heading out.

"And suit up!" he called after us. "No lounging around!"

"Tell that to your cousin!" I called back.

We meandered back to the "storage shed," which was actually a cabana for *stuff,* hidden among shrubs and palms. "I feel like I'm at a resort," Dot said when I handed her the plastic tub of blue and red water polo skullcaps. "And everyone's being so *nice.*"

I grinned over my shoulder as I reached for the hoop, which is a mesh net lashed inside a kind of floating pyramid. "Enjoy it while you can—in a few hours it's back to the real world."

Holly accepted the bulky hoop and murmured, "Hard to believe that for them this *is* the real world."

Dot laughed. "How easy would getting used to this be, huh?"

We both agreed, "Very!"

Anyway, we gathered the stuff and were leaving the "shed" when I noticed the faded purple water hoops ball. "Hey, the ball!" I said, grabbing it off the shelf.

"That's it?" Holly asked. "I thought it'd be a basketball."

"It's weird-looking," Dot said, taking it from me.

I remember thinking the same thing the first time I saw

it. It's only about eight inches across, and it's rubbery and squooshy, with long tunnels of air running through it.

"Won't this sink?" Dot asked.

"Oh yeah," I laughed. "And the color makes it hard to see underwater."

We went back to the pool area, and the first thing I noticed was that Marissa was no longer on the lounger.

And neither was Heather.

I chucked the hoop in the water near the middle of the pool, then started sorting the skullcaps into red and blue piles. "I can't believe they have their own skullcaps!" Holly said. "But I'm glad." She held one up—they were the tie-under-the-chin-with-*ear*-holes variety. "Can you imagine you know who putting on one of these?"

"No!" I grinned at her. "See? It'll definitely be safe in the water."

"Poor Marissa," Dot whispered. "She told me all about the kiss."

"The kiss? What kiss?" Holly asked.

So real quick I caught her up on our little spying fiasco, and then Dot added, "I wish she'd just forget about Danny. I don't like him."

Holly frowned. "Yeah. He's too slick."

We'd finished sorting the caps, so I scanned the backyard for Marissa.

"I don't see her, either," Dot said. "Maybe she's getting changed?"

Just then one of the cabana doors opens, and out steps the lime green two-piece.

Really, that's all I see at first—the suit.

For one thing, it's really bright.

For another, it's definitely the suit Marissa used my money to buy at the mall.

Ruffled top.

Wide-belted bottom.

Only as the suit moves away from the cabana, I'm having an awful time making sense of what I'm seeing. It's like one person's head has been put on another person's body. But as hard as I blink, the image doesn't change.

And finally it hits me that I *am* seeing what I can't believe I'm seeing.

It's Marissa's bikini, all right.

But it's wrapped around Heather Acosta's body.

TWENTY-EIGHT

"Isn't that *Marissa's* suit?" Dot asks when she hears me gasp. "She showed it to me on the way over!"

And I'm sorry, but my own advice about ignoring Heather was now out the window. I got immediately *fried* over Heather's unbelievable nerve. I mean, stealing someone's swimsuit and faking like it's yours might be insane, but for Heather it's a typical stunt. And good luck getting it back. She'll just sneer at you and whisper, "Got a receipt, loser?"

So while I'm getting madder and madder and my mind is flashing with all the dirty, rotten, *unbelievable* tricks Heather has pulled on *me* in the past, another cabana door opens.

An identical lime green bikini comes walking out.

And this time, Marissa *is* inside it.

My jaw drops.

My eyes pop.

Dot whispers, "Whirling windmills! They're wearing the same suit!"

Now, if this had been two *guys* in the same swim trunks, no one would have cared or even noticed. And if the swimsuit had been, you know, some happy Hawaiian

215

print or something, maybe it wouldn't have been so glaring. But this suit was neon-bright and not exactly risqué but kinda . . . *daring*.

And on top of not wanting your fashion statement stolen, who wants to be twins with Heather Acosta?

Not Marissa, that's for sure. The minute she realized what was walking a few yards ahead of her, *her* jaw dropped, and behind the movie-star glasses she was still wearing, I'm sure her eyes popped.

Heather must've picked up on the fact that something weird was going on, because she looked over her shoulder through *her* movie-star glasses and instantly skidded to a halt.

Holly summed up the situation nicely: "Uh-oh."

We were around the pool and at Marissa's side in no time, but Heather was already facing off with her, pointing at the cabanas. "Go back in there and take that off right now!"

Marissa just stood there.

"Why would you *want* to wear it?" Heather said, looking her up and down. "You must be so embarrassed!"

And then does she follow up by saying something about looking like twins or even copycatting?

No.

She wobbles her head and says, "It looks *so* much better on me."

Which was a big steamy pile of manure—it actually looked way better on Marissa.

Holly steps forward. "Get over yourself, would you, Heather?"

"Stay out of it, would you, Trash Digger?"

Well, *I'd* been trying to stay out of it, but this was too much. "Go back to your sticky little web, Heather. So you guys have the same suit. So what?"

Heather sneered at me, then turned it on Marissa. She pulled the sunglasses down low on her nose. "Why don't we ask Danny who looks better, huh?" Her sneer grew bigger. "Oh, never mind. I *know* what he'll say." She gave an evil grin. "He *kissed* me, you know."

This was obviously meant to light Marissa's fuse, but before Marissa could react, I rolled my eyes and said, "Yeah, yeah, we know." I snorted. "And then you dumped him out the window into the mud and made him crawl home. Must've been some kiss."

Well, that totally lit *Heather's* fuse. Her firecracker eyes sparked as she tried to figure out how we knew about her little kissing calamity, and the conclusion she jumped to did not happen to involve us spying through her window.

"That sneak!" she snarled. "I'm gonna *kill* him!" Then she stormed off, most likely in search of someone *I'd* been kinda looking out for since we'd arrived.

Casey.

I tried to push him from my mind, and I focused on Marissa. "Now will you *please* go put on your one-piece? We're here to play water hoops, not fight the Great Bikini War."

"I didn't even bring my one-piece," she whimpered. And as we followed her back to her lounger, I could tell she was about to break into tears. "First Danny, then my suit?"

"You look way better in it than Heather," Dot told her.

"Way," Holly confirmed.

"But you'd be having way more fun in the water," I said. "Come *on*, Marissa. Take off those glasses, get in the water, and just be you!"

Just then Brandon hoisted a megaphone and called, "Time to do battle! If you're playing, come on over here!" He slung his arm around a very tan, very blond guy, obviously also a high school swimmer. "I'm Red leader. Andrew here is Blue leader. To make it fair, we'll pull players by age—youngest first."

I tried to drag Marissa down to the gathering, but she refused to go. "Maybe later," she finally said, shaking me off.

So the rest of us went over, and after the dust had settled, Holly and I were on Brandon's team, and Dot was on Andrew's.

As usual, we were the youngest players.

And three out of only five girls willing to get wet.

The rules of McKenze-style water hoops are easy—anything goes. The exact number of players doesn't matter, as long as it's pretty even. There are no timed periods—you play until you're exhausted or famished or both. There are no "handling" rules—you can move the hoop. You can *submerge* the hoop. You can even get out of the pool, just as long as at least one foot stays in the water.

What you're *not* allowed to do is hold on to another player. Latching on to the *ball* while another player is holding it is fine. You just can't latch on to the player.

So there's basically just one rule: Don't drown or cause to be drowned.

Anyway, all the players strapped on team caps and got in the water, and then Dr. McKenze came out for his annual water hoops toss-up. "You kids ready?" he called, holding out the squooshy purple ball.

"Ready!" we all roared.

Up went the ball. "Let the games begin!" he roared back.

I held back while Andrew and Brandon battled it out for the toss-up, and when I saw that Andrew had possession and was making a break for the net, I did a move I've perfected over the years—I dived down and came up *inside* the hoop pyramid, sticking a fist straight up through the net.

Sqooosh went the ball right on my fist, and it punched back out.

I came up, gasping for air, and heard Andrew sputter, "What!" while Brandon whooped and cried, "Way to go, Sammy!"

That was it for me. I didn't think about Casey, I didn't think about Heather, and since Holly and Dot were playing, I didn't really think much about Marissa. I just *played*.

And yeah, maybe that wasn't very nice of me, but the rapid-fire pace of the game just sort of blasted away everything else.

Besides, Holly was great at receiving passes and moving the ball forward, and Dot turned out to be a fierce competitor. At one point it was her and me wrestling like mad with the ball, and she flipped me completely upside down and *over*, and when we came up for air, she said through gritted teeth, "Give up, Sammy. I've got *brothers*," and around we went again. I finally got water up my sinuses and just let her have it.

People subbed in and subbed out as they got tired or hungry or whatever, so I didn't really notice the new person on my team until we collided going after the ball. "Casey?" I said, letting him have the ball. "When'd you get here?"

"Just now," he said, panting a little. "Billy couldn't find his suit."

"Billy?" I asked, but I wasn't thinking about Billy.

Or the ball.

Or the game.

I was just soaking in Casey: His hair curling out from beneath his cap and out of the ear holes. His lashes, so long and clumped together with water. His teeth, so shiny and . . . smooth. His shoulders, so surprisingly muscular. . . .

And then he was gone, passing the ball, shouting, "Billy! Under! Under!"

It was the most breathless I'd felt the whole game.

And after months and months of running from it or fighting it or thinking the time wasn't right, I finally couldn't deny it any longer.

I really wanted to kiss Casey Acosta.

TWENTY-NINE

When Casey took a break to eat, I took a break to eat. When Casey sipped a soda and watched the game from the sidelines, I sipped a soda and watched the game from the sidelines. And even though Holly and Dot and Billy and Danny were doing the same thing, I felt like a little shadow. Like a pathetic little puppy dog shadow.

I acted like the same old Sammy, but I didn't *feel* the same.

And the awful thing is, I wasn't the only one who felt different—Casey did, too, but in the opposite way. Oh, he talked to me, but there was a distance. An uncomfortable, stomach-squeezing distance. From the outside everything probably *looked* normal, but inside I could tell he was pulling away from me. He was way more interested in joking around with Billy and Danny than he was in talking to me. Here I'd finally fallen right out of my little security tower of caution, or fear, or whatever, only he wasn't there to catch me.

I felt like a giant splat of regret.

Why had I held back for so long?

I tried to act like nothing was wrong. I laughed and talked with the group and listened to Holly and Dot

221

whisper about Heather and Marissa, but it was like an out-of-body experience. Like I was floating through the motions of having fun.

And while I was having this out-of-body experience, *in* my body I was feeling small and alone and dorky. I probably looked like a drowned rat with my hair all matted, a towel wrapped around my shoulders. I started feeling totally self-conscious. About *everything*. Casey probably thought I looked like a scrawny little kid.

Then to cap off my self-confidence crisis, Heather sauntered over. "Hi, guys," she said, all sweetness and light, looking revoltingly stylish in her lime green suit. She sat down next to Danny and gave him an adoring smile. "What a bunch of monkey boys you were out there!"

Danny smiled, but it was a kinda uncomfortable smile.

Like he was afraid of being found out.

Afraid of being *caught*.

I gathered my garbage and stood up. "I'm ready for round two!"

"Me too!" Holly and Dot said.

Then the guys stood up, and pretty soon we all had our caps on and were back in the water. "Marissa!" I shouted. "Get *in* here!"

She nodded and finally, *finally* took off the sunglasses and got up. "We've got Marissa!" I called, but Andrew protested. "No way! We're down two players—she's ours!"

Now, maybe most high school swim stars wouldn't have cared what side a gonna-be-eighth-grade girl played on, but Andrew's team was losing 18–26, and a lot of that was because he'd kept underestimating what scrappy dogs we junior high schoolers were in the water. So he demanded Marissa, and for the first time in all the summers I'd been playing water hoops, Marissa and I were on opposing teams.

And two-piece or not, she was on me like white on rice.

Like green on beans!

We wrestled and charged and dived and battled for the ball, laughing and panting and half drowning, then clung to the side next to each other, catching our breath and just smiling at each other.

I didn't have to say it.

She didn't have to say it.

It was there like the sunshine, like the happy laughter of summer—no matter what happened, no matter what *guys* came into the picture or left the picture, we were friends.

Forever.

"To the death!" she panted, and dived back into the game.

Now, because the ball sinks, Marissa and I have learned to do underwater reconnaissance. By the time other players have done their little dive to get under the surface, we've snagged the stray ball and are moving away from the center so we can pass to someone near the goal.

And in years past it's worked really great because we worked together. But now suddenly I was battling against her and it wasn't working at *all*. One of us would get the ball, and instead of bringing it out for a pass, we'd be stuck wrestling the other one for it. So I finally decided to let her have the deep end—I was going to work the shallow end.

It didn't take long for Danny to make a move toward the deep end. And forget about them being on the same team; to me it was obvious he was there to hang with Marissa.

She was all smiles.

He was, too.

And part of me was happy for Marissa, but most of me was ticked off.

Danny Urbanski is like the charmer and the snake packaged as one.

"Oh boy," Holly said, noticing it, too.

"At least she'll be happy," I said with a frown. "Until he breaks her heart."

The ball came flooping through the air, so I jumped up, snagged it, and called to Billy, who was wide-open. Billy called, "Case!" after he'd caught it, then flung it at Casey, who was near the hoop.

Immediately about six strappin' blue-capped guys dived on him like sharks on a baby seal. One of them came up with the ball and dunked it.

"Twenty-*four*, twenty-six!" Andrew crowed. "We are makin' a comeback!"

Casey looked at Brandon. "Sorry, man."

Brandon laughed, "Like you had a chance?" He put his hand in the air and called out to another red cap. "Scuffy! Over here!"

But Casey swam out of the thick of it, and I could tell

he was feeling kind of defeated, so I worked my way over to him and said, "That's why I don't play the net. They're hard-core!"

He nodded, then smiled at me, and a crack suddenly appeared in the wall he'd put up. I could see it in his eyes.

"I'm sorry things are weird," he said.

I was so relieved that he was saying things were weird and that it wasn't just my stupid paranoid imagination or something that I reached over and touched his arm. "Me too."

Now, I'm not a gooey-eyed person. Touching *hands* makes me nervous. So facing someone and going gooey-eyed is definitely not part of my repertoire.

But there I was, totally gooey-eyed.

How embarrassing is that?

Especially since he didn't exactly go gooey-eyed back. He just said, "I've got to go redeem myself—we'll talk later, okay?" and swam off.

So okay, fine. I slapped my gooey-eyed self upside the head and joined the game, this time doing what Marissa and I call the Crocodile Creep. It's where you get right up behind someone on the opposite team and just sort of hover with only your eyeballs above the water, and when someone passes them the ball, you snap forward and intercept it. They don't know you're there, their teammate doesn't know you're there . . . you just sort of lurk and wait and then attack!

Marissa and I are big fans of the Crocodile Creep.

So that's what I was doing around the pool—trying to find a good lurking prospect. I tried Dot, but she was onto me, and besides, it's more fun to surprise a larger opponent. So I lurked behind Andrew for a while, but he was too much in the middle of the action, where lurking is not really possible.

And then it hit me that it would be really funny to sneak up behind *Marissa*. I mean, she and I are the Crocodile Creepers. How funny would it be if I did, like, a Creeper double cross?

So I head for the deep end and sneak around the fringes of the action, searching blue-cap faces for Marissa, but I can't find her.

So I figure she's probably busy doing some underwater reconnaissance, waiting for the ball to plunge down in the deep end. So I dunk under and look around for her, but all I see are legs treading water.

Only just as I'm bobbing back up for air, the corner of my eye catches something.

Something way down at the bottom of the pool.

Something lime green.

I take a quick breath and bob back down, and sure enough, it's Marissa at the bottom of the pool, curled up like a ball.

I come up long enough to shout, "Help!" and take a deep breath. Then I swim down as fast as I can, my heart pounding in my ears, my ears screaming from the change in pressure as I go deeper and deeper. All I can think is, Marissa! Oh God, no! Marissa!

When I reach her, I grab her by the arm and push off the bottom of the pool, but she's heavy. So heavy.

And then I realize that she's holding on to *me*.

At first I'm ecstatic.

She's alive!

But all of a sudden it feels like she's going to drown *me*. She's pulling on me, digging her nails into me, trying to *climb* me.

And I know she's panicked and out of air and afraid of drowning, but now *I'm* panicked and out of air and afraid of drowning!

So I struggle with her and somehow manage to grab her wrist and twist her arm behind her back. I crank it up hard so she can't get away or try to latch on to me again, then kick like mad to get us both up to the surface.

When we pop through, I screech in air, Marissa coughs and sputters and gasps and hacks, and all of a sudden we're surrounded. Brandon's there, Andrew's there, Casey and Billy and Danny and Holly and Dot and all these high school kids are there, and people are helping us over to the edge of the pool, going, "What happened? Are you all right?"

I hang on the edge, panting for air as Brandon pulls Marissa so she's half in and half out. Marissa's head is turned away from me, resting on the cement as she coughs and sputters and gasps and hacks.

Brandon asks me, "What happened?"

"I don't know," I pant out. "She was at . . . the bottom . . . of the pool."

And then, from behind me, a voice says, "Sammy, are you all right?"

It's a voice I'd know anywhere.

A voice I've been sharing secrets with since the third grade.

My head whips around, and there, looking right into my eyes, is Marissa McKenze.

THIRTY

It was like somebody had dropped a live wire into the water. My head whipped back toward the body half in and half out of the pool as what I'd *really* done jolted through me.

I'd saved Heather Acosta's life.

And for once in her life, she was not faking. She was wiped out and barely able to answer questions.

"Heather," Brandon finally said, squatting beside her after they'd pulled her the whole way out of the pool, "do you want us to get you to the doctor?"

She shook her head.

"You're breathing okay? Your lungs feel okay?"

She nodded.

"Did you get hit?" he asked. "What happened?"

She choked out, "I had a cramp. I couldn't *move*."

"Ah," he said, like he could totally relate. "Yeah, they're wicked."

She propped up a little and turned to face him. "Did *you* . . . save me?" she asked, like she was still in a watery daze.

"No, Sammy did," he answered, all matter-of-factly.

Heather propped up a little farther. "Wh-who?"

"Sammy." He pointed at me. "Right next to you."

Heather turned to face me, and when she saw it was really me, her head thumped onto her arm and she started sobbing. "No! No-oo-oo-oo-oo-ooooo!"

Brandon looked at me like, What's up with that? but I just gave him a shrug and climbed out of the water. All of a sudden I wanted to get away from the whole scene. I was wiped out and feeling really weird.

How many times had I wanted to kill this girl?

And here I'd gone and *saved* her?

I felt like I was in emotional warp speed. In less than a minute, I'd gone from panicking that my best friend might die to realizing that I'd saved my archenemy.

Shoot, my archenemy who'd become my best friend's archenemy, too.

And what somehow completely exhausted me was knowing that even after everything Heather had done to me and my friends, I was glad I'd saved her.

Like I'm gonna just let her drown?

Okay, so maybe I'd have sent *Brandon* to rescue her if there'd been time, but still.

Marissa wrapped a towel around me as I staggered away from the pool. "Are *you* all right?"

I nodded, then whispered, "I thought she was you. Where *were* you?"

"In the bathroom. I came back and all of a sudden you're popping up with Heather. She must've gotten in when I got out so she could make a move on Danny." She leaned in really close. "I can't believe you saved Heather's life!"

Holly and Dot were there now, too. Holly whispered, "Heather is freaking out! You've got to look, Sammy. She is totally losing it!"

But I didn't want to look. I didn't want to see. All I wanted was to collapse on Marissa's lounger.

"You are *shaking*," Dot said. "Sit down!"

I did, and a minute later Casey came hurrying over. "I called my mom. She's on her way."

"Is Heather all right?" I asked, and it sounded weird coming out of my mouth.

It sounded like I actually cared.

He nodded. "I'm pretty sure, yeah. We're gonna take her to the doctor anyway, and once she recovers a little, I'm sure she'll milk it for all it's worth." He sorta grinned at me. "I don't think she'll ever recover from you being the one who saved her, though."

I snorted. "Oh, she'll find a way."

He shook his head. "Too many witnesses to rewrite history on this one." He glanced over his shoulder, then said, "Look, I've got to go get her stuff and help get her to the doctor."

I nodded.

He started walking away, but turned back. "I know she's a monster, but thanks."

I nodded again, and as he hurried back to his sister, I closed my eyes and took a deep, aching breath.

Why did life have to be so complicated?

With Heather gone, the party should have been a lot more fun. And for Marissa, it definitely was. She hadn't been playing all that long, so she was full of energy, making great plays in the pool, and Danny paid a lot of attention to her.

But I was wiped out, and as I lay there on the lounger, I couldn't help obsessing over Heather and Casey and my mother and his father and . . . well, the whole Acosta/Keyes mess. I mean, Casey thinks Heather's an annoying, embarrassing, manipulative liar—I know he does—but how much he cares about her was written all over his face when he realized she'd almost drowned.

So I couldn't help wondering . . . Why? Why are blood ties so strong?

And *that*, of course, made me think about my mother and her sneaky ways and how she's so self-centered and doesn't seem to consider how what she does totally messes with my life and how much I *say* I hate her . . . but if something happened to her, I'd be really, really upset.

Scratch that.

I'd be devastated.

There's that tie to her that isn't rational or even explainable.

It just is.

So thinking about all that brought me right back around to thinking about how messed up things were with Casey and me. My standing up to Heather is what brought us together, but it didn't really matter that we thought the same thing about her—in some weird way, she would always have a power over him, just like my mother had over me.

And the longer I lay there stewing about the whole

mess, the more one question kept popping back inside my head.

It wasn't about whether Casey and I would ever get together.

It wasn't about whether my mom and his dad were already together or going to *stay* together.

It was about Heather.

I couldn't help wondering . . . If it had been *me* at the bottom of the pool, would Heather have saved me?

When the party was winding down, Dot called her dad and he gave us all a ride home. "It was fun, *ja*?" he asked when we piled inside the truck.

"It was the *best*," Dot said. "Unbelievable fun." Then she went on to tell him every little detail of *everything*. By the time he was pulling up to the Pup Parlor, he must've felt like he'd actually been to the party.

"Thanks for the ride," Holly and I said, getting out together.

"*Ja*, happy to do it," he called across Dot and Marissa.

Marissa scooted over to the window. "I'll call you later, okay?" She'd been quiet on the ride home, and even though her hair was still wet and matted, she had the warm glow of someone who's been basking in the rays of L-O-V-E.

I nodded, and after they drove away, Holly turned to me and said, "Thank you *so* much for making me go. That was the most fun I've had in my entire life."

I gave her a tired grin. "Told ya."

"Well, you were right!"

So I jaywalked across Broadway, dragged myself up to the apartment, and had the calmest, quietest night of my life. I gave Grams a quick overview of what had happened at the pool party, but that's really all we talked about. She didn't quiz me about anything, Mrs. Wedgewood didn't fall off the toilet or make any demands, Dorito didn't pounce on any mice, no one knocked on the door . . . no one even called.

It was unbelievable.

And exactly what I needed.

I should have known it was the quiet before the storm.

THIRTY-ONE

The next day started off strange. Not because of phone calls or pounding walls or neighbors causing earthquakes; no, it started out strange because I slept until eleven o'clock.

"Grams?" I said all groggy-like when I saw the clock. "Grams?"

"Right here, dear," she said, coming out of her bedroom with a book in her hands. "My! You must've been exhausted."

I rubbed my eyes and sat up. "Wow." I looked at her. "Why didn't you wake me up? You always wake me up. . . ."

She stroked my hair. "I tried. Twice. You obviously needed to rest."

I took in her soft eyes and her sweet smile and felt a surge of love for her. I may have the flakiest mother in the world, but my grandmother's a rock. "Have you heard from Mom?" I asked.

"You mean Lady Lana?" She dropped her hand. "Yes."

"And?"

"And she's back in Hollywood, denies any wrong-doing, says she's been 'embarrassed and unfairly maligned' by you, and expects an apology."

"She expects an apology from *me*?"

"That's right."

"Did she give *you* one?"

"Of course not." She took a deep breath and shook her head. "I was happy for her success, I really was. And I had thought that it would make her easier to be around. After all, she's living her dream—what more could she want? But instead, her success is making her look down her nose at others. The airs she puts on! What makes her think she can act like royalty?"

"She's been like that forever, Grams."

"Maybe a little bit, but now she's phonier than a three-dollar bill."

I laughed and said, "You can say that again," because really, my mom's always been a bit of a diva—which is why I call her Lady Lana—but hearing Grams put it that way just tickled me.

But after I got through laughing, the tickle seemed to move into my brain. It didn't make me laugh, either. It was like a little itch on a hard-to-reach part of your back. You contort your arm like crazy trying to reach it, and you seem to scratch all around it but never quite *get* it.

All through breakfast, I tried to scratch it.

And since it was almost noon and a bowl of reheated oatmeal was just not cutting it, I made a monster sandwich for lunch. And as I sat at the kitchen table scarfing it down, thinking about the pool party and Heather and Casey and Marissa and Danny, my subconscious was back there, reaching for the itch.

And then out of the depths of Grams' room came, "Oh my *word*."

"What, Grams?" I called.

She came into the kitchen area with her jaw dangling. "Look what I just found in my winter coat!"

She had a fistful of crisp, clean twenty-dollar bills.

The tickle in my brain was suddenly . . . ticklier.

I tried to ignore it. "That's great," I said. "But why were you looking in your winter coat?" I chomped down on my sandwich. "It's gotta be ninety degrees outside."

She ignored the question. "I am so careful with money. I never put it loose in a pocket. Am I losing my mind?"

I snickered and took a gulp of milk. "If losing your mind means finding money, I hope I lose mine soon!"

"I feel like I'm dreaming," Grams murmured. "Like this isn't real."

And that's when the itch turned into, like, poison oak of the brain.

I knew she wasn't talking about the actual money—she was talking about *finding* the money.

But . . . not real?

I sat up a little straighter. Maybe that was why Buck Ritter from Omaha, Nebraska, had wanted me to chuck it overboard.

Maybe I'd been going around town buying cameras and art and bikinis and pretzels with money that was . . . fake?

I suddenly lost my appetite.

I reached out for Grams' wad of cash and said, "Let me see."

She handed over the money and sort of jelly-kneed into the seat across from me. "Those are brand-new bills," she said. "Did I go to the bank? Did I . . . ?" Her voice trailed off as I took one of the twenties and felt it between my fingers. I turned it over and over and over. I snapped it. I had no idea what I was looking for, but it sure looked real to me.

And then I remembered Grams telling me that T.J. had used a counterfeit pen on the money she'd spent at Maynard's Market. It had passed that test just fine!

I handed it back. "Definitely not Monopoly money," I said.

"I know it's *real*," Grams said. "Obviously, it's real. How did it *get* there, that's what I want to know."

I shrugged. "Maybe Lady Lana left it for you."

"Hrmph!" she said, standing up. "That would be the day!" Then she shook her head. "Maybe I should go see a doctor."

I laughed, "Grams!"

"I'm serious." She gave me sort of a bewildered look, then handed me a twenty. "Here. You never have any spending money."

I put up a hand. "No, that's okay."

She wagged it at me. "Take it!"

So I took it.

And when she wasn't looking, I checked it over again and again. It felt real. It looked real. It *smelled* real.

But still. I had this little seed of doubt in my mind.

Could it possibly *not* be real? Could T.J. have checked money that wasn't the money I'd slipped her?

The more I thought about it, the more worried I got.

"Uh, Grams," I finally said, trying to come up with an excuse to get out of the apartment. "I think I should go over to Marissa's and see how she's doing."

Grams was at the sink, doing dishes. "Shouldn't you call first? That's a long way to go if she isn't home."

"Uh, yeah. I guess I will."

So I gave the McKenzes' house a call, thinking I'd go over after I was done doing what I was planning to do, only Grams was right—Marissa wasn't even there.

"She went to visit Michael," Mrs. McKenze informed me.

"At Hudson's?" I asked.

"That's right."

I got off the phone feeling totally surprised by that. Only then it hit me that Mrs. McKenze probably *made* her go visit Mikey. So I said to Grams, "She's at Hudson's."

"Because of Mikey?" she asked, wiping her hands on a dish towel. "That whole situation is so . . . unfortunate. I blame the money, you know that? Look at the dysfunction it's caused that family. Glass furniture? Priceless art? What good does that do them?" She came over and gave me a kiss on the cheek. "It's nothing compared to what I have."

I felt a sudden sweep of sadness.

Of *guilt*.

What she had was a lying, deceiving granddaughter. And if I'd go through all this to hold on to three thousand dollars, what would I do to hold on to three *hundred* thousand dollars?

What about three million?

And then a nauseating thought hit me—how was I any different from Lady Lana? I was sneaking around and lying. . . . I was actually *worse* than Lady Lana!

Grams was moving toward the bathroom, saying, "Tell that old hound dog I say hello."

"Huh?" I said when it registered, and then my jaw kinda hit the floor. I mean, if you know Grams, you know she just doesn't say stuff like that. She's, like, too *proper* to say stuff like that. "You mean Hudson?"

She gave me a mischievous smile. "Of course Hudson." Then she closed the bathroom door.

So I grabbed my skateboard, shoved the twenty bucks Grams had given me into my pocket alongside some other bills I had left over, and took off.

The first place I went was definitely not Hudson's.

It was the Office Emporium.

I found the security products section, snagged a three-dollar counterfeit-detector pen, and got in the shortest checkout line. There was a middle-aged woman getting rung up, then a tall baldish guy in an old stretched-out T-shirt, then me.

Now, at first I was pretty busy studying the directions on the back of the package: *Identify phony bills easily with a swipe of the pen. Pen leaves a brown mark on suspect bills (light yellow on genuine bills) so you know right away when to decline payment.*

But when the lady getting rung up started arguing about the price of the software she was buying, the bald guy in front of me got antsy. He shifted from side to side and sighed loudly, and just as I was thinking his head looked like a giant mottled egg poking out of a nest of gray feathers, he scratched the back of his neck.

And *that's* when I noticed the faded tattoo peeking out of the neck hole of his T-shirt.

It was the tops of wings.

Angel wings.

My heart started thumping faster. I mean, I couldn't see the whole tattoo, but I could see that there were letters arching over the tops of the wings.

Obviously, Buck Ritter from Omaha, Nebraska, hadn't risen from the dead, lost fifty pounds, and grown six inches. But the tattoo sure looked like the one Grams had described.

I moved a little closer and tried to make out the letters.

T O L M E R V P A R.

Tol Merv Par? Tolm Erv Par? Maybe it was Latin or Greek . . . ?

"I'm sorry, ma'am," the cashier was saying to the lady buying software. "Let me call the manager."

All of a sudden Mr. Wing Tattoo's head turns, so I jump back and act like I hadn't been doing anything snoopy, like, say, trying to read his neck.

We're in the farthest lane to the right, so he turns his head pretty good, looking at the other registers, then says, "Excuse me, miss," to the cashier. "All I have is this roll of tape." He picks up some flattened cardboard boxes he'd rested against the counter. "These are discards from your warehouse."

"I'm sorry. This transaction is already in progress, and I can't ring you up until it's complete. It'll be just a minute."

"Can I just leave you the cash? I'm in a hurry."

The cashier shakes her head. "I'm sorry, sir. We need to scan your item for inventory purposes."

Now, I'm dying to ask him about his tattoo, but I'm also thinking that his voice is familiar.

Really familiar.

Then he takes the stack of flattened boxes, turns, and bumps right into me.

"I'm sorry!" he says, his neck craning clear around to face me. "I didn't see you there!"

Now, I may have been behind him, but I wasn't *invisible*. And in the few seconds he's facing me, excusing himself out of the lane, I notice that there's something odd about his eyes.

About his left eye.

And it's not that it looks clouded or bloodshot or, you know, *blind*. It looks totally normal, except that it's a little bigger than his right eye, but it seems kinda . . . paralyzed. Like it's not moving the way his right eye is.

"Give up on this lane now," he whispers to me. "You'll be here all day."

The whispers send an eerie tingle through me, and that's when it hits me why his voice is so familiar.

It's the voice I'd heard over Mrs. Wedgewood's rigged phone.

Well, my heart was beating pretty fast before, but now it's *pounding*. And I do hesitate for a second, but then I follow him to another lane, making big waving motions over by the left side of his head.

Does he turn to me and say, What are you doing flapping in my ear like a big ol' bird?

No.

He just keeps on walking like I'm not even there.

My mind flashes back to Rex Randolf not seeing me as he stepped out of the fourth-floor elevator, and it now makes total sense.

The guy's got a fake left eye!

And the clothes he wore to Mrs. Wedgewood's made total sense, too.

The beret hid his bald head.

The tinted glasses hid his fake eye.

The scarf hid his angel wings tattoo.

I stared at him a minute as he put his packing tape on the checkout counter.

It had to be him!

Then I ditched it back to the first lane we'd been in.

There was no way I wanted the Jackal to notice I was buying a counterfeit pen!

THIRTY-TWO

The Jackal made it through his line before I made it through mine, so after I paid for the pen with the miscellaneous bills I had in my pocket, I ran outside and spotted him putting his boxes in the back of a white van.

Now, I've been accused of having a "vivid imagination," an "overly active imagination," a "wild imagination," and a "destructive imagination."

These have come from principals, vice principals, and policemen.

Oh.

And my mother.

I've never mistaken any of these as compliments—probably because of the sneer or frown or eye roll that went with it. And I have to admit that it's kinda true. My brain can get really spun up in thinking things are connected when it turns out they're not.

So even though I'd convinced myself that this bald, one-eyed guy with the angel wing tattoo is the Jackal, as I'm watching him drive away, I'm thinking, What if he's not? What if he's just some old guy buying tape at the office supply store?

How will I ever know?

And then I start kicking myself. Why didn't I have my camera with me? Why was it zipped inside a couch cushion? Why did I even *have* a camera if that's where I was going to leave it? I could have taken a picture of the bald, one-eyed guy! I could have zoomed in and snapped his license plate! I could have had something to work with!

But I didn't have the camera, so instead, I tossed down my skateboard and chased after the van.

Now, if he'd been going clear across town or out to the highway, there's no way I could have tailed him. But with downtown traffic and him sticking to downtown streets, I managed to keep him in view.

It involved some illegal street crossings and grabbing my skateboard and *running* a couple of times, but I never lost sight of him.

And you know where he went?

Straight to the Senior Highrise.

Most of the people who live at the Highrise don't drive. And most of the ones who do probably *shouldn't*. But the point is, there's no garage or any, you know, parking *structure* for the Highrise. There's just a parking lot tucked around back and street parking.

The one-eyed bald guy pulled into a place on Main Street, took his boxes, and went in the front door.

I waited a few minutes, then jaywalked across Main and went straight for his license plate.

Trouble is, the license frame said BUDGET RENT A CAR.

I memorized the plate anyway, then went in the front door.

"Sammy-girl!" Mr. Garnucci bellowed from his desk.

"Hey, Mr. G.," I said, hurrying up to him. I kept my voice real low as I asked, "You know that guy who just came in? The one with the boxes?"

"Sure do!" he shouted.

"Shhhh!" I looked around. "Don't you think he's kind of . . . you know . . . *scary?*"

"Jack?" he said, his eyebrows reaching for the sky. "Jack's a great guy!" His eyebrows ease down as he leans back in his chair. "Ohhhh. It's the eye. He can't help that." He shrugs. "But I can see how it might give a kid the creeps."

"So he's okay?" I ask, trying to fish out some more information.

"Sure he is."

Now, since he's not volunteering any details and I don't want to seem like I'm actually *snooping,* I just say, "Okay, well, thanks. I feel better."

"I keep a good eye out, don't you worry." He chuckles, "No pun intended." Then he adds, "Your grandmother's safe here."

So I start for the door, saying, "Thanks, Mr. Garnucci." But after a few steps, I backtrack and say, "I feel bad. I thought for sure he was, you know, *shady.*"

He laughs. "Trust me. Jack Allenson is a good man. A very good man."

I nod and smile, but my body's shivering with the heebie-jeebies.

Jack *Allenson?*

Jack-Al!

I left there wondering what Mr. Garnucci would say if I told him his "very good man" had been sneaking around the Highrise in disguises and breaking into fat ladies' apartments.

When I was safely across the street again, I found a quiet place near the mall, parked myself on the ground, and finally ripped open the counterfeit pen package. Then I pulled out the twenty Grams had given me, uncapped the pen, and swiped.

I waited and waited for the swipe to turn dark, but nothing happened.

I swiped again.

And again.

On the back, on the front, everywhere.

All the swipes stayed yellow.

"Yes!" I whooped. "Yes, yes, yes!"

I jumped up, feeling like a million bucks. The money wasn't fake—it was the real deal!

I toed my skateboard around, pushed off, and flew to Hudson's house. "Sammy!" he said from the porch, where he was all by himself, reading the paper.

"Hey!" I called, picking up my skateboard. "I heard Marissa's visiting."

He kicked his boots off the railing and said, "She's playing catch with Michael in the backyard."

That stopped me in my tracks. "You're kidding, right?"

He shook his head and hitched a thumb around back. "Take a peek. They've been at it quite a while."

What I saw when I looked around the corner was roly-poly Mikey waddling after a softball, scooping it up, and hurling it to Marissa.

"See? You've got a good arm," she called. "You just needed practice!"

My jaw dropped.

Marissa *complimenting* Mikey?

These were definitely strange new developments.

"Pssst," Hudson said, motioning me over. "Let them play."

So I tiptoed back and sat down in the chair next to him. "Did you have a talk with her or something?"

He folded up the paper and tossed it on the table between us. "She just showed up on her own. Said she'd had a bad dream about him drowning. I assured her there was nothing on the premises he could drown in, but she wanted to see him anyway." He smiled at me. "You seem full of vim and vigor today."

I laughed. "I ought to be. I slept 'til eleven."

His bushy eyebrows reached for the sky. "Oh?"

So I told him all about the pool party and saving Heather's life and being totally wiped out and all of that. And when I was done, he sort of grinned and shook his head.

"What?" I said, 'cause I could tell he was thinking *something*.

"You know why Heather broke down and cried, don't you?"

I just looked at him.

"She's beholden to you." He eyed me. "Forever."

"What do you mean?"

"You saved her life! That's no small thing. In some cultures, if someone saves your life, you become their servant for the rest of your life." He smiled. "After all, you wouldn't have a life without that person."

I snorted. "Well, Heather's not about to become my servant. I'm sure she'll keep right on plotting ways to *kill* me instead."

He wagged his head like, Nuh-uh-uh, you are so wrong. "She may *act* like she hates you for it, but there's no denying what you've done. It'll have a deep psychological effect on her." He shrugged. "How that plays out will be interesting to see."

As I rolled my eyes and told him, "Whatever," that counterfeit pen sort of jabbed me. So I pulled it out of my back pocket and was about to shift it to a front pocket or something when Hudson zeroes in on it and says, "Is that a counterfeit-detecting pen?"

Now, there's nothing unusual-looking about the pen. It does say COUNTERFEIT DETECTOR on it, but it's not real obvious. It just looks like a random highlighter or marker, so Hudson spotting it for what it was surprised me.

But then I remembered that Hudson Graham has a kind of secretive past.

Not *bad* secretive.

I don't think, anyway.

More CIA or FBI or, you know, Undercover Guy secretive. Like maybe he was a spy at one point. He never talks about it, but sometimes something happens that sort of gives away that he's got secrets, and this was one of those sometimes.

"How'd you know that's what this is?" I asked. Then, because *I* had secrets to cover up, I said, "I thought it was just a regular marker when I found it."

He gave a little smile as he took the pen and turned it between his fingers. "It's very plainly a counterfeit pen."

I didn't want to push it, so instead, I asked, "How's it work?" as I pulled Grams' twenty out of my pocket. "I marked this and it just stayed yellow. That's 'cause it's real money, right?"

He nodded.

"Why does counterfeit money turn brown?"

"There's starch in standard paper, that's why. It reacts with the iodine in the counterfeit pen's ink and turns from yellow to brown."

"So . . . real money doesn't have *starch* in it?"

"Correct."

I thought about this a minute, then asked, "Why don't counterfeiters use paper without starch in it?"

"Some do. *If* they can get their hands on it without raising suspicion."

I blinked at him.

I blinked at him some more.

Finally I choked out, "They do?"

"Sure."

"So . . . one of these pens wouldn't work on it?"

He shook his head. "But there are other ways of determining whether a bill is real or fake."

"Like . . . ?"

He took the twenty from me and rubbed it between his fingers. "Aside from the paper, which has a distinctive feel, there's the security thread, the watermark—"

"Wait—what security thread? What watermark?"

"Well, look," he said. "It's been a while since I've really analyzed a bill, but see this eagle here behind the Federal Reserve stamp? See this wavy TWENTY USA behind the Treasury Department seal? See how the art is made of incredibly fine lines? All these things are very hard to duplicate, but the security thread and the watermark are the real giveaways." He held the twenty up to the sunlight. "See this?" he said, pointing out a faint, smudgy-looking vertical line that ran through the upper and lower number 20s on the left side of the bill. "That's the security thread."

"Is it a *thread* thread?" I asked, looking up through the bill.

"No, it's the currency denomination printed in a line, but it's called a thread." He pointed to the right edge of the bill. "Here . . . can you see the watermark? It's a smaller picture of the president, which you can only see when you hold it up to the light."

"Yes!" I said, taking the bill away. "Wow! I had no idea."

He stood up. "Let me get you a loupe. You'll be able to see everything a lot more clearly."

So he brought out a little pyramid magnifier, and when I held it up to the twenty, I could see all *sorts* of detail. And that security thread was just what he'd said—a repeating USA TWENTY in teeny-tiny characters.

"There's one more thing," he said, easing the bill out of my hands. "See this number twenty?" He was pointing to the one in the bottom right corner. "When you look at it straight on, it's gold. When you look at it sideways, it's . . ." He hesitated. "That's odd."

"What?"

"Maybe it's because it's the newest series? In the older issues, the gold twenty appears green when you view it from the side." He slid his wallet out of a back pocket and removed a different twenty. "See this one?" he said, passing it over. "It's an older issue—it changes color."

I looked at his gold twenty face on and then from the side. It definitely turned from gold to green. "Wow, that's cool," I said, but my heart felt suddenly lumpy. Like the blood inside it was thick and having trouble pumping through.

"Here, this one does it, too," he said, handing over another bill. "And this one." He inspected my twenty again. "I wonder why this one doesn't."

"Can I keep all these?" I joked, taking my twenty back.

Just then Marissa and Mikey came around the corner. "Sammy?" Marissa asked.

I shoved Grams' twenty and the counterfeit pen in my pocket and handed the other bills back to Hudson. "Hey!" I said. "I heard you were here, so I thought I'd swing by."

"Cool!"

Hudson smiled at Mikey. "You ready for lunch, slugger?"

252

Mikey was red-faced and sweating, but he panted, "Do I get to light the grill?"

"Yes, m'man." He turned to us. "Girls, do you want to stay for shish kebabs? Michael and I will cook for you."

Marissa looked at me, so I shrugged like, Whatever you want, and to my surprise, she blurted, "That sounds *great*."

So while we kept half an eye on the wonder that was Mikey *cooking*, Marissa talked and talked and talked about Danny and the pool party and all her long-range projections for everything that had happened. "Heather made such a fool of herself, don't you think? First she nearly drowns, then she has a complete meltdown. Who wants to go out with that?"

But while she's talking, what I'm really thinking about is how the gold twenty on Grams' bill didn't change colors.

Why didn't it?

One of the other bills Hudson had handed to me had been the new style, just like Grams'.

It changed colors.

Why didn't mine?

And despite the fact that the bill had passed the watermark test and the security thread test, despite the fact that it felt like real money and passed the counterfeit pen test, the gold twenty staying gold bothered me.

Why would my bill be different from any other?

Plus, other things were creeping into my head, haunting me.

The bundles of cash I'd found had all been so *new*. So crisp and clean and . . . *perfect*. If the money was stolen, it would be, you know, *varied*. Some worn, some crisp, most in between. Right?

The amazing sketches that I'd found in Buck Ritter's desk drawer at the Heavenly also spooked around in my brain. The ones of birds and faces, done in fine lines made out of dots.

Just like the art that's on money.

And that dream I'd had about the money disintegrating haunted me. Maybe it hadn't disintegrated into sand.

Maybe it had disintegrated into *dots*.

Marissa's words were a blur. And no matter how much I tried to focus on how the bill I'd shown Hudson had everything *right* about it except for one tiny detail, it was that one tiny detail that I couldn't get out of my mind.

Why didn't the gold twenty shift colors?

The more I thought about it, the more this icky-sicky feeling grew in my gut. I hadn't just stumbled onto three thousand dollars. I was in the middle of something deep and dark.

And—I could feel it now—dangerous.

THIRTY-THREE

My problem was, I wasn't sure I had a problem. Maybe the twenty I'd been checking was some brand-spanking-new issue where they didn't use color-changing ink. Maybe I was totally worried over nothing.

What I needed was more information. So I started thinking that if I could get my hands on a bunch of money—you know, just to *look* at—maybe I'd see other bills without color-changing ink.

I thought about going to the bank, but figured that no matter what story I tried, they'd never let me near their stacks of cash. I thought about going to Maynard's Market, but the only one who might help me out there was the Elvis impersonator, and he only seems to work nights. And I thought about going over to the Pup Parlor, but Meg and Vera are kinda paranoid about their money. They keep it locked up tight in a thick cast-iron safe, and it's this big ordeal any time Holly needs a little money for something.

Besides, I didn't want to have to explain what I was doing, and I didn't want to feed them some lame *story* about what I was doing.

So I went to the only other place I could think of.
The Heavenly Hotel.

As usual, André was behind the counter, chomping on his cigar. And he was making like he was reading the paper, but what he was really doing was keeping his eye on me.

"You're back," he growled.

"Happy to see you, too," I said, then did something I'd never done before—I walked behind the counter like I worked there.

One of his eyebrows arched waaaaaay up. "What are you doin'?"

I grinned at him. "Let me see your money."

He pulled the cigar out of his mouth. "What is this, a stickup?"

"Oh, right," I laughed. Then I came as close to the truth as I dared. "My friend just taught me how to spot a counterfeit bill. I'm here to do you the favor of checking your money." I smiled at him. "No charge."

His eyebrows did a sort of rolling wave. Like a little hairy sea of suspicion.

The cigar floated back to his mouth.

Finally he growled, "I know how to check for phony cash."

"Watermark? Security thread? Color-shifting ink? All of that? Or do you just swipe with a pen?"

He studied me. Then without a word, he popped open the ancient register and pulled out a ten. "Show me."

"It's easier with twenties," I said, still smiling.

He switched the bills and grumbled, "What in the world are you up to, girl?"

"Trouble—what else?" I laughed, trying my best to

sound like I was definitely *not* up to trouble. I gave a sad little shake of my head. "Why are you always so suspicious?"

He grunted. " 'Cause I work in *this* joint."

"Well, lighten up!" I pointed out the security thread, the watermark, and how the number twenty shifted colors as you looked at it from different angles. "Isn't that cool?"

"I had no idea."

"So let's do another."

One by one, we went through all the twenties, fifties, and even tens in his drawer.

Every single bill had color-shifting ink.

"Looks like you're all clear," I said, like a cheerful little do-gooder.

"Uh, thanks, Sammy," he said, and for the first time ever, his voice didn't sound like a growl. It sounded almost . . . *soft*.

"No problem," I called over my shoulder as I headed out. But the fact is, there *was* a problem. There was a problem with the way I felt. I felt sneaky and creepy and kinda sick to my stomach.

Why couldn't he have growled at me?

Why couldn't he have told me to quit wasting his time?

Why did he have to sound so *grateful?*

And there was another, bigger problem.

A big color-*not*-shifting problem.

A problem tucked neatly away inside my pocket.

And, I was afraid, tucked away inside the cushions of my grandmother's couch.

I hurried home, and when I discovered Grams wasn't there, I felt so relieved.

Until I found the note:

GONE SHOPPING—BACK SOON.

I felt panicky all over. She was probably spending the cash I'd slipped her. What if it *was* fake? What if she got caught?

I hurried over to the couch, unzipped a cushion, and started inspecting the gold number twenty in the bottom right corner of every bill.

I checked nearly two thousand dollars in twenties.

Not one of them shifted colors.

"Oh no!" I whimpered. "Oh *no*."

My mind began a complete free fall about the money. If it *was* fake and I got caught, would they throw me in jail? Would they make me pay for everything I'd bought with it?

How would I ever do that?

I didn't have any money!

And I sure couldn't borrow from Grams!

Which made me start panicking about Grams. Besides her being out on a possibly-fake-money spending spree, there was the Jackal to worry about. He knew there was some sort of connection to our apartment—what if he and the Sandman and Buck Ritter from Omaha, Nebraska, were, like, old Mafia guys? The Jackal was sure smooth enough to be a Mafia guy.

And what if some head honcho Mafia guy was putting

big pressure on the Jackal because the money was supposed to get *laundered* first.

What did laundering money mean, anyway?

Washing it?

Making it less crispy?

I shook off that thought because what did it matter
what laundering was? It was something they did to dirty
money or fake money or whatever! The problem wasn't
that, it was what the Jackal might do to get his money
back. He'd already been pretty over the top. I mean, come
on—he'd broken into Mrs. Wedgewood's apartment!

Wait. Worse than *that*, he'd pretended to want to go
out with her!

If he was *that* desperate, what if he forced his way into
our apartment and then, like, tied up Grams and . . . and
ransacked the place!

What if he found the cash and the digital camera with
the picture of him and he put the whole thing together . . .
only he thought *Grams* was the one behind it all?

What if they *killed* her to keep her quiet?

I tried to tell myself to get a grip. I tried to say, Mafia
guys laundering money in the Senior Highrise?

Please!

Like the Nightie-Napper wouldn't foil their evil, sudsy
plans?

But I couldn't shake the image of Grams all roped to a
chair being tortured by a one-eyed Mafia guy.

As I stuffed the cash back inside the cushion and
zipped it up, I was completely panicked and desperate to
do *something*.

But . . . what?

My brain started Dumpster-diving for a plan. Any plan. And after inspecting a few ideas that were total garbage, what it came up with was one that at first seemed like junk, but the more I dusted it off and looked it over, the more potential it seemed to have. Because right now all I had were hunches and guesses. I had to *know* if there was really something going on before I . . . what? Before I called the police or the FBI or the CIA or whoever you call to report that a one-eyed Mafia guy is laundering money in the Senior Highrise?

But—like Officer Borsch had told André—to get a search warrant, they had to know what they were searching for. And I knew Officer Borsch well enough to know that my hunches and guesses were not enough for a search warrant.

But if I could somehow see inside the Jackal's apartment, I might be able to pick up some clues that would help me figure everything out *and* give me something besides hunches and guesses to tell Officer Borsch about.

The more I polished the idea, the more I liked it.

But I didn't know where the Jackal lived, so the *Sandman's* apartment was actually the one to try. It was on the fourth floor—the same floor where I'd scared Buck Ritter to death. The same floor where the fire escape door had been rigged not to lock. It was the place where the Jackal had used his secret knock.

The Sandman's apartment seemed like headquarters.

But how was I going to see inside? I couldn't just go up, use the secret knock, and say, Hey, dude. Are you in the Mafia? Are you laundering phony money? Are you planning to tie up my grandmother and torture information out of her?

But then it hit me that there *was* someone who could go up and ask a bunch of questions. Maybe not about laundering money, but that didn't matter. The point was, she could snoop. Maybe even get inside!

The minute the idea hit me, I knew I had to give it a shot. It was risky. It was iffy. But I had the thought in my head, and at this point, I was desperate to do something, *anything,* to figure things out and fix the mess I was in.

So this was it.

Time to pull out the wig.

Time to put on the glasses.

Time to turn into Old Lady Superspy!

THIRTY-FOUR

I grabbed a notebook and pen, snuck out of the building, and went straight to the bushes where I'd stashed my sack of old-lady stuff.

It was still there.

So I hurried around the building to the back side of the Dumpster and got busy—tummy bulge, flowery dress, sweater, earrings, ugly shoes, wig. . . . This time was a lot quicker than the last time 'cause I knew what I was doing.

I had to put on extra makeup because even with sunblock I'd gotten a lot of color at the pool party. When that was finally done, I did my lips way outside the line, popped on my granny specs, and stuffed my regular clothes inside the bag.

While I was shoving in my jeans, the counterfeit pen fell out of them and onto the ground. I picked it up and was about to put it inside the bag, but at the last second I stopped, thought a minute, then slipped it inside my little granny purse.

Now, in all the times I've gone up and down the fire escape, I've only had problems outside the building twice. Well, that's not including scaring someone to death. I'm talking *normal* problems.

Anyway, both times were with the gardener going back and forth on his riding mower near the fire escape, and both times I just waited him out.

So when I heard the purr of an engine getting closer and closer, I just backed up a little, making sure I wasn't visible from the lawn area.

But the sound got even *closer,* and then I saw something driving across the lawn that made my heart skid to a halt.

A van.

A *white* van.

I edged out and peeked around the corner, watching as it parked right beside the fire escape. And sure enough, out of the driver's side comes one bald, glass-eyed Jackal.

I duck back quick, my mind scrambling for a reason he'd be driving a van up to the fire escape of the Senior Highrise in the middle of the day.

Was he making the Big Escape?

Was that why he'd gotten boxes and tape at the Office Emporium?

Is that why he'd been in such a hurry?

Whatever the reason, I don't have time to hang around and spy on him. Obviously, something's going down, and I've got to get *moving.* And since I sure can't go up the fire escape, I ease out of my little changing area, sneak around some bushes, and hurry over to the main entrance walkway. I'm moving *fast,* too, but before I get to the door, I make myself slow down and creak along. "Hello, dearie," I say under my breath. "Isn't it a heavenly day, dearie?"

And that's when it hits me that the last time I was Old Lady Superspy I had a name. Only . . . I can't really remember it. The last name was Florentine, but the first name? Was it Mary? Margaret? Millie? None of those seem quite right, but I can't put my finger on what *is* right.

I don't have time to waste thinking about it, though, so I finally just go inside and creak my way past Mr. Garnucci, who's playing with one of those handheld electronic poker games.

"Hello there!" he calls out.

I give a creaky little hunched-over wave.

"We visiting someone today?" he asks.

"Eh?" I warble, cupping my ear.

"Who are we visiting today?"

I stand there and just blink at him a minute. "Are you coming with me, sonny?" I ask, acting confused.

"No, no," he laughs. "Who are *you* visiting today? I'll call them and let them know you're here."

"Now, don't ruin it, dearie," I tell him, then put a finger in front of my big orange lips. "It's a surprise."

"Ah," he says. "Do you know your way?"

"I do, indeed," I tell him.

And just like that, the interrogation's over. "Well, enjoy your visit," he says, and turns back to his electronic poker game.

Now, as I creak my way over to the elevator, it hits me that it would be very helpful if I knew the Sandman's real name. So I take a little detour over to the mailboxes, find number 427, and see the name T. Egbert.

And while I'm at it, I find J. Allenson, too.

He's in number 298.

That actually made me feel safer. If the Jackal lived on the second floor, maybe I didn't have to sweat him going up to the Sandman's on the fourth floor right away.

'Course, then again, maybe I *did*.

I hobble over to the elevator and ride it up to the fourth floor. And before I can talk myself out of it, I go up to apartment 427, knock four times, and pause, but before I can even finish the secret knock, the door swooshes open and I find myself face to face with a stout old guy sporting a buzz cut. He's also sporting a ruddy, sweaty face and a dingy wife-beater T-shirt. "Oh!" he says, obviously surprised I'm not someone else.

I don't really like the looks of him, but I glance down at my notebook like there's actually something written in it, then say, "Mr. Egbert?"

He wipes his forehead with the back of his hand. "Yes?"

"I'm here about the problem with mice."

"I don't have a problem with mice," he says.

But in a sort of pushy-old-lady way, I move past him and into the apartment anyway. "They're coming in the building through plumbing crevices, so we're checking under the sinks of all the apartments. It won't take long."

"Wait just a minute!" he says, coming after me, only he's not moving as fast as I am 'cause he's got a serious limp. "I did *not* say you could come in here!"

But I'm already in, and what I'm seeing by the kitchen

table are packing boxes stacked up and ready to move out. I'm also seeing fat rolls of paper. They're like butcher paper, only . . . cleaner. Whiter. And more *transparent*.

And there are what I think are computer printers—*three* of them.

And a large plastic high-tech-looking paper cutter.

"I have to do all the apartments or I don't get paid," I tell him, but my heart is pounding and my hands are sweating and all of a sudden I've got the urge to get *out* of there.

"Look," he says, not knowing what to do with me, "just make it quick, all right? I'm actually very busy right now."

But then, when he turns around and hobbles back toward the door, I see that he's got the same tattoo on his neck that the Jackal and Buck Ritter had on theirs. And I want to scream, What's the deal with that tattoo?! but I more want to get *out* of there. So real quick I take out the counterfeit pen, tag one of the rolls of paper with it, and pop it back in the purse.

The yellow streak doesn't turn brown.

It doesn't even turn *orange*.

It stays a light, clean yellow.

And as the pieces scattered all over my brain come together in a loud, solid *clank,* my knees start shaking and there's no doubt in my mind—I've got to get out of there *now*.

"You!" a voice booms from behind me, and without even looking, I know who it is.

The Jackal.

I turn around and I don't even have to pretend to be an old lady anymore. My joints are all wobbly, and my voice is all warbly as I say, "Hello there," like he's a total stranger, 'cause the last time I was Old Lady Superspy, he was in his Suave Guy disguise.

I turn to the Sandman and say, "I took a look under the sink and it's fine—everything's sealed up tight."

Now, as I'm talking, I'm trying to ease my way out because the Jackal is not looking too friendly, let me tell you. As a matter of fact, he's studying me *verrrry* closely, and his eyes are all slitty and slanty and suspicious-looking. He starts wagging a finger at me slowly, and I can see him putting the pieces together. And before I can get past him, he blocks my way and mutters something in the Sandman's ear.

The Sandman looks at him like he's crazy. "*She* did?"

"Uh-huh." He gives me a biting look. "And I can assure you she's not here looking for *mice*." He moves in closer to me, saying, "As a matter of fact . . ."

He reaches for my wig, so I jump back and try to buy a little time. "Gentlemen, please! Call Mr. Garnucci. He can explain everything. He's the one who sent me."

"Drop the act," the Jackal says, coming toward me. Then he calls to the Sandman, "Block the door!"

"Stay away!" I tell him, and then since he's coming at me and I'm totally desperate, I swing at him hard with my pea green granny purse, trying to bean him in the head.

Trouble is, it's a dumb little pea green granny purse with no weight to it, and he manages to grab it and twist it out of my hand. "Got your camera in there?" he asks. He

267

reaches inside the purse, watching me the whole time, but instead of finding a camera, he pulls out my counterfeit-detector pen.

His jaw drops and he hurls the purse aside. Then he tosses the pen to the Sandman, calling, "This is worse than I thought!"

I jet away from him, but really, there's no place to go. The Sandman's apartment is just like every apartment in the building. There's no way out except through the front door.

Now, it does flash through my mind that if I can get to the bathroom, I can lock myself in there, but all they'd have to do is snap the chintzy knob off with some pliers.

Piece of dead-granny cake.

And since going into the bedroom or kitchen is like backing myself into a corner *away* from the front door, I scramble into the living room while the Jackal comes at me, muttering, "Domino's Pizza. What kind of police department puts together a ridiculous surveillance like *that*?"

And that's when it hits me—he thinks I'm a *cop*.

I look left and right, trying to find a way out of the corner he's backing me into. "I have no idea what you're talking about, sonny."

"Classic line," he mutters. "I couldn't figure it out, because the woman who lives there was out of the apartment that night. But *you* were staked out there, weren't you?"

"Please," I warble, "you're scaring me."

"Oh, knock it off. You're not even old," he says, then lunges at me.

Now, if I *had* been old and stiff, I definitely would have

been toast. But he's got me cornered by a *couch,* so when he lunges, I jump onto the couch, run *across* the couch, and charge for the door.

"Stop her, Tommy!" the Jackal cries.

The Sandman's standing in front of the door like a big ol' sand*bag,* but all I can think is that I've got to get past him or that one-eyed Jackal is gonna kill me. So I hunker down with my head tucked and my shoulder forward and charge him like a linebacker, thinking I'll knock him aside and get out the door.

Trouble is, shoulder-slamming him is *exactly* like charging into a big ol' sandbag—he doesn't even budge. And as if the pain shooting through my shoulder isn't bad enough, the next thing you know, *I'm* off my feet and flat on the ground.

The world starts spinning around me.

The Jackal and Sandman are waaaay up above me, looking down.

Old Lady Superspy is in serious trouble.

THIRTY-FIVE

I hear the Sandman saying, "What now?" but it sounds like it's underwater.

"Whaaaaat naaaaaaooooooowwwwww . . ."

The Jackal says something to Sandman, but I can't quite make it out. It has to do with killing me, though, I just know it. And since the world isn't spinning quite so much now and I definitely don't want to die, I take a deep breath and *focus* while they argue back and forth. Then, when I feel like I've got enough strength, I concentrate every ounce of energy I have, whip my left foot in front of the Sandman's ankle and my right foot behind his knee, and—*whack*—I scissor-kick him as hard as I can.

Trouble is, it's like scissor-kicking a rock. My ankle screams at me, my shin goes into shock, and while I'm busy having spasms of pain, the Sandman just sort of teeters above me—he's off balance, but he's not exactly crashing to the ground.

So I grab his ankle and *yank,* and all of a sudden he takes a complete nosedive.

All of him except his leg.

I've somehow broken it off his body.

"Aaaaaaah!" I scream, 'cause there I am with a *leg* in my hand—the shoe, the sock, and a big ol' calf.

Only the calf's got no hair.

Or veins.

Or skin.

It's, like, *plastic*.

"Aaaaaah!" I scream again, 'cause I'm plenty freaked out by the leg, and the one-eyed Jackal is coming at me like he's gonna kill me.

So I twist up onto my knees and do the only thing I can think to do.

I swing that fake leg like a baseball bat and hit the Jackal in the head as hard as I can.

He staggers, and his *eye* pops out and lands in my lap.

"Aaaaaaah!" I scream again, 'cause now there's a glass eye staring up at me from the skirt of my granny dress, and I am totally freaked out about everything—the eye, the leg, these old guys who are falling apart in front of me . . . everything!

And falling apart or not, these geezers are *tough*, and they're not giving up. The Sandman's crawling toward me, and the Jackal's pushing up from the floor, where he fell when his eye popped out—they're like old-geezer ghouls, and they're definitely out to get me!

So I start bashing on the Sandman with his own leg. *Whack! Whack! Whack!* But as he's rolling away from me, the Jackal's coming *toward* me.

"Stay back!" I yell. "Stay back or I'll . . . I'll . . ." I pick up his glass eye. "Or you'll never see your eyeball again!"

He comes at me anyway, but the Sandman's not blocking the door anymore, so I dive for the knob, yank the door open, and stumble into the hallway. "Help!" I shout. "Help!" And I run to the inside stairs and start bounding up to the fifth floor, hauling the leg and the eyeball with me.

When I get to the fifth floor, I go flying down the hallway, skid to a halt in front of Grams' apartment, and dive for cover inside. "Grams! Call the police! Call Officer Borsch!"

So there I am, in my granny disguise, holding a fake leg and a glass eye, panting like mad, when all of a sudden I see that Officer Borsch is already there.

Sitting in our living room.

With a picture in his hands.

A sketch, actually.

Of *me*.

"Samantha?" Grams asks, coming toward me. "Sa-*man*tha?"

"Uh, yeah, it's me," I say, my eyes darting from her to the sketch, then back to her. And then I just blurt it all out. "I'm sorry, okay? I'm really, really sorry. I had no idea it was fake. But we've got to do something to stop them quick! Do you have a gun, Officer Borsch? 'Cause you're gonna need it. They're *tough*. That's why I took their leg and their eye . . . to slow them down! How can you run with only one leg, huh? How can you see with only one eye? Well, I suppose you *can* see with only one eye, but your depth perception is totally whacked. Of course, his depth perception is probably *always* totally whacked 'cause it's just a *glass* eye and he can't really see out of it anyway and—"

"What are you *talking* about?" Officer Borsch says, coming toward me.

"The counterfeiters! Their headquarters is apartment four-two-seven. They have rolls of paper and printers and boxes of . . . stuff! Their names are Tommy Egbert and Jack Allenson and—"

"Tommy Egbert?" Grams says. "That's Tommy Egbert's leg? Oh, Samantha!"

"You know him?"

"Yes! He's a very nice person! And he lost his leg serving our country!"

"What?" I shake my head. "No. He is not a nice guy. He's a counterfeiter! I checked the paper with a counterfeit pen! I . . . I . . . The pen's at their headquarters 'cause the Jackal snatched it away from me. But I did have one! And the paper stayed yellow!"

Grams is looking very worried. "The Jackal? You are making no sense, child! What paper?"

"The rolls of paper they've been using to make counterfeit money! It doesn't have starch in it!"

"Starch?" But then she's off and running with a new batch of questions. "Why in heaven's name are you dressed like that? That was *you* coming out of Rose's the other night? What were you *doing* there?" She shakes her head. "And where did you get those *shoes*? They are the ugliest shoes imaginable!"

Well. I'm obviously getting nowhere with her, so I turn to Officer Borsch. "They're bustin' out of here!

They've got everything packed up! Probably 'cause you visited them before and they thought you were onto them. They've got a van parked on the lawn by the fire escape. You've got to do something quick or they'll be *gone*."

Officer Borsch pinches his eyes closed. "You're telling me there's a counterfeiting ring inside the Senior Highrise?"

"Officer Borsch! You *know* me! I'm not making this up." I shake the fake body parts at him. "Why else would I have this leg and this eye?"

He holds his forehead and takes a deep breath. "I'm afraid to speculate." Then he adds, "The reason I'm here is because someone's been spending counterfeit money around town—"

"I know!"

"But the composite sketch they came up with looks like *you*."

"I know!" I pull a face. "It could also look like Grams."

"What?" she says, finally tearing her eyes away from my shoes.

"You know that money you found in your coat and checkbook?"

Her eyes got really big behind her glasses. "Yes . . . ?"

"*I* put it there."

She gasps. "You slipped me counterfeit money? Samantha!"

"I didn't know it was counterfeit! I was trying to be nice!"

"But . . . where did you *get* it?"

I look down. "It was Buck Ritter's."

Grams gasps again. "The man on the fire escape? You didn't—"

"Stop!" Officer Borsch cries, covering his ears. "I don't want to know any more. I *can't* know any more! I'm an officer of the law, for cryin' out loud!"

"Officer Borsch, really," I plead. "I didn't know it was fake. He told me to get rid of it, but I didn't know why! So I was getting rid of it by *spending* it." He's just staring at me, so I say, "You've got to get *moving,* and you've got to be careful! They thought I was a cop and—"

"They thought *you* were a cop? Dressed like *that*?"

"An undercover cop! And I swear they were going to kill me! They're probably making their getaway right now!"

He frowns at me. "Two seniors. Making a getaway. One with one eye, one with one leg . . ."

I stomp one rubbery tan foot. "Officer Borsch! They're counterfeiters! And they're *good*. They've got the watermark and the security thread and the . . . and the everything! Everything except color-shifting ink."

He studies me a second, then gives me a pained squint. "You look like Tweety Bird's granny, you know that?" He looks at my feet. "And those *are* amazingly ugly shoes."

"Officer Borsch!"

"All right, all right!" he grumbles. "I just can't believe I'm talking to a Tweety granny look-alike about one-eyed, one-legged counterfeiters."

"Just *do* something!"

"I'm goin', I'm goin'," he gripes, "but this whole thing's unbelievable."

So he radios for backup, tells Grams and me, "Don't leave this apartment!" and heads out.

The minute he's gone, Grams turns on me and says, "You have some explaining to do, young lady."

"I know," I whimper. "And I'm really, really, *really* sorry. I was just afraid you'd make me give it back! I'd never had money before—it was really *fun* to have money. I could buy anything and *do* anything. . . . And it's not like I was being selfish! I gave you money, I bought stuff for Marissa, I bought Hudson a surprise. . . . If I wanted a pretzel at the mall, I could just buy a pretzel at the mall—"

"How much did you *spend*?" Grams gasps, sinking into a chair.

I look down. "About a thousand."

"Dollars?"

"Well, Hudson's present was over five hundred—"

"Five hundred dollars? Five hundred dollars? No wonder the gallery was able to give a description of you."

"The gallery did?"

Her head wagged from side to side. "It's a lot of cash for a young girl to hand over."

"Oh," I said, feeling suddenly very stupid.

"Oh, Samantha! How are we ever going to pay all of it back?"

"Maybe they won't make us?" I asked, but my voice sounded really small. Like I was talking from way down at the bottom of a big muddy pit.

"And if those men get away . . ."

"They won't!" I gave a halfhearted hoist to the fake leg and the eye. "They can't see, and they can't run."

Grams held her forehead like she was holding back a migraine. "I can't believe Tommy Egbert is a counterfeiter!" She looks at me. "Are you sure you've got this right?"

I pull off my wig and set it on the coffee table along with the leg and the eye. "Yes! And he and Jack Allenson both have angel wing tattoos on their necks. With letters arching over the wings."

"They do?"

"Do you think they're in some kind of counterfeiting cult or something?"

"A counterfeiting cult? Samantha, really!"

"So why would they all have the same tattoo in the same place? Maybe they're in some kind of underground moneymaking association, or something! Like the winged-neck Mafia!"

"That's the most ridiculous thing I've ever heard." She thinks a minute, then shakes her head. "But why would two seniors in their condition, living *here*, counterfeit money? Were they expecting to start living the good life?"

I blink at her as this queasy feeling slowly tide-pools in my stomach.

"What's the matter, Samantha? What are you thinking?"

"Buck's daughters said something about him living in a trailer—that he deserved better. And he was a war vet, too!"

"Buck's daughters? When did you talk to Buck's daughters?" Her brow pinches down. "What *else* have you not told me? How long has this been going on?"

"Uh . . . sorry, Grams, but I have to make a phone call."

"To whom? Samantha, get back here!"

I race over to the phone. "I promise I'll tell you everything, but first I've got to call André."

"André? At the Heavenly? What does *he* have to do with this?"

"I'll tell you in a minute!"

I whip out the phone book, look up the number for the Heavenly, and dial. "André?" I ask when he answers the phone. "It's Sammy. Do you still have Buck Ritter's daughter's card?"

"Uh, I might. . . ."

Through the phone, I can hear sirens wailing in the distance. "Can I, uh . . . can I have the phone number?"

"Is this another one of those don't-ask-questions situations?" he growled.

The sirens are getting louder—I can hear them in one ear through the phone and also kinda muffled through the apartment. "It's actually an extension of the same one," I tell him. "And I really need to come over and explain a bunch of stuff, but it won't be for, you know, a while."

"Hmm. Well, I got the card right here. You ready?"

So I scrawl down the information, get off the phone, and get right back on again.

"*Now* who are you calling?" Grams asks.

The phone's already ringing, so I hold up my finger,

and when a woman answers, I say, "Hi. Is this Buck Ritter's daughter?"

"Why, yes. Who's this?"

The sirens are suddenly quiet.

"A friend of Jack Allenson and Tommy Egbert's."

"Oh my!" she says. And after a short eye-opening conversation with her, I get off the phone feeling totally shaken. And now I don't know *what* to do.

So I do the only thing that seems to make any sense—I run back to the coffee table, wrestle on my granny wig, grab the leg and eye, and race for the door.

THIRTY-SIX

"Samantha, wait! Where are you going? Why are you taking those . . . body parts?"

"I have to find Officer Borsch!"

"Just let him handle it! He said not to leave the apartment."

"You don't understand!" I cry, and take off running for the fire escape.

I'm feeling so strange. Completely confused. And when I pass by the fourth-floor landing, I get all choked up. "I'm sorry," I whisper. "I'm so, so sorry."

Officer Borsch is at the white van, all right. So are two squad cars, which are parked on the lawn and aimed at the van like black-and-white cannons.

The Jackal's and the Sandman's heads are bowed, and their hands are being cuffed behind their backs by Squeaky and the Chick.

"Officer Borsch," I cry, flying off the last few steps of the fire escape. "Officer Borsch, wait!"

He takes one look at me, grabs me by the arm, and yanks me aside. "What are you *doing*? And why are you carrying those things? Why are you here at all? Go home!"

"I have to give them back! I . . ." I tear away from him

and run over to where the Jackal and Sandman are looking totally defeated. "I'm so sorry," I tell them, and I'm trying to return their body parts when it hits me that the Sandman is standing on two feet and the Jackal has two eyes.

Apparently, they have backup body parts.

Anyway, I'm just gawking at them like an idiot, holding out a leg and an eye, when the Jackal says, "Who *are* you?"

Squeaky and the Chick are obviously wondering the same thing, because Squeaky pipes up with, "Excuse me, ma'am, but your presence here is not constructive or warranted," and the Chick is blinking her ultra-tarred lashes at me like she can't believe what she's seeing.

Officer Borsch tries to pull me away, but I wrestle my arm back and say to the Jackal and Sandman, "Buck's daughter told me about you guys. Said that your whole platoon got killed except for the three of you." I turn to the Jackal. "That's how you lost your eye." I look at the Sandman. "That's how you lost your leg. And that's why you have those tattoos on the backs of your necks."

Everyone goes dead quiet.

Finally the Jackal sort of nods and says, "That's right."

"Buck's daughter said you had the tattoos done at the same time. She said those letters are the initials of your friends who died."

The Jackal and Sandman exchange looks, and finally Sandman says, "It's been forty years of nightmares. You think you'll get over it, but you never really do."

"Please try to understand," the Jackal says. "We felt . . . disposed of. And we all thought Uncle Sam owed us more than he was willing to pay." He shrugs. "So after forty years, we came up with a way to *make* him pay. We weren't trying to get rich, we just thought we deserved better."

"Poor Buck," the Sandman says in a really heavy-hearted way. "He was nervous about it the whole time."

The Jackal rolls his good eye my way. "I know you thought we were going to hurt you, and I'm sorry. We just wanted to restrain you until we could leave town." He frowns. "I know it didn't look that way, but that's the truth."

I look at Officer Borsch and whisper, "Can't you just let them go?"

Officer Borsch pulls me aside. "I understand why you want to, but the answer's no. They broke the law. They were skipping town with big duffel bags of counterfeit money."

"But—"

"Look, it's not really Uncle Sam who pays—it's the people who get stuck with the phony cash." Then he drops his voice even further and says, "Now *please*. Go home. And don't use the fire escape. These other officers are witnesses to everything, you got that?"

I nod, and after a little more shooing on his part, I trudge around to the front of the building and head for the front door.

My feet are killing me in my rubbery old shoes, but my heart feels even worse. It's like a lump of cement in my chest. I mean, usually a bad guy is just that—a bad guy.

Or a psycho sicko.

Or, you know, just plain *crazy*.

But it wasn't so cut-and-dried with these guys. It *didn't* seem right that they were stuck living in the Senior Highrise or some trailer park in Omaha, Nebraska. But I knew that Officer Borsch was right—counterfeiting cash wasn't right, either.

And even though I had really thought that I was in, you know, mortal danger, I was feeling really, really bad for ripping off a war vet's leg and using it to pop out another war vet's eyeball.

Not to mention having scared the third one to death.

So I didn't go in the front door right away. I just sat down on one of the wooden benches by the walkway to the Highrise entrance and felt miserable. My feet were hurting, my tummy padding was itching like crazy, and I knew I *looked* ridiculous in my stupid granny getup, but I didn't care.

All I could feel was my block-of-cement heart, pulling me down, down, down, making it hard to breathe, hard to want to do *anything*.

Which is why I didn't hear the *clickity-clack* of the skateboard right away.

Why I didn't notice that it was actually coming up the Highrise walkway.

Why I didn't even look up until it was clickity-clacking right past me.

All of a sudden my heart forgot about being a lump of cement and started bouncing around in my chest. "Casey?"

He stopped and looked around, and when all he saw

was a crazy-looking old lady on the Highrise bench, he pushed off again.

"Casey!" I called, and when he stopped again, I started laughing.

His face went all funny as he cocked his head.

I waved him over. "It's me!"

"No way . . . ," he said, coming toward me. "What are you *doing*?"

"What are *you* doing?" I laughed, because he'd never come to the Highrise before and something about him being there made me feel all bubbly inside. All bubbly, and light-headed, and *happy*.

He moved closer and sort of *peered* at me. "Is that really you?"

"Yes, sonny," I warbled.

He looked over both shoulders. "Do you *always* wear a disguise when you're here?"

"No!"

Now, I've been in some pretty embarrassing situations with Casey before, but this was on beyond embarrassing.

It was totally absurd.

Laughable, actually, and boy, did I laugh.

He sat next to me on the bench and shook his head. "Man, you've got that lipstick thing down, that's for sure. My grandmother used to wear hers just like that." Then he whispered, "So why are you in an old-lady disguise?"

I made my voice all quivery as I said, "It's kind of a long story, sonny."

"Well?"

So I started at the beginning and told him everything.

About scaring Buck Ritter to death, about taking the money, about . . . everything. And when I was all done, I came up for air and said, "I dug myself in pretty good, huh?"

He let out a low whistle. "Wow." Then he kinda grinned at me. "Who says living with old people is boring? Man!"

I snorted. "Yeah. Well, this was a little *too* much excitement." I shook my head. "I wish I hadn't found the money or gotten nosy or tried to figure it out. I'm all, like, confused." I looked at him. "I know that counterfeiting money is wrong, but I still feel really bad for them." I took a deep breath. "And I'm gonna be in total hot water with Grams."

He nodded, then reached over and held my hand.

My very spotty, very ugly hand.

I looked at his hand on mine, then looked into his beautiful brown, caring eyes.

It was a perfect moment, us alone on the bench, holding hands, looking into each other's eyes.

Trouble is, I looked like Tweety's granny, and *he* looked like a kid making eyes at an old lady.

After a few seconds of this, his mouth twitched.

My big orange lips pinched down a smile.

He snickered.

I snorted.

And then we both just busted up.

When we were all done laughing, he said, "I actually did come over for a reason." He pulled a square yellow envelope out of his pocket. "Here. It's from Heather."

My eyebrows shot up. "Really?"

The flap was licked to death. It took me forever to peel it open, and when I finally got the note out and unfolded it, I found myself face to face with three bold blue words.

I HATE YOU!

"Gee, thanks," I said, handing it back to Casey.

"What!" He jumped off the bench. "She was supposed to *thank* you. Even my mother said she had to!"

I shrugged. "All the more reason for her to hate me."

"Man! I can't *believe* her." He grabbed his skateboard. "I'll call you later, okay?" Then, when he was a few yards away, he grinned at me over his shoulder. "Go do something about those lips, would ya?"

I laughed and blew him a great big granny kiss.

THIRTY-SEVEN

Apparently, the only one who actually laundered any of the counterfeit money was me. Well, Grams did, too, but that was *thanks* to me.

Laundering, it turns out, has nothing to do with washing machines. It means exchanging fake money for real money. Like, if you go spend a fake twenty and get back fifteen dollars in change, you've just laundered a twenty.

Who knew I'd been laundering more than blackmailer briefs?

Anyway, Officer Borsch says that the Jackal and Sandman's lawyer will probably argue that making fake money is not a crime if you keep it in your house. He says that it *is* and that they were obviously *planning* to spend it, but he also says that, considering all the circumstances and that they have no "priors," they'll most likely get off easier than they might have.

Unfortunately for *me,* I'm in some pretty hot water. Not as hot as it could have been if Officer Borsch wasn't helping me, though. "Can't have a criminal in my wedding," he grumbled. "We're gonna have to get you out of this."

Saved by the wedding bells.

I turned over all the leftover money to him, and he helped me return everything I could return. No pretzels or Juicers or pool party swimsuits, but he gave back the camera and the clothes, and we even bagged up my Old Lady Superspy disguise and left it on CeCe's Thrift Store doorstep after hours.

For the rest, he's arranging to have me do community service. I don't quite know what that means yet, but I have a feeling it's going to involve an orange vest and a big trash bag. I don't mind, though. Even if I have to pick up trash for a year, I know I'm getting off easy. The way Officer Borsch explained it was, "Passing around counterfeit money is like playing old maid."

"Huh?" I said, and I guess I was squinting pretty good, 'cause he said, "You've never played old maid?"

"Uh . . . yeah. You saw me . . . ?"

"No! Not dress up! I mean the card game. Your grandmother never taught you old maid?"

"Uh . . . no."

He let out a puffy-cheeked sigh. "I am getting so old." But then he went on to explain how in the card game old maid, the person who gets stuck with the old maid card loses. "Counterfeit money is like that. It passes around from person to person, but eventually someone realizes what it is and doesn't accept it, and the person holding it loses. They get nothing for it."

"Even if they turn it over to the police?"

"What are *we* supposed to do about it? Millions of dollars of counterfeit money are confiscated every year. We can't pay for that!"

"*Millions* of dollars?"

He nodded. "Besides the jokers in this country, rogue governments in other countries print up our money."

"No way!"

"It's a big problem that hurts the whole economy. It waters down the actual value of our real cash. If people don't trust their country's money, they lose confidence in the economy, and the finances of the whole country are affected."

I just looked at him and said, "Wow." I mean, who knew that buying pretzels with fake twenties could bring down the whole economy?

Not me.

Anyway, Officer Borsch was actually really great about the whole mess. The only thing I didn't let him help me with was getting the "secret admirer" gift back from Hudson. I had to do that myself, and let me tell you, it wasn't easy.

"My," Hudson said when I'd finished telling him everything. "That is some story." Then he went inside and got the photograph and handed it over. "It was a very nice gesture, Sammy. I'm touched that you did it." He gave me a one-armed hug and said, "But don't you know? Your friendship, *that's* what's valuable. No gift can compare."

And the interesting thing is, I'm seeing that for myself now. I'm back to having nothing, but I don't really mind. And Marissa still doesn't have a cell phone or a credit card or even spending money, but she seems to be getting used to it. We just hang out with Holly and Dot, toss the softball around, and talk about stuff.

Like Danny and Danny and Danny and Danny.

Actually, there is another boy she talks about.

Mikey.

Ever since she found out about Jab-the-Flab and the other things kids at school have done to Mikey, she keeps wanting to "check on" him. She hangs out with him, laughs with him, does stuff with him. . . . She's actually *nice* to him and totally behind Hudson's Boot Camp. "It's working," she told me. "His attitude is *so* much better, and he's lost ten pounds!"

The situation with their parents is still a mess. I have no idea where that's going to wind up, but seeing things change between Marissa and Mikey has been like witnessing a little miracle on Cypress Street. Who'd have thought losing money and Mikey living in a kind of foster home would make those two get along?

Again, not me.

Anyway, I also took a chance on André and told *him* everything and explained that the Jackal had confessed to ransacking Buck's room to get the rest of his counterfeit money stash. André didn't know that I live illegally with Grams, so it was a big leap of faith for me to tell him, and André knew it. "How am I supposed to tell you to scram now?" he said, his cigar stump wagging away.

I grinned at him. "Guess you're stuck with me as a friend, huh?"

"Guess I am," he growled. "So, when ya gonna clean this place, huh? It's filthy."

"Uh, *later*," I said, heading for the door.

"Figures," he grumbled, but right before hoisting his newspaper, his eye twitched a wink at me.

So I was feeling really good about all of that as I eased back into the Highrise. Then came my encounter with Mrs. Wedgewood, which, believe me, can totally blow a good mood.

I hugged the wall quick when her door opened up, but she whispered, "It's okay, sugar." Then she clanked out a few steps and asked, "Why are you always so skittery?"

I felt like saying, 'Cause I'm living next door to a big ol' blackmailing, slave-driving whale! but I bit it back and sighed, "What do you need, Mrs. Wedgewood?"

"Need? Why, sugar, who says I need anything?"

Yeah, right. Like vampires don't need blood?

"Come in, come in!" she says.

"Uh . . ."

"Oh, come on. I've got something for you."

So I followed her, wondering what it was this time. Garbage? Laundry? Cans to recycle? A shopping list?

But she stopped at her table and picked up a plate of cookies. "I baked these for you." Her eyes twinkled as she added, "Not that I didn't eat a few myself."

I eyed the cookies suspiciously.

She must've read my mind. "I'm not looking for something in return. I just got to thinking—you've been so helpful, and with that prima donna mother of yours and everything that's gone on here this week . . . why, I just thought you could use some appreciation. So I baked these as a little way of saying thank you. I wish

I could pay you or do more in return, but as it is, I'm not able to." She pushed the plate of cookies on me. "Go on, sugar. They're chocolate chip with creamy fudge centers. They were my all-time favorite when I was your age. It's been years and years since I've made them, but"—her eyes twinkled again—"they're every bit as good as I remember."

I left there completely stunned.

And she was right about the cookies.

They were *amazing*.

Anyway, it was actually Grams I was most scared of facing. I mean, how many times have I been down this same dumb road? In my gut, I knew there was something wrong with keeping the money, so why didn't I listen to that? Why didn't I confide in Grams? How could I have let things get so out of control?

There were a lot of details I could have kinda glossed over, but in the end, I wound up telling her everything anyway. I wanted to come totally clean, but since it was after the fact, it was too late—I'd lost her trust and she was fuming. And since Lady Lana was still on her high horse about being "unfairly maligned" and refused to have me shipped to Hollywood to stay with her, Grams finally just told me, "You are grounded, young lady! For the rest of summer!"

"Yes, ma'am," I said.

I mean, what else was there to say?

But after a week of being cooped up with me, she finally let me out, grumbling, "Just try not to scare anyone to death on your way down, would you?"

I actually laughed, and it was the first time she'd smiled at me in a week.

So even though I've got a lot of community service hours looming in my future, I know that overall I'm lucky to have gotten off so light. And maybe someday I'll have some *real* money of my own, but in the meantime, I've got my friends.

And my grams.

And a boy who might someday kiss my cleaned-up lips.

Which, now that I think about it, are all things even real money can't buy.

Yeah, maybe I've just been looking at this the wrong way.

Maybe it turns out I've been rich all along.

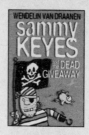
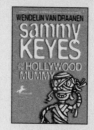

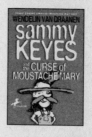
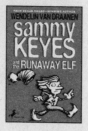

Have you read
SAMMY KEYES and the WEDDING CRASHER
yet?

Turn the page for a sneak peek.

PROLOGUE

In the beginning I thought it was funny. I mean, having Mr. Vince for a teacher is not exactly a sunshiny way to start your day. It's more like being trapped in a room with a dark, threatening cloud rumbling around you.

It's not just that Mr. Vince acts like he hates us, it's also that he's gross. Everyone knows he chews tobacco because we've all seen him add to the little cup of nasty brown spit that he keeps in his desk drawer. Plus, he has a disgusting scratching habit. You name it and we've seen him scratch it—his head, his neck, his stomach, his crotch. It's unbelievable.

So when the pranks began, I had to laugh. But pretty soon I realized that the prankster was serious.

Serious and dangerous.

ONE

I was almost looking forward to eighth grade starting. Not because I missed getting up early or couldn't wait to get saddled with homework again.

Please.

No, I was looking forward to school starting up again for the only reason anyone in junior high looks forward to it.

I'd get to see my friends every day.

My best friend, Marissa, was ready, too. Her family is in crisis mode, and I think going back to school seemed like a way for her to escape all that. Plus, we'd be eighth graders instead of lowly seventh graders, and last year's stress of being at a new school would be totally gone.

But then the first day of school arrived, and I got my final schedule.

"No!" I cried when I saw it.

"What?" Marissa asked.

"I've got Mr. Vince! For homeroom *and* history!"

"Eew," she said as she inspected my schedule. "Bad way to start the day."

Then I leaned over to see her schedule and saw that

we only had one class together—drama, at the very end of the day. "No!" I cried again. "This is the worst schedule ever!"

Our friends Dot and Holly joined us, and I found out that they had three classes the same as Marissa . . . and that all of them had some guy named Mr. Jefferson for history instead of Mr. Vince.

"This is so unfair!"

"Maybe you can get switched?" Marissa said.

So I marched right up to the office. It wasn't *just* that I had only one class with Marissa, it was that I had only one class with Marissa *and* they'd stuck me with Mr. Vince.

Mr. Vince!

Let's just say that there was no way I would survive the year with Bad Mood Bob. And that's not just because he hates kids. He may teach history, but he and I *have* history. Last year he covered up a total sabotage of my softball team by one of his players so his team could make it to the Sluggers' Cup. That may not seem like a big deal to you, but in Santa Martina, the Sluggers' Cup is *huge,* and since I was part of why his little shenanigans backfired, anywhere near him is now definitely enemy territory.

So, yeah. As Grams would say, I had good grounds to demand a change. Trouble is, when I got to the office, I found out from the office lady that my counselor couldn't see me. "She's swamped, sweetie," Mrs. Tweeter said with a tsk. She leaned forward and whispered, "She's new this year, so have a little patience, all right?"

"But she put me in Mr. Vince's class!"

Her eyes did some rapid-fire blinking over the tops of her reading glasses, and I could tell she was remembering the Sluggers' Cup fiasco. "Oh my."

"Exactly!"

She took a prim breath and a little step back. "Well, Mr. Vince *is* a professional, dear. And if you stay on your best behavior—"

"No! This will never work!" I looked past her to the vice principal's office door. "Can I please see Mr. Caan? He'll straighten this out."

"Hmm. I *would* see about that," she said, drawing out the words, "but Mr. Caan no longer works here."

"He what? Wait. Why not?"

"Didn't you read the August newsletter, dear? He's now principal at the high school. Mr. Foxmore is the new vice principal here."

"Mr. Caan is at the *high* school?"

"That's right, dear." She gave me a cheery smile. "So you'll reunite with him next year."

"Well, what about Dr. Morlock?" I asked. "Can I see him?"

She looked at me like, You're kidding, right? because Dr. Morlock is a totally absentee principal. I only saw him about three times last year, but one of those *was* at the Sluggers' Cup tournament, so he knows about me and Mr. Vince.

"He's not even here?"

"He was, dear, but he had a meeting." She reaches to answer the ringing phone. "I'm afraid you'll have to wait your turn to see Miss Anderson, just like everyone else. I'm sorry."

I left there so frustrated that even the janitor noticed. "Hey, hey, hold on now, Sammy," he said, catching up to me. "What's wrong?"

"Oh, hi, Cisco," I said, feeling bad for blasting right by him. I mean, Cisco may be "just" a janitor, but he's the coolest adult at school. He can talk about music or movies or sports, and he knows all the kids by name. So instead of answering "Nothing" like I would have with most other people, I said, "They put me in Vince's class, and nobody in the office seems to get why that's a disaster."

"Oh boy," he says, and I can tell that he *completely* gets it. He glances back at the office. "A lot of changes around here, man. Not all good, that's for sure. I coulda told them what to prune and what to transplant if they'd asked me, but of course they didn't."

I laugh and tell him, "Thanks," and just knowing he understands why I'm unhappy makes me feel better.

A lot better, actually.

"Don't worry," he says with a wink. "Things'll work out."

After that I just tried to tell myself that my schedule *would* get changed. Things *would* get better. After all, they couldn't get much worse, right?

But when I walked into history third period, I found myself face to face with Heather Acosta.

"Hey, loser!" she sneered.

I stepped around her and found a seat, but wow. Talk about a rash of bad luck. I mean, being anywhere near that vicious redhead is like being surrounded by poison oak. Get too close and your life will be covered in itchy, oozy bumps. Stumble in and you might actually die. The only real solution is to avoid her, but she makes that difficult.

Very difficult.

For one thing, she's sneaky. Some days she's shiny and green, and people think she's, you know, a blackberry plant or some sweet little meadow clover.

Don't let her fool you. She's always poison oak, and when she finally shows her true colors, you'll just want to go drown yourself in calamine lotion.

So I steer clear.

Really, I do.

Trouble is, she likes to brush up against me.

Likes to camouflage herself in front of our teachers.

Likes to surround me and make my life as painful as she possibly can.

So after she calls, "Hey, loser!" she says, "I saw my brother hanging out with a hot girl at the high school yesterday. He is *so* over you!"

See? It's hard to ignore her. Especially when she says things you're secretly worried about. I mean, Casey isn't *officially* my boyfriend, but Marissa has been saying it for so long, it was inevitable that I'd started to believe it.

I *wanted* to believe it.

But he's in high school now.

And he's still my archenemy's brother.

Whose dad is secretly going out with my soap-star mother.

Which makes everything . . . complicated.

And messy.

And not at all inevitable.

And on top of all that, I haven't heard from him since he called me during his high school orientation, and that was over a week ago.

Anyway, as if having Heather in Mr. Vince's class wasn't painful enough, it turns out I also have her in science and drama.

Half of my classes!

Why not just move her in with me?

But after two weeks of trying to get my schedule changed, Miss Anderson told me that there's nothing she can do about it. Dr. Morlock is never around, and the new vice principal refuses to see me, which makes me really mad. I thought about following him to his car after school and making him hear me out, but I don't even know what he looks like!

Grams tried talking to him on the phone, but she couldn't get anywhere with him, either. And when Mr. Foxmore began asking questions about why *she* was calling instead of my mother, Grams gave up. "Why didn't I say I was Lana?" she moaned. She fluttered around the kitchen like a trapped little bird. "I'm sorry I botched that, Samantha. He made me so nervous! Maybe you can get your mother to call?"

I just rolled my eyes and snorted.

Like Lady Lana would want my sorry little scheduling problems to interfere with her soap-star life?

No, the bottom line is, I'm stuck with Mr. Vince for homeroom and history, and I'm stuck with Heather Acosta in history, science, and drama. "Oh, that's harsh," Cisco said when he asked me how things had turned out. "But that's what's happening around here, man. People don't *listen*."

"It's nice that you do," I told him.

"Too bad that's all I can do." He smiled and pushed his cleaning cart along. "Except clean up your messes."

"Hey! I throw out my own trash."

He laughed and waved. "I know you do, Sammy." Then over his shoulder he called, "Believe me, I pay attention!"

Now, there *is* one good thing about my schedule, and that's Billy Pratt. Billy is also in history, science, and drama and totally makes those classes. For one thing, he's a good friend, but he's also like a chimp in a cage of hyenas.

A macaw swooping through a murder of crows!

A clown fish in a school of sharks!

He's so . . . Billy.

And although most teachers don't appreciate his hyper sense of humor, I sure do. Especially after it finally kicked in again during the third week of school.

"Are we gonna reenact battles in here?" he asked Mr.

Vince on Tuesday.

"No, Mr. Pratt," Mr. Vince said with a frown.

"Are we gonna set up encampments in here?" he asked on Wednesday.

"No, Mr. Pratt. But you can set up camp in the principal's office, if you'd like."

"Are we gonna have guest speakers in here?" Billy asked on Thursday. "We could *really* use some guest speakers in here."

This made Mr. Vince scratch his hip and eye Billy with a frown. "Are you implying that my class is boring, Mr. Pratt?"

Billy gave a little shrug. "I'm implying that we could *really* use some guest speakers in here."

Mr. Vince scratches his other hip as he looks around the classroom. "How many of you think we need guest speakers?"

Billy's hand shoots up, but everyone else just looks around at everyone else.

"Aw, come on," Billy says to us. "Flap your chicken wings in the air already. Don't you want to listen to some old Civil War dude? Or Rosie the Riveter? Or slaves that were hunted by hounds?"

Jake Meers's hand inches up. "I would."

David Olsen's follows. "That would be cool."

Soon almost everyone has their hand up, including me.

Well, not Heather Acosta, but that's because she's being her sneaky little shiny-leafed self.

Mr. Vince shakes his head and mutters, "I'm dealing with a roomful of retards." Then his face pops full of blood, and he screams, "Those people are all dead! Dead, you hear me? They've died! They're DEAD!"

Billy jumps out of his seat. "We should have a séance!"

"GET OUT!" Mr. Vince yells, pointing an angry finger toward the door. "Go to the office, NOW!"

So while Billy collects his stuff and trudges out the door, Sasha Stamos turns around in the seat in front of me and whispers, "I can't believe he called us retards. Doesn't he know that's offensive?"

I smirk. "He *lives* to be offensive." Then I add, "This place takes some adjustment, huh?" 'Cause Sasha was homeschooled until just this year.

"Well, my little brother's autistic, and I shouldn't have to *adjust* to such an ignorant teacher." Then she gives me a we'll-just-see-about-*this* look and turns back around in her seat.

The trip to the office doesn't seem to dampen Billy's spirits, though, because on Friday he comes into history wearing a hodgepodge of clothes that sort of adds up to a Civil War soldier's uniform, including a blue hat with crossed rifles on it.

The hat comes off when Billy notices a short man with soft features and receding red hair standing in a back corner of the classroom.

I catch Billy's eye and grin like, Guest speaker? But he shakes his head and gives me a warning look that means one definite thing.

Be good.

The tardy bell rings, and Mr. Vince immediately clears his throat. "I'd like to apologize," he says, looking down at his shoes, "for using the word *retard* yesterday. It was in poor taste, and I shouldn't have done it."

He glances up from his shoes and sort of vultures a look at the class.

We just stare at him, not making a peep.

"I'd like to put the incident behind us, so please accept my apology."

We just stare at him some more.

Then suddenly he calls, "Mr. Foxmore, stay a minute, would you?"

We all whip around to see that the man with the receding red hair is in the middle of slipping out the door.

Now, through my head are flashing a million thoughts.

That's Mr. Foxmore? The new vice principal? The new discipline guy? The new Mr. Caan? The guy who flustered Grams and refused to see me?

It can't be!

He seems so . . . soft.

And he's *short*.

And his suit is all rumply!

I mean, if he can't even control his suit, how's he ever going to control eight hundred junior high kids?

But then it hits me that he just got Mr. Vince to do something that Mr. Caan—who looks and acts like a pro wrestler—had a really hard time getting him to do.

Apologize.

Sasha Stamos whips around and whispers, "My mom called the school about it yesterday!" She seems very proud and super-excited, but then hesitates and adds, "Don't tell anyone, okay?"

I nod, and as Mr. Foxmore comes back inside the classroom, Mr. Vince reaches for the rope at the bottom of the projection screen, which is pulled down in front of the whiteboard. "I'd like to know," he says, looking around the classroom, "which one of you thought you could get away with this?"

Then he yanks the rope, rolling up the screen and exposing a big, bold, red-lettered message on his white-board.

A message that says, DIE DUDE!